C000002998

A captivating thriller to rival any B

Biological Deception

Geoffrey Bott

Solihull Publishing

Biological Deception
All Rights Reserved.
Copyright © 2020 Geoffrey Bott
v3.0

This is a work of fiction. Names, characters, businesses, places, events, locales, and incidents are either the products of the author's imagination or used in a fictitious manner. Any resemblance to actual persons, living or dead, or actual events is purely coincidental.

The opinions expressed in this manuscript are solely the opinions of the author and do not represent the opinions or thoughts of the publisher. The author has represented and warranted full ownership and/or legal right to publish all the materials in this book.

This book may not be reproduced, transmitted, or stored in whole or in part by any means, including graphic, electronic, or mechanical without the express written consent of the publisher except in the case of brief quotations embodied in critical articles and reviews.

Solihull Publishing

ISBN: 978-0-578-24034-3

Cover Photo © 2020 Geoffrey Bott. All rights reserved - used with permission.

Copyright Registration, Certificate of Registration # TXu 002194583

PRINTED IN THE UNITED STATES OF AMERICA

Acknowledgment

Publishing Uphill last year gave me confidence to craft another story. Lockdown from COVID-19, as it would later become known, afforded me the luxury of freedom and time to write Biological Deception.

Several who read Uphill told me to write a thriller. I would be remiss, therefore, if I didn't mention names here. James proctor, my longtime lawyer and friend, was the first to encourage a second book. Lorie Chapman, the lovely wife of my realtor, also encouraged me after being enamoured with Uphill. As I started to compose the chapters, I would send them to her. Lorie's response was to tell me to keep writing. Rich Kondrat, a friend for decades, was the first to read the finished manuscript. It needs to be a James Bond movie, was his response. Rich' gifted attention to detail aided in the chapter titles, whose importance I hadn't fully recognised. Diana Zupkus who advised me on the political layout regarding which state the US senator should come from. My sister in England Jennie Gillyon, who wanted to edit it and ensure it was published in English, and not American English. There is a difference and I feel the main character being English helps with this directive.

There were others who added some input and I will always be eternally grateful to them.

Finally, to my children whom have supported my endeavors and encouraged the writing.

1

Windhoek, Namibia

Cross grabbed a satchel containing the essential technical equipment required for this job, vacated the hotel room and walked downstairs to the lobby. He had selected the Am Weinberg Boutique Hotel because it was a convenient distance from downtown Windhoek, the capital of Namibia. He was there on a specific assignment and then vowed to get the hell out of there as fast as possible.

Robert Mitrovic had called him two weeks earlier with an urgent request. Christmas was approaching and he was enjoying an evening in his California home in Tahoe when the call came. He knew it was coming. Igor, his closest friend, had informed him a day or two earlier. He had polished off his first libation of Macallan 18 so poured himself a second when the phone rang.

"Hello, this is Daniel," as he recognised the number given to him.

"Hello Mr. Cross, this is Robert Mitrovic. I was told to call you and really appreciate you taking the time to discuss my business proposition," he replied in a strong Serbian accent.

"Please, call me Daniel," he kindly responded, trying to diminish the formalities.

Mitrovic was polite and had a reasonable command of English

but the accent reminded Daniel of someone.

"Igor filled me in on what you are looking for. I have a scientific background and was brought up and educated in England. I feel these attributes will help you significantly, especially on the African continent."

"Well, thank you, yes. I was also given your dossier and I did some research myself. You are highly respected in the scientific community."

"Thank you."

Mitrovic filled him in on what he had already been told. He wanted to purchase a special diamond but needed someone to test the veracity, authenticity and quality. He needed someone he could trust to fly to Namibia. If Cross agreed, he would have him fly with Robert's girlfriend Cassandra Mikhailov.

The details were laid out once he had confirmed his intent to do this. During subsequent conversations the details were further augmented and payment for services was tendered. A few days prior to departure, Mitrovic had sent a device, as promised, for testing the diamond with instructions.

Cross walked down to the lobby and met Mikhailov. She was a stunning Russian brunette. Long dark brown hair complemented her emerald green eyes, but Russian ladies knew how to dress.

A taxi had been ordered and when it arrived they jumped into the back. It exited the hotel on Jan Jonker Road and then turned left on B6 road towards downtown. Cross was a tad apprehensive but hid it well. He was on a mission, one he had never experienced before, but he had failed to observe a non-descript Toyota that took interest in their movements.

The taxi pulled up outside a prominent diamond outlet and they exited.

"Please wait for us. We will not be long," Cross told the cab driver.

Two tall dark men exited the building and greeted them.

"Hello Mr. Cross and Ms. Mikhailov. I am Mr. Ndumbo and this is Mr. Beukes, head of security. Please call me Abraham."

"Nice to meet you, Abraham. Please call me Daniel and this is Cassandra," as they exchanged pleasantries and shook hands.

"Please follow me."

They did as instructed and entered the store and were immediately taken to a private room located at the back. The door was closed behind them. They each seated themselves on expensive leather-backed chairs surrounding the substantial oak conference table. Abraham took some keys and opened the safe that was situated behind a large, original sailboat painting on the wall. Out came a wooden box that was also sealed. Placed on the conference table, it was unlocked and opened. Inside the mahogany box was an opulent diamond. Its beauty had not been properly conveyed.

Cross carefully put his bag on the table and removed some testing utensils. As he started to perform the first rudimentary tests, something seemed odd. Diamond is one of the strongest substances on earth and this was allegedly a multimillion dollar specimen. It passed some of the initial tests, it was a fine sample, but they weren't convincing. His heart-rate changed and he moved off to the side with Mikhailov.

"This isn't the diamond Robert is buying, Cassandra," he said leaning over and whispering in her ear.

"What do you mean?" she responded, in her strong Russian accent.

"I have one final test to perform but the rudimentary tests are inconclusive. This isn't a multimillion dollar hydrocarbon," sounding like a scientist.

Cross laid out his final test, more elaborate and scientific in its determination but again, the result seemed inconclusive. He confirmed his suspicions using a large hand-held magnifying glass.

"Abraham, I have determined the results and I need to convey them to Mr. Mitrovic back in LA before we commit to its purchase. Can we step outside so I can make the call more privately?"

"Of course, of course. I understand," seeming a little agitated.

Mr. Ndumbo led the way to the front door.

"Thank you."

As Cross and Mikhailov stepped outside, a Toyota appeared from nowhere and shots rang out. Cross saw the splinters and dust as they ricocheted off the street and buildings. He ducked, felt the whizz of the bullets passing his head but heard Cassandra scream and then drop to the pavement. He observed blood starting to flow and quickly knelt down lifting her head.

"Daniel, I am hurting. I didn't see who it was but I need help," gasping for her last breath.

He motioned to the taxi and the guy cranked his engine. Cross picked up Cassandra and carried her, placing her on the rear seat cradling her head. It sped off.

"Don't worry, I will get help."

"Please find out who did this. Tell Robert I love him," were her last words as she closed her eyes, rolled her head and passed away in his arms.

Now partly soaked in blood, he needed an escape plan.

"Get me to the nearest rental car company."

He spun his head around looking for the Toyota he observed that had housed the murderer. The street was busy with cars and pedestrians. He couldn't find it. What the fuck. Where did it go?

The taxi pulled up outside Drive South Africa and he jumped out.

"Wait for me please."

A few minutes later he pulled around from the rental car lot and parked next to the taxi. He carefully picked up Cassandra's lifeless body and laid her on the back seat of the rental. He extracted some money from his wallet and gave it to the cab driver who immediately took off.

Cross' head was spinning. He called Mitrovic who was waiting for the call.

"Cassandra is dead. The diamond wasn't the one you wanted to purchase and the shooter disappeared. What are you into?" Panicked, he continued, "I didn't sign up for this," he yelled and clicked the phone dead.

What the hell do I do now? he said to himself.

Now being more vigilant and using the phone's GPS, he took the back roads to the hotel. He grabbed a change of clothes, a blanket and then quickly left. The airport would likely be monitored so that was a no-go. Who was after him? Was he really the target? After covering Mikhailov's body with the blanket, he navigated the streets of Windhoek and found B1 road which would take him south to South Africa. No one would suspect that.

He didn't have much time because the Namibian border closes around midnight and it is a long drive. He needed to dispose of her body somewhere, somehow. He couldn't just toss her out. His anxiety level was creeping up to the danger line.

Mitrovic called him several hours into his escape.

"I have someone helping me. They will have a person meet you along the way and provide new identity. My people know where you are and who you are. What are you driving?"

"What have you got me into? This is insanity."

"I will explain later," he said, not with any conviction though. He cared little about his girlfriend too. What was her part in all this?

An hour or so later south on B1, a car flags down Cross and he pulls off at a convenient place. A big African gentleman approaches.

"Here are your new passport, visa and a credit card, Mr. Cross," he says in a thick South African accent. "These will get you across the border, even if it is closed, and to Cape Town. There you will be assigned a flight through Frankfurt back to California. Mr. Mitrovic will contact you when you get home. I cannot say anything more. Take my car. You cannot be seen in this rental."

"Are you home, Mr. Cross?"

"Yes, I arrived a few hours ago. I am desperate for sleep."

"Make your way down to LA after some sleep," Mitrovic explains and provides the details.

I fucking didn't sign up for any of this…

2

Insurance Policy

Daniel didn't sleep much. He couldn't. His agitation level was too high and his brain couldn't turn off. Not waiting for a decent social hour, he called his Russian friend Igor, fully anticipating him to be awakened from his sleep.

"What is going on? Who is Robert anyway? This was a simple request to test a diamond," obviously pretty irritated, upset and frightened.

Igor Verenich had moved to California after the collapse of the Soviet Union, as did a lot of people from that part of the world. His expertise was in resource management, international communication and business relations. They had become friends from an impartial love, some would say insane love, of British Rover cars. He knew Mitrovic through a friend of an ex-girlfriend which, admittedly, wasn't a flattering endorsement.

"What happened, Daniel?" he answered, recognising his voice.

"The diamond wasn't perfect. It had been switched although only an expert and scientific tests would reveal that. I was prepared but not for what happened. Cassandra Mikhailov is dead. I was given fake identification and flew home yesterday. My phone died so couldn't call you. It is likely being tracked anyway."

"Oh my, I didn't suspect a thing. I did a background check on Robert and nothing came up untoward. His purchase seemed legitimate and he had a contract he told me." He continued. "Let me get back to you. Can I use this number you are calling on?"

Damn it, kicking himself. He thought he had turned off the phone's identity. Now I will have to find another phone, he told himself.

"Yes, but not for long."

He had been asked to head to Los Angeles area and visit Mitrovic. He was unsure of this move but he had to meet up with him to find out what is going on. He got cash from an envelope in his home, called Uber and headed to a nearby car rental. He couldn't fly so sourced a bland AWD, navigated through South Lake Tahoe, up and over Kingsbury Grade and eventually headed south on 395.

The drive was a long eight hours. He stopped once for gas and coffee but the events were rattling in his head. He was trying to recite the experiences from only a few days ago. The sight of a beautiful Russian lady, now dead, he had met only two days before her death had unnerved him. The shock was still wearing off. Who was she?

395 took him south past the turnoff for Yosemite, route 120, then past Mammoth Ski Resort, through Bishop and down to Route 14 intersection. He forked right and headed through Lancaster and onto I5. Now he was heading into the sprawling LA-area's concrete jungle where he could hopefully be hidden. Traffic was relatively light as he had timed his arrival to perfection. Leaving the Tahoe area at lunchtime meant he had massaged the drive down to avoid the nonsensical rush hour mayhem. He was in familiar territory having done work down here for decades.

I5 took him through the San Fernando Valley, past I210 and Burbank, then Hollywood and into the monolithic nightmare known as LA. Daniel knew where he was heading having worked at USC's East LA campus. Years earlier he had convinced them to purchase an upgraded triple quad mass spectrometer when they were pursuing their first instrument purchase. They never looked back on their purchase.

He hadn't made hotel arrangements because he didn't want to alert anybody, if anybody knew that he was coming down. He had no idea. Approaching the I5/I10 interchange, he exited right which looped him up and over the freeway and merged onto I10 east. Through a convoluted series of turns to get back heading west, he then exited I10 west at N. Soto Street and executed a left turn at the stop light. There were plenty of low-end motels in the area and he checked himself into one.

A quick shower, a change of clothing and he was approaching starvation levels. Cross knew of a nice bar just west of I5 near the USC campus. He had enjoyed the company of a client there a few times. A quick drive north on N. Soto and then west on Valley Blvd sent him in the direction of Moulton Ave. It was a secluded, dead-end street that afforded the luxury of being concealed from anyone, or so he imagined.

The restaurant was a converted warehouse and he walked up the small flight of stairs and into the bar area. Cross had traveled around the world on his own for decades so knew exactly where he would sit. He found a table opposite the bar but facing the door through which he had entered. Never did he sit with his back to any establishment's front entrance. He was always vigilant but for reasons unknown he felt he needed to be even more so down here. He ordered a locally-brewed light pale ale, having vanquished IPS's long ago, and fish and chips from the bar, opened a tab and returned to his table, beer in hand.

Half way into his food, he watched as an attractive, slender and beautifully dressed blonde walk in. She surveyed the patrons languishing at the bar before focusing her attention on the seating areas. She then motioned towards the dining area but returned to the bar.

She appeared to be looking for someone. Cross immediately caught her attention and she walked over.

"Hello, are you Daniel Cross?" she asked, surprising him. Her perfume gravitating into Cross' sensory glands.

"That depends who you are and why you are asking," he replied cautiously, rising from his chair.

"My name is Ms. Dunhill but please call me Chantelle."

She held out her hand in anticipation of Cross taking it. He didn't disappoint. How could he, whoever she is. She was an American and wore expensive earrings and necklace. Her long curly blonde hair had just been bleached, it looked like anyway because there were no indications otherwise. It was parted to one side as it flowed across her face and down. She wore facial blush, eye-liner, red lipstick and her finger nails had been manicured. Her green silk dress was simple but elegant and slid a few inches above her knees. Her legs must have been contoured by hours a week in the gym, he thought. It was evident she was here for a reason and must have known of Cross' reputation for elegant ladies. She knew what she was doing. No wedding ring.

"It is very nice to meet you Ms. Dunhill."

"Please call me Chantelle. May I be permitted to call you Daniel?"

"Of course, please do."

The pleasantries over with, she continued.

"May I sit down? I have some important business to discuss."

Ignoring the obvious, he was now mesmerised by her presence.

The table was square with four chairs. He courteously pulled the chair on his left away from the table and offered her the seat. Her back now purposely facing the bar, he asked if she would like a drink.

"Yes, please. I would like an aged Scottish whiskey, neat. You decide which preference." Perhaps she also knew his drinking habits.

"Are you hungry?"

"The calamari appetizer would be fine," without even observing the menu, he noticed.

Cross returned with the aged whiskey, neat, and presented it to her. She grasped it, thanking him in the process.

"Now, what is it you would like to discuss with me, Chantelle?" avoiding the question about how she knew he was here. He would get to that later, he suspected.

"I understand you just returned from Namibia. I am sorry about the death of Ms. Mikhailov. You must have been frightened but you handled it very well."

What the hell is going on, thought Cross, but he kept his cool. He was incredible under pressure.

"I was asked to perform an assignment the details of which you are evidently already aware. I don't understand what happened but I intend to find out. Now how may I help you?"

"I am from the insurance company, Daniel. May I call you Daniel?" asking a second time, seeming a tad nervous. Cross confirmed with a nod so she continued, "I was asked to insure the transaction, shipment and eventual delivery of the diamond."

Cross now sat for a moment to ponder and digest what she just said. Just as he did, the calamari arrived. Chantelle thanked the waitress and picked up a breaded tentacle, dipped it into the marinara source provided and took a bite. She was so beautiful. Her legs were crossed and the knees were perfect. The dress had ridden a little exposing more of the naked, toned legs. She was surreal, eating finger food with such dexterity and elegance, trying to avoid damaging those manicures. He was amused now but had to stop himself.

"How did you know I was here?" he finally asked.

"I cannot divulge that information yet. I am here to tell you to be careful. A Russian cartel is involved with this along with some Jewish enterprise and perhaps the Asians also. We don't know yet.

Mr. Mitrovic inadvertently got involved in some racket that even he doesn't understand. Evidently someone else wanted the diamond. My company is at a loss as to who took it. Since we insured it, we need to find out. I may need to ask your help."

"Honestly, what can I provide? I am a scientist who was asked to perform a simple but, in hindsight perhaps, dangerous mission. What do I know? I cannot be involved in something of this nature. I don't know anything," he professed.

"That is precisely why you are perfect. The people involved will not suspect you. They will not care about you. As a consequence, they will not know you will be trying to help me."

"I am also dispensable, Ms. Dunhill. I serve no purpose to the crime lords and so can easily be removed."

"Yes, you are unfortunately correct. That is why you need to be very careful. I am kindly requesting your assistance. I need your help."

With that she finished the second breaded octopus tentacle, uncrossed her legs and moved closer. Goddammit, Cross was incredulous. Why do beautiful women do that to me, he wondered. He saw further up her legs but returned his gaze to focus on her staring into his eyes. She was smiling at him now. Oh God.

Cross had been married a long time to an Asian beauty queen. It ended in heartache and the loss of significant financial holdings. He had bounced in and out of relationships in the ten years since his horrific divorce. He couldn't handle them primarily because his ex-wife had taken most things. He was afraid now. It really didn't help when about to tie the knot a second time, his fiancée walked away. Bewildered and shocked, he decided escorts were to be his source of satisfaction. He could deal with them and knew how to. He had even dated a few. No emotional ties anymore. But he had a weakness.

"Please, Daniel. I beg you," staring at him with those salient Caribbean-blue eyes.

It was sealed, and most likely his death warrant too.

3

The Buyer

Cross woke up the following morning. No wake-up aids were needed since he has an internal alarm. It was 7am and the winter sun was slanting in through the half-draped curtains.

Dunhill had captivated him. They had another round of drinks and continued their discussions. She gave him her contact information before they hugged and departed. He did manage a kiss on her cheek and could still smell her perfume wafting in the air. How can he trust her?

Gathering his thoughts, he called Mitrovic from a smart phone he had purchased on the way down yesterday. Mitrovic was expecting his call but hesitated when he saw no caller ID.

"Robert, this is Daniel. I will take a shower and eat some breakfast before heading your way. I will wait for the commuter traffic to die first. I am not on enough medication to navigating that mess."

"Good morning Daniel. That sounds fine. I am at the address I provided you. Where did you stay?" Mitrovic responded.

"Ok, sounds good. I should be there around 10am," ignoring the question.

He now had three hours to kill. He had brought his laptop so opened it up and signed onto the motel's WiFi network. Typing in

Chantelle Dunhill, he googled her. He had access to other lesser known but more powerful data bases so he dived into those too. She did in fact operate her own insurance company but he needed to be careful about her also. In her mid-40's, no children, she had been married twice and now divorced a second time. Oh, shit, her second ex-husband is Russian. Well, that explains a few things. He planted that note into his head. Another one to extract later.

He searched for a Denny's and found one on E. Cesar E. Chavez Avenue. This would make it easy to get to Santa Monica, north on I710 and west on I10.

Cross closed his laptop, removed the briefs he had slept in and turned on the shower. He was 55 but didn't look it. Surgical nightmares some years ago meant he had to work out to keep his leg muscles strong. He had astonishing legs for his age but marred by the onslaught of knives and a bone saw to his left knee. Spinning hard in winter and cycling up huge mountain passes in the summer, he was fit and strong. He kept his weight to around 180 pounds in winter. At 5'10", he was powerful and athletic. He lifted weights to keep his upper body toned and didn't dress like a middle-aged gentleman either.

Cross once entered a local hairdressing boutique in Tahoe and the cute owner refused to cut his naturally-curling silver hair. He left smiling, holding a bottle of lotion to highlight the color. It was beyond his shoulders now and he was getting used to the look and liked it, despite pleas from some. He was beyond caring what others think. He was his own man and could walk into any room anywhere in the world and take it over. People found him fascinating with his personal stories and views, partly biased from years of experiences not many could match. He had started from nothing and turned himself into an internationally respected engineer/scientist. He really didn't give a damn what people thought of his hair. He had accumulated a few days of grey facial stubble which added to his debonair looks. The English accent just reinforced it and ladies couldn't resist him.

After the shower, he put on some grey ribbed Hudson stretch jeans, a black Merino wool long sleeve Italian sweater and black Cole Haan leather casual shoes. He stood in front of the mirror and donned his Ray Ban sun glasses. Excellent, he mused. He put on a custom-made tan linen jacket and checked out of the hotel.

Breakfast at Denny's comprised of bacon, sausage, eggs and French fries along with the cursory coffee. He loved dipping the fries in the runny yoke, something he remembered from his days growing up in England.

He liked to catch up on news events which he did using the phone whilst digesting the breakfast. Glancing at his watch, it was time to head west.

Cross followed instructions given to him by Mitrovic and arrived at his home. It was a good size and had balconies overlooking the Pacific Ocean. Cross pulled into the driveway and extracted himself from the car. He rang the front doorbell.

"Good morning, Daniel. It is nice to finally meet you. Welcome to my abode," Mitrovic injected once he opened the door.

"Good morning Robert. A pleasure to meet you too. Nice location," Cross humbly replied surveying the area.

They shook hands and Cross was led down a small hallway and into the kitchen. He parked himself on a chair at the granite-covered breakfast counter.

"I have made some freshly ground coffee. What would you like with it?"

"Brown sugar and cream if you have those. If not, white sugar and milk will suffice. Thanks."

"A man of taste."

"Sometimes. Some might question that with my choice of women." They both laughed.

Cross needed to break the ice and was good at it. A joke here and there lightened things up. Obviously there was some tension that could be sliced with a chainsaw but he had to be cordial, at least to start the conversation. Mitrovic's alleged girlfriend was dead. He had escaped a foreign country using fake ID and credit card. Dunhill last night just added to the chaos being tossed around his head.

Mitrovic handed Cross his coffee comprising the specific request for cream and brown sugar. He took a sip. A tad different to Denny's coffee, he thought. Mitrovic walked around the kitchen and sat next to him at the counter.

"I am sorry this didn't go as planned," he started in with his thick Serbian accent. "I never expected anything at all. I have a buyer for the diamond already and all I had to do was have you verify it and then bring it to LA."

Cross was curious about his tone and matter-of-fact manner. He was surprised he didn't mention Cassandra since she was supposed to have been his girlfriend.

"I am not made for this nor did I sign up for it. I didn't expect it at all. I went in with an open mind ready to do the job I was well paid to do."

"Yes, it got messy and complicated very quickly. I wasn't expecting to avoid any altercation. This is a rare diamond worth substantial monies to the buyer. I am glad you escaped unscathed."

The last comment irritated Cross.

"Unscathed? I am trying to purge the memory of Cassandra dying in my arms. Who was she anyway? You haven't mentioned her at all yet," and was now becoming a little agitated.

"I had known Cassandra only briefly, perhaps a few months or so. She knew the purported buyer but I wonder that myself now. I never met him but we have a buy/sell contract signed ready. He was a Russian oligarch. I did wonder how Cassandra knew of him." He paused and then added, "Wait a minute. Let me go check on something. I will be right back."

Cross sat and drank the breathtaking coffee. Nothing could capture the unmistakable essence and smooth taste of Kopi Luwak coffee. He looked around and surveyed the expensive furnishings, artwork and paintings. He wasn't an expert but had purchased original artwork for his home in Tahoe. He knew the difference and admired the choices currently gratifying his visual sensors. He got up and walked into the living room area. He looked out of the grand window and could see the ocean waves rolling up onto the busy sandy beach. Mitrovic re-entered the kitchen so Cross walked back to the counter.

"I tried to call the buyer but his receptionist told me he had returned to Russia. Just out of curiosity I asked if I could speak with Ms. Mikhailov. The receptionist put me on hold for a few minutes and then told me she had left with Mr. Romanov."

Cross was speechless, almost anyway.

"Then who was with me in Namibia?"

"I haven't the faintest idea," was Mitrovic's honest reply. His expression confirmed his retort. "It should have been Cassandra and perhaps was. I told you what she looked like and sent pictures before you met her at LAX."

Attempting not to divulge too much information and ignoring the Mikhailov disaccord for now, Cross needed to know about Ms. Dunhill.

"Did you go through the motions of having the transaction insured?"

"Yes I did. I used a company recommended to me by someone Mr. Romanov knows. I contacted this company and had all the pertinent information written into another contract. Let me go find the information."

"Who was the name of Mr. Romanov's contact?"

He had to hide the shocked look on his face when Mitrovic told him.

Again, Mitrovic departed the room leaving Cross to admire the surroundings. How did this guy get into this mess in the first place, he asked himself. Who is Cassandra? The shot that killed her was obviously done by a trained sniper. It was meant to look like they were after him but he wasn't involved in the gory details of the diamond. The shot, the one directed at her, penetrated the chest where the heart was situated. The memory of that event coming to the forefront as Cross was piecing it together with the little information he had so far.

Mitrovic returned with a business card and handed it to Cross. The name on the card he was expecting but didn't show it. Chantelle Dunhill was prominently displayed but the contact number on the card was different to the one she had given him. Neglecting to pass this information on, Cross finished his coffee and pronounced that he had things to do and must head back up north to his office. They made their way to the front door and shook hands.

"I am sorry for all the pain this has caused you Daniel. I had no idea. Please forgive me. I need to move on. I loved Cassandra but now I don't really know who she was anymore. I am confused."

Clearly this was affecting him. Cross was just surprised he hadn't done more homework on such a rare diamond or the people he was dealing with.

"Thank you. I appreciate that. I need to get back home so that I can recover from the shock. I have my own work to do and prepare for more overseas trips. I have seminars and lectures to give."

With that they said their goodbyes.

4

The Diamond

Cross drove around the corner and parked at the side of the road. He picked up the phone and dialed the number that was scratched on a piece of paper.

"Hello Daniel. I wondered if you would call me."

"How did you know it was me? My identity is not shown."

"You are the only person who has this number. I told you I want you to be careful."

Hiding his surprise, he continued.

"The diamond was insured by Mr. Mitrovic for the buyer, Mr. Romanov, correct?"

He needed to piece and confirm some details for clarity. He was forming a network of facts in his head but really needed to get home.

"Yes, it was."

"Who was Ms. Mikhailov?"

Now Dunhill hesitated slightly but enough for an alert Cross to detect.

"She was dating Mr. Mitrovic but she was Mr. Romanov's mistress," she finally said.

"But she was killed by a sniper bullet in Windhoek."

Now he was revealing information to test her. He needed to trust her but not sure he could. He didn't know what side she was playing. Again, he noticed she hesitated to carefully craft her answer.

"She was the target, yes," she truthfully answered. She had to because the shot was to perfection and the sniper could easily have chosen Cross. She was most definitely the target. "It seems that way from the information I have been given."

"Now it is time you told me the truth, Ms. Dunhill," he said with some authority. "Mr. Romanov had a very close Russian friend did he not? And who really was the lady killed in Windhoek? If it was Ms. Mikhailov, then who flew back to Russia with Mr. Romanov?"

Clearly Dunhill will be aware what information Cross has gathered. His questions were staged but if she was to be trusted, then he needed to test her. He needed answers to questions that some of which were rhetorical. He knew some answers already.

"Mr. Romanov's close friend is Vladimir Kuznetsov. He is my ex-husband, and the right hand man of large but ruthless Moscow enterprises. Vladimir and I started the insurance company together but in the divorce he let me have the company. We have been divorced three years."

Dunhill was confirming details Cross had found in his data base search that morning. He already knew all this and it is possible she knew this, or suspected he knew.

"Ms. Mikhailov was indeed Cassandra and was Mr. Romanov's mistress for a time. She left him and started dating Mr. Mitrovic, but mistresses don't leave oligarchs. He must have left her. However, it looks like she kept seeing Mr. Romanov, at least from a business relationship standpoint. I don't know who left for Moscow with him but she may be playing a role in this if she has adopted Cassandra Mikhailov's name and credentials."

"Where do you stand on this insurance policy, Ms. Dunhill?"

"I have been asked to pay if off. It is valued at $25M."

"So, the policy is put into place and the premium paid. The

diamond was determined not to be the real McCoy, shall we say, and never arrives in the US. I am guessing you weren't supposed to know it wasn't real but someone got killed. Perhaps I wasn't supposed to know it wasn't the diamond Robert was buying. It was a close call but signs were evident that it wasn't."

"It was supposed to be a simple transaction," Dunhill added. "The difficulty was getting it into the country but that had been taken care of and assurances made. If the diamond has been stolen, then it goes onto the black market and its value doubles or triples. It could fund massive military equipment for what whomever took it has in store next. It could be a game-changer. Mr. Mitrovic was going to use the proceeds of the sale to fund a network of cannabis grow houses in California."

"What has your ex-husband got to do with the insurance company you now own?"

"He provides me some clients and resources for policies. The company is legitimate, I promise you that, but my ex-husband is a very dangerous man which is why I divorced him. Unfortunately I couldn't fully extricate myself from his grasps and control."

"I am seeing that now," feeling unsure of what he had agreed to do for Dunhill last night.

Cross was done, for now. He needed to leave Santa Monica and get home. All this was bringing him mental fatigue and he needed to digest it all.

"I am heading back to Tahoe. If I have any more questions, I will call you."

"If it continues to snow up there this winter, perhaps I can come on a ski trip and stay with you. I would use your guest room of course, if you have one."

Cross didn't think that was a very good idea at all. In fact it could create a situation that would add to his already dangerous plight.

"You are free to stay any time you wish. I don't promise being there since I have travel coming up," he replied, trying to convince her to stay away. It didn't work.

"I will call when I think about visiting. I am a really excellent skier." So was Cross, or used to be.

With that the line went dead and Cross pushed the start button in his rental car and navigated back onto I10 east to the I405 north.

5

Emergence of Ruthless Interests

The following morning Cross brewed some fresh ground coffee and sat at his kitchen counter. He had started to compile all the information garnered the last few days and was composing a story. He needed to fit all the pieces together. Many questions were coming to the foreground but he didn't have any answers to them, yet.

He glanced at his watch. It was now 9:42am and he needed to make calls. He dialed the first number and recognised the voice.

"Hello, this is Igor."

"Good morning my friend, how are you?"

"Daniel, where have you been? I have been worried about you. Tell me something new? Where did you go?"

"I went to meet your illustrious friend Mr. Mitrovic. I spent the last two days down in LA. He brought me up to date on some things I didn't know but also opened up a whole can of worms. I am unsure if he knew what he was into."

Verenich was a contractor for federal and California state governments in some legal capacity. Cross wasn't fully versed on what he actually did and really didn't need to know. However, his friend had access to government data bases and information he didn't. He needed that access and fast.

"Mr. Romanov was the buyer of the diamond. Robert had a contract with him."

Cross filled him in on most of the details but kept some information to himself. Verenich didn't need to know about Dunhill yet. He told him about the Russian involvement, the ruthless enterprise Romanov ran with his right-hand man Kuznetsov. He needed to know more information on these two and their businesses in Moscow. He explained the possibility of Jewish and Asian interests in the diamond and how it could fund military armaments. He finally explained Mitrovic's reason for purchasing the diamond in the first place and why he needed the proceeds. He laid it all out and asked that his friend make copious notes and kindly salvage more information.

"Why are you doing this Daniel?" his friend asked. "You are dealing with some serious people here. You could be signing your own death warrant."

"I am fully aware of that Igor. Thank you for the concern. I don't know what I am going to do yet but the information will help me digest what I know. Ms. Mikhailov was Romanov's ex-mistress but remained in some business capacity in his life. She was singled out and killed with one precision shot to the heart. She died in my arms Igor."

Verenich knows how that feels so had sympathy for his friend. His girlfriend had a heart attack and died in his arms a decade ago. Cross knew by telling him that Verenich would follow through on his request. He was also a very handsome man, with elegance and class in abundance, and ladies loved him. Cross knew it was a tug at his heart but Verenich understood him. He knew the why now.

"Please let me know what you find Igor. I am at home for a few days at least," and gave him his unlisted number.

He called his office on Industrial Avenue. Brandy, his office manager, answered. She was excited to hear his voice.

"Where have you been boss? We have been worried here. How was the trip to Namibia? Did you verify the diamond? How were the accommodations? I tried your cell phone but it didn't ring and went into voicemail. We didn't know what else to do. We tried email also."

"Good morning Brandy," now happy to hear her cheerful yet obviously concerned voice. "I am really sorry. Something happened on my trip and I lost the phone. I had neglected to check emails for a while also."

"Well, I am glad to hear you are ok," but she sensed something in his voice. "There was no phone ID so how can I reach you? Where are you?" she added, calming down a little and back to her bubbly self.

"Look, I am home but have a few things to sort out that may involve travel. I will be out of the office for a little while but you can use this number." He then proceeded to give it to her. "I will explain this all later. I have things on my mind Brandy. Something came up and I cannot tell you what yet. I cannot involve you or anyone in my company. Please trust me on this. Can you please cancel plans for the next two weeks?"

"Of course. If I need anything, I will call or text," and didn't question anything he just said.

Brandy had seen Cross go through his precedent-setting divorce. She had seen his new home burn down in Tahoe's forest fire back in 2007. She had seen him being dragged down into a very deep abyss and haul himself back up. She had witnessed it all but she had never seen him cry. He must have, she thought often. She waited for him to crack and break but he never did. She trusted and admired him. Cross knew this as he ended the call.

Verenich called that afternoon.

"Daniel, I don't know what you have gotten yourself into but you need to come down to Sacramento tomorrow morning. Meet me for breakfast at the usual place. I need to go over what I have already discovered. I will do some more research between now and breakfast."

"Wait a minute, Igor. Might I remind you that you got me involved in this assignment in the first place."

"I was hoping you had forgotten that part," he said chuckling.

"Is this as bad as it feels?" Cross venturing his own perception.

"See you tomorrow morning. The usual place then, say 9:30 to avoid traffic."

6

The Russian Connection

Citizen Hotel was on J Street and 10th. Cross didn't valet-park in case he needed to escape for whatever reason he couldn't immediately think of. He must have put his investigative hat on or something or now thinks he works for MI6.

He walked through the hotel front entrance and the restaurant was off to the left. Verenich was already there. Dark grey pants complemented his black Calvin Klein shirt over the top of an expensive black linen jacket. He looked Russian, thought Cross, with his shaved head and well-manicured facial hair. He was situated at a table away from other patrons but overlooking the street.

"Good morning Daniel," as he stood to take his hand and hug him. "How was the drive down from the mountains?"

"доброе утро, как дела?" Good morning, how are you, he responded in perfect Russian with a smile.

He liked to impress his friend once in a while with his Russian vernacular. He wanted to pose relaxed but he wasn't at all.

"The drive was good. As you know, I like driving the mountain roads in my Range Rover Autobiography."

He also knew Russians trust men with expensive automobiles and a Range Rover was highly regarded. They were very close friends separated by different cultures, history and thousands of miles of real estate.

"Let us order breakfast and drink some coffee before I get into the research you asked me to do."

Cross was beginning to relax a little. After eating, their plates were dispensed with and the table cleared so that documents could be laid out.

"Romanov worked for the KGB and then was high up in the Russian federal government. Like all the oligarchs, he was in the right place at the right time when the Russian Empire collapsed. He was offered shares in a national oil company that went private and he made several billion dollars. Kuznetsov was his right hand man for many years and he also profited from being offered favourable shares in a company the government knew was going to be liquidated. He faired very well and came out with several hundred million dollars. Not bad for being a half-assed Russian government employee."

He stopped and let Cross make notes. They both sipped the fresh coffee. Verenich didn't mince words when discussing such matters. His home country had been systematically decimated and pilfered by greedy, powerful men. He continued.

"These two now operate many businesses in and around Moscow, mostly essential imported materials for manufacturing and construction. However, they operate a cartel that is known to have ties in ex-Russian Republics such as Georgia and Chechnya.

"Romanov owns homes in several countries including down in Beverley Hills. He is married and is known to have mistresses and perhaps other wives outside of Russia. Kuznetsov also owns several homes including the LA area. He has a wife in Russia but was also married to a Chantelle Dunhill who originally came from Miami. They actually met in Miami and then moved to LA. They opened an insurance company that Ms. Dunhill operated but she never actually changed her last name." Looking at Cross, he added with a smile, "Perhaps she knew something wasn't right. It was her second marriage and it lasted five years. She was awarded, or perhaps Kuznetsov agreed, to let her keep the company once they divorced.

"I have verified also that Cassandra Mikhailov worked for Romanov in his Moscow office and then became his mistress for a while. She allegedly broke it off but that doesn't usually happen with oligarchs. The interesting aspect of all this Daniel is that Robert just wanted the diamond. He wasn't aware of all this other crap. He had the buyer, Romanov, in contract and all he had to do was validate its' authenticity and bring it to LA."

"I sensed at his home he didn't understand much. He seemed a tad naïve which is weird for a Serbian," explained Cross.

"I have looked into the specifics of the diamond also. It is rare and large, obviously from a mine in Namibia. People die to obtain such a specimen. It is difficult to get a lot of information because the diamond industry hides behind a lot of bullshit. They want to keep diamonds off the market to purposely elevate their trading prices. Most of them as you may know are sold to men who feel the need to spoil their wives, girlfriends, family, mistresses," he added the latter chuckling, "Since they demand expensive diamonds to keep them materially content, which allegedly helps to support and confirm their partner's love. Or perhaps as a gift to repay for something stupid the husband, fiancé, or boyfriend had done." He was now laughing along with Cross. "Price of diamonds is kept artificially high by keeping them off the market. This is done on purpose. I wouldn't rule out the diamond industry keeping it hidden. However, Cassandra's death limits that opinion to a very low percentage.

"The other interesting aspect of my research is that a cartel in Taiwan and a Jewish entity here in California kept coming up. I haven't quite figured out why yet. Romanov might have ties to both or he has infiltrated them. I need more time to look into this aspect.

"Daniel, you need to pay serious attention to what I am about to say and promise to stay calm." He placed his hand on Cross' arm. "When I was researching all this, I got a call from a gentleman at the CIA. They have been monitoring Romanov for some time so my research sent alarm bells off. I had to explain why, sort of, and I kept you out of it, sort of. I obviously neglected to mention the death of Ms. Mikhailov and your venture into Namibia. Cassandra's death may have been because she left Romanov and nothing else. He was angry. Oligarchs don't like being embarrassed and to leave him for a Serbian would have truly pissed him off. But she remained close with business dealings which is also strange." He removed his hand.

"Someone from CIA headquarters in Langley is coming to see me tomorrow. They fly out in the early hours on one of their private jets. This has reached a serious level. I will likely have to involve you."

Cross sighed and sat back in the chair. He looked out over J Street and watched as the people mulled around. Men in business suits and women in professional office attire were everywhere, all running to get somewhere fast as if the world was ending.

"You need some more time to research the other entities Igor?"

"Yes. I can do that this afternoon. I am free. I need to be prepared. Umm, **we** need to be prepared for the visit tomorrow from Langley. Perhaps you should contemplate hanging around Sacramento tonight. Go buy some clothes and things."

"I came prepared already. I have a suit in the car," replied Cross. "I had suspicions this was going to get a tad testy."

"Damn Brits," Verenich retorted, laughing so hard. "That is a gross understatement. My guess, you may be asked to pursue leads the CIA will provide. You are about to get a taste of counterespionage."

"Why, I am only a scientist. What the hell do I know about spying and dealing with oligarchs and their bands of merry men?" Cross casually countered.

"Because you are expendable Daniel and no one will suspect your involvement at this level."

"Прощай мой друг" said Cross, in perfect Russian. Goodbye, my friend.

Verenich and Cross said their goodbyes but it was only temporary. Verenich was going to continue his research and they would connect later on in the day. Cross walked outside the restaurant and into the lobby. Whilst he had waited for his friend to pay the bill, confirmation of his reservation for the night was made via the phone. I guess his fake ID and credit card still work, for now.

Around 7pm, Verenich called and they went over what he had managed to find that afternoon. This was all becoming absurd.

At 9:26, as he was beginning to crash, his phone buzzes. He leaned over and answered without looking to see who it is.

"Hi Daniel."

"Hello Chantelle. How are you?" he recognised the voice.

"I am fine. I went over a few things after you left LA. I think we should talk."

"Where are you? I am out of town and have a meeting in the morning."

"I am down in the lobby."

Startled, he sat up. What the hell. The fake ID and credit card, who actually provided those he wondered. Dammit, I need to teach myself some new techniques, he said to himself. Why didn't I use cash for the reservation?

"Give me ten minutes to freshen up and I will meet you in the lobby. There is a bar down the street," and he clicked the phone dead before she could answer.

7

A Beautiful Agent

Cross walked down to the lobby and saw Dunhill sitting on a chair. She stood up and walked towards him. They hugged. Her makeup was fresh and now he remembers the other 'why'. She wore tight-fitting designer jeans, an Egyptian blue Italian sweater that color-coordinated her sparkling eyes and sexy laced high-heel sandals. She carried a Louis Vuitton handbag.

"I know a small bar a block down the street. It is usually quiet at this time of night," Cross gestured towards the exit.

She placed her arm in his as they walked down J Street. Cross was comfortable with this but he didn't know her motives yet. They stepped off the sidewalk and into the purveyor of alcoholic beverages. A small table was nestled in a quiet corner so they took it. Cross ordered two Balvenie 21's, neat, from the bar and returned to the table, ensuring he picked the seat facing the front door. Reading his mind, Dunhill started the conversation.

"I had the fake ID and credit card prepared for you. I had the South African gentleman process them. Once you made the hotel reservation this morning, I booked the next flight up to SMF."

"I don't know what side you are on or if I can trust you," Cross replied. "I need to be in that position to do so if we are to divulge certain topics tonight."

"The CIA is flying someone from Langley in the early hours to see you and Mr. Verenich in the morning. They have been monitoring me for some time, along with Romanov and my ex-husband. These are dangerous people which I have already alluded to. I asked for your help for two reasons. I need it for one but the other is I need to escape from my ex-husband's grasp. He controls me and monitors everything I am doing. I have struggled even dating after the divorce."

Cross saw the hurt in her eyes. She conveyed information he had only learnt in private that morning, but suppressed his astonishment at her knowing. Her perfume was distracting him again and emanated from her personality. God, she was stunning.

"I don't know what the CIA is going to tell us. This is becoming absurd. I am not in a position to guarantee protection or results. I am a scientist," which is something he seems to keep repeating as if trying to convince himself.

She placed her hand on top of his. It was soft and warm.

"My life is also in danger. Vladimir has people watching me but I was very careful coming up here. I have learnt how to avoid them when I feel the need and they aren't that smart. I too have alternative ID's and credit cards, along with wigs and all," she said smiling.

Cross' imagination jumped a few steps and he smiled at her and winked. However, when he saw her in the hotel lobby his heart-rate quickened a little. There is no question he has an attraction to her. It is incredibly rare he has emotions towards a beautiful lady anymore. He thought those feelings had dissipated when his fiancée left. He rotated his hand so that he could hold hers. He pressed tightly.

"Cassandra died in my arms and I cannot get that image purged from memory. I have woken up a few times in deep sweat and shaking. I still feel her blood on my skin. It seems Romanov and your ex-husband may have orchestrated her slaying, but I don't know that for sure either. This web is being strung out and becoming internationally complex. I want to wait and see what the CIA has to say."

With that he lifted her hand and kissed the back of it. With their free hands, they clanked the glasses and enjoyed the acquired taste of aged Balvenie single malt whiskey.

"для вашего здоровья." To your health, he said in Russian.

He glared into her eyes. She was so beautiful but looked so angelic and scared. He wanted to help her, hold her, protect her, but how? What the hell did he know about any of this?

"I feel safe being with you," she added, her incredible voluptuous red lips breaking into a smile that melted his heart.

Dammit, she did it again, Cross thought and sighed. They talked some more, ordered a second round and enjoyed the relaxation and genuine calmness of each other's company.

They eventually left two hours later and headed back to the hotel, still holding hands.

"Where are you staying?" Cross asked.

Dunhill didn't answer. She walked towards a car parked on the side of the street and pressed a key fob Cross didn't see. The lights turned on and the sound of door locks opening punctuated the muffled Sacramento evening. She opened a rear door and grabbed a small bag. She returned, grasped his hand and continued walking into the hotel.

The elevator doors opened and she followed Cross to his hotel room. Door open, he let her proceed first and then ensured the door was locked and the safety click was latched behind them.

"I need to freshen up first," she said and headed into the bathroom.

Cross' heart was beating fast and was nervous. He hadn't dated for a few years now and was used to ladies from agencies. He could handle them.

A few minutes later Dunhill opened the bathroom door and headed towards the bed. She wore a white laced negligee that allowed

Cross to see the matching stockings, white G-string and the laced bra holding her perfect natural breasts. He couldn't believe the sight he was seeing. She lay on the bed next to him and started kissing him.

"I have been all over the world and you are the most beautiful and striking woman my visual senses have ever reacted to."

"Please don't talk."

She carefully pulled off his Italian linen pants, removed the Egyptian cotton shirt and ripped off his silk briefs. God, her hands are incredibly soft as he rolled his head back, his heart now beating even faster to help keep up with the blood-flow now being demanded.

8

CIA Come Calling

His phone jingled at 7am sharp. He was lying on his back with Chantelle's head on his chest. Their arms were wrapped around each other. The love making had gone on for hours.

He lifted her arm and carefully slid from underneath her, gently replacing his chest with a pillow. He snatched the phone. It was his friend.

"Good morning Igor. You are up bright and early."

"Good morning Daniel. Yeah, something about the CIA visiting kept me awake most of the night."

Cross had nearly forgotten all that as the events of the night sent him off into some dreamland.

"Let us have breakfast. Shall we say 8:30am at the hotel?" Verenich inquired. "I have some things to go over. David Granfield has arrived from Langley and he will meet us at the FBI's office on Freedom Way in Roseville around 10:30. I told him I had a prior meeting this morning downtown and he was fine with that."

Cross looked at his watch.

"8:30 is fine. I will have someone with me."

Oh God, thought Verenich, but kept his mouth shut. He wondered which agency he found this one.

Not waking Dunhill, he shaved before he jumped into the shower. He dried off and put on his Italian double-breasted purple suit, one of his favourites. Dunhill was beginning to show life and was stretching.

"Good morning honey. Rise and shine. We have breakfast in an hour downstairs and then a meeting at the FBI building in Roseville at 10:30."

He leaned over and kissed her forehead. The bed sheets were around her waist but he couldn't do anything about it. They didn't have time so she jumped out and leapt into the shower.

Cross and Dunhill were already seated when Verenich entered the restaurant. He looked over at Cross and the lady sitting next to him. He remembers her photo whilst doing his research. He walked over to the table. Cross stood up and they hugged.

"Good morning Daniel and Ms. Dunhill," surprising his friend. Verenich doesn't forget faces.

"You know each other?"

"No, Daniel. She is Vladimir Kuznetsov's ex-wife. She owns the insurance company. Why didn't you tell me and how can we discuss my findings with Ms. Dunhill here?" He was clearly irritated.

"Good morning Mr. Verenich. Daniel has told me all about you. Please call me Chantelle and may I be permitted to call you Igor?" She extended her hand to shake his and he nodded his approval. "I know about the meeting this morning. David Granfield called me. You are correct. I was married to Vladimir but the CIA has been monitoring him and, consequently, me for some time. His association with Mr. Romanov put us in their crosshairs. They approached me with conditions I am not permitted to discuss when we divorced.

"Daniel was provided fake ID's and a credit card in Namibia which were supplied through my contacts. I saw he used his credit card to secure the hotel reservation so I flew up from LA yesterday."

Verenich looked over and Cross saw him staring. Cross gave

him the 'I know I fucked up' look.

"Daniel was kind enough to have drinks with me last night and we discussed some details about this case and why the CIA is interested in Romanov.

"Please, sit down and let us order breakfast. I want to add to this discussion."

After calming down, Verenich opened up and went through the findings about the Taiwanese connection and the Jewish enterprise based in Tahoe.

"Did you know South Lake Tahoe used to be the drug capital of California? It was so far off the beaten track that they thought authorities wouldn't find them. Eventually they did and a sheriff, high ranking government officials and other parties were implicated including motel owners who were laundering money. It was quite the scam in its day."

Dunhill added her knowledge to all this and they were piecing together a complex network of unscrupulous individuals and their ruthless organisations. After about an hour of this and copious cups of coffee, they had established quite a record.

Verenich looked at his watch. Time was of the essence. Telling Granfield about a meeting helped him delay it but they couldn't be late for the adjusted time slot. Granfield would get pissed and that wouldn't be beneficial.

Cross and Dunhill had already checked out so they jumped into Verenich' black BMW X5 that the valet had waiting outside. Verenich navigated through Sacramento and then headed east on I80.

"Good morning madam. We are here to see Mr. Granfield from the CIA," said Verenich to the receptionist.

The FBI building was fairly recent and looked modern. Quite a big difference from the former Soviet-era grey non-descript building Cross had visited in Moscow only a few years ago. He had been invited to a government facility by a Russian chemist whilst he had been working with a client south east of Moscow. The FBI building in Roseville was light, bright and welcoming.

"Can I have your names sir?" asked the receptionist.

Verenich obliged. A few minutes later Granfield came bounding down the stairs to greet them. He was tall, late 50's, perhaps 6'2", weighed around 200 lbs and was athletic. He had short brown hair and was handsome, in a strange way. His suit was nothing special, even government-issue, but he looked smart and professional. He had energy.

"Good morning Mr. Verenich, Mr. Cross and Ms. Dunhill." He extended his hand. "Follow me but please leave your cell phones with the receptionist. Unfortunately we have rules we have to obey, particularly with what we are about to discuss."

They followed him through a metal detector, past security guards and upstairs where he led them into a conference room. A notice on the door explained pretty well their circumstances:

This is a secure location. No cell phones permitted. It has been screened for listening devices and other external obstructions and interferences.

Several other staff members sat waiting for them to arrive. Through with introductions and pleasantries, Granfield started the conference. He had a laptop attached to a large screen.

"This is the Romanov Empire."

Pictorial presentations showed vast business enterprises. He explained one after the other. Most were import companies for essential goods into Russia. Essentially he controlled large swaths of materials and resources. He explained who Kuznetsov is, without divulging Ms. Dunhill's connection. It wasn't important for this purpose. Then it got interesting as he went into the connections in Georgia and Chechnya. Those connections were part of a clandestine military group bent on destabilising the countries. Pictures of shooting victims, murders, hangings were graphic and horrific. Cross sat motionless. What the fuck, he thought. What is he doing here? Dunhill looked over at him. I am a scientist, he lipped to her, but he was losing his battle with that title. She tilted her head and shrugged her shoulders.

It was an extensive presentation, around ninety minutes long, before Granfield stopped. Clearly this had been well prepped. They had been working on this for some time and wasn't put together for the early morning flight over from Langley, Cross knew.

"Where does Mr. Mitrovic come in?" asked Cross.

"He doesn't really," answered Granfield. "He was a man with no affiliation it seems. He wanted the rare diamond for his own business needs in California. There is no evidence that supports association with Romanov's businesses. Ms. Mikhailov, his girl-friend, was the conduit that led him to it, for reasons that are not clear to us yet," he looked over at Cross, who was focused, and taking mental notes.

"She was Romanov's mistress, one of a few we gather. One is hard enough. I am not sure how he handled several," he looked over at Dunhill and then the other women in the room. The men laughed, but the women not so much. He coughed and continued, "She left with Mr. Romanov a few days ago from LAX on a private jet. Their final destination was a military field north east of Moscow."

Cross looked over at Dunhill. They knew something even the CIA didn't know. Perhaps best they kept it that way for now.

Granfield continued his presentation.

"There is a Taiwanese connection in Kaohsiung. This is Taiwan's second largest city and was one of the largest ports in Asia. It is situated south west of the island. A Mr. Wu is the head man who controls large swaths of the shipping industry over there. He and Mr. Romanov have met but then things went south. Mr. Wu wanted to get into Russia and started stepping on some toes. Not the way to do things in Russia apparently," adding his sarcastic and humorous opinion.

"We have located a Jewish enterprise in Tahoe that wants to establish their control over the new cannabis grow businesses being implemented in California. They were also after money. Understanding the Jews, they wanted to use someone else's money despite having their own. We have yet to determine if Mr. Mitrovic was beginning to stand on their projected empire. This is too new and we are still researching names and establishments."

Again, Cross locks his eyes on Dunhill. Something else they have information on the CIA doesn't. Intriguing, Cross is getting into this now. Granfield continued.

"The stolen diamond is of course at the epicentre of all this but we lack concrete evidentiary support backing that statement. It was a Namibia-mined diamond and typically people die to obtain such a rare and large specimen. I am sure some young miners who mined it don't exist anymore and their bodies buried.

"Romanov knew about it because he was in contract to purchase it from Mitrovic. At least in legal terms. Reality may be considerably different, however, as it usually is in these cases. We believe he wanted the monetary conversion on the black market to fund his cross-border destabilising excursions.

"The Taiwanese wanted it because it would have funded their desires to move into Russia without using their own resources.

"Does anyone have questions?"

A few were presented but the conference and presentation died down. Cross got up, stretched and grabbed a paper cup and poured some tea that was on a cabinet at the side of the conference table. He stuffed a chocolate cookie into his mouth. He poured a second for Dunhill whilst Venerich poured his own. He was fascinated with it all. It seemed exciting until he remembered the whistles as bullets went flying past his head.

Granfield excused the other federal employees and asked Cross, Verenich and Dunhill to remain.

"Mr. Cross, you are now being contracted to be a consultant for the CIA. In a few minutes you will be presented with several fake ID's and credit cards.

Cross tried to protest but it was futile.

"We request your cooperation. Romanov, Kuznetsov and others will have no idea who you are. You will not appear on any US federal employee data bases. If they do eventually check you out, you will show as a renowned engineer/scientist.

"We did some background checks and see you have many convenient and impressive attributes. You have a client already in Kaohsiung, a client in Rural Russia and I have information that suggests you want to open a cannabis testing laboratory in South Lake Tahoe. You gave a highly technical presentation a few years ago at a local council meeting. We had someone who was there," he winked at Cross.

"You already have an open visa into Russia. It would look fishy if we suddenly started requesting new visas for people. Taiwan requires no visa and your records will show four visits there, three since 2014. None of what I have said will set off alarms.

"We asked your friend, via his known contacts of course, people he trusted, if he knew someone who could help us. He immediately brought your name up. When things went down the way they did in Windhoek, your response was incredible and masterful. Trained FBI and CIA agents could not have handled it the way you did. It was staggering."

Cross was stunned.

"We realise and appreciate this is a shock but take that as a massive compliment and commendation. Ever wonder how you escaped South Africa? Come on, you are good, but not infallible. Ms. Dunhill did in fact obtain the necessary passport, visa and credit card but she used CIA resources. The South African gentleman was a CIA operative."

Cross sat speechless and he looked over at Dunhill.

"The death of Ms. Mikhailov was not part of any plan. However, as you do, we suspect that Romanov wanted her gone and that was a perfect place. No strings attached and no records. Someone else dying on the streets of another African city just added to a mundane statistic."

"Wait," said Cross. "You said Ms. Mikhailov left with Romanov on a flight to Moscow but now you tell us she died in Windhoek. So which is it?"

"Excellent, Mr. Cross. I wanted to see if you are taking mental notes and listening attentively. Obviously you are so well done. You passed my litmus test. We believe the lady who left with Romanov is the real Ms. Mikhailov. We don't know who the lady whom was shot is, yet."

"But Mr. Mitrovic confirmed her identity with pictures. I knew who I was meeting at LAX before departing to Namibia through Europe."

"That could well be Mr. Cross, but did he really know who she was?"

Cross didn't know who he could trust anymore. It was all surreal. He had risked his life but people knew he had. It was all planned, except for Cassandra, or whoever she was. Watching her take her last breath haunts him. That part was real. He didn't know what to say.

"Mr. Cross, you have a few days. We understand you have another city council meeting presentation next Tuesday. We suggest you keep that to avoid any unnecessary suspicion. It will also help your office staff to keep status quo. We want you to spend a few days here to go over some training. Money will be provided for clothing and necessary supplies for that period. A downtown hotel has been set up already. Take the rest of the afternoon off and be here at 9am tomorrow. How is the knee by the way? I understand you were in a serious accident and had it rebuilt several times. I cannot imagine all the surgical problems and then three years of physical therapy."

"Thank you Mr. Granfield. I keep my legs strong to keep the knee pulled together. It really helps. I have a good mental take on it which aided the recovery," Cross replied with sincerity.

Granfield handed him a package. In it were passports, documentation, driver's licenses and credit cards. He also saw a separate envelope for cash. There was a bank account too with an ATM card and a hefty balance.

"Use the cash and bank account for expenses. Soon you will be asked to visit Taiwan and Russia. We want some insider knowledge on these enterprises. Ms. Dunhill has been asked to be your liaison and organiser. The diamond isn't going anywhere fast. We have people all over the world looking for it but it is a hot ticket item now so it needs to stay off the market for a while."

Granfield asked to be excused for ten minutes and vacated the room. Cross turned to his friend.

"Why?"

"They, some federal officials I know, asked and you were the best person I know. They wanted someone with integrity and ethics, someone they could trust. You are brilliant Daniel. I didn't know anything about this until you asked me to research it two days ago. Honestly, I didn't know the CIA was involved until Granfield called me. I am a contractor for the government. They trust my judgment and need my expertise for certain applications. I have never entertained anything of this nature."

"Chantelle, what do you have to say?"

"The CIA came after me when I divorced my husband. They told me to cooperate or they would lock me up. They had enough information on my insurance company and this they held to my head.

You used a credit card for the hotel in LA and at the bar. I knew where you were and followed you. I did insure the diamond. I had to. Romanov through my ex-husband demanded it be insured. It is a legitimate policy but I didn't expect the diamond not to be perfect. The $25M payout is a real request I need to document for legitimate insurance reasons.

"I met Mr. Mitrovic. He was very nice but very naïve, as you thought he was. His girlfriend, whoever she was, wasn't there at the time but she helped facilitate the signing of the policy. All legitimate.

"I am in trouble. Mr. Kuznetsov does control my company and what I can do. I was honest about that. I asked you to help me because I need you to. I need you to accept this assignment, not that the CIA is going to give you a choice I don't think. You now know too much.

"Last night was real. I have feelings for you. I know your history and I am sorry. I have been married twice but neither husband made love to me the way you did."

Verenich' eyes lit up. He knew it, he thought. Cannot keep the bugger tied down, he mused. Like a bloody rabbit he is, and chuckled to himself, but loud enough that Cross and Dunhill heard unfortunately. Cross saw Venerich' grin and knew what he was thinking.

"Cycling at high altitude in the mountains, my friend," he said with a huge grin, "Keeps the heart pumping and blood flowing."

Dunhill slapped his arm and smiled. She kissed him on the lips. Granfield returned.

"This is my direct contact info. Use it any time of day. We will not assign anyone to guard you but as this gets going, I may make adjustments to that decision. I am of course presuming you are agreeing to help us," and passed him a piece of paper. "This is the amount of money we are contracting to pay you. The first installment of four will be transferred into your account tomorrow. I will have a document for you to sign tomorrow also. Igor has his own contract."

Cross' eyes lit up. Holy shit.

"Of course expenses will be in addition. Just call me or text/email the details but you have an account for those already."

"Now, I will fill you in as needed and when needed. For now, check into the hotel you have been given a reservation at, go buy some clothes and toiletries, and we will see you tomorrow at 9am."

With that, Granfield shook hands and departed. A young lady who had followed him in told them to follow her. She led them out to the front entrance.

Cross gasped when he was finally outside.

"What the hell just happened in there?"

"I have things to do Daniel. Let me drive you back to the city so you can find your car. I don't know what you are doing Chantelle. We can meet up later for dinner if you wish, but I need to continue with my research. This is getting crazier and crazier. I believe they put you in the Holiday Inn adjacent to I5 downtown."

"I will stay with Daniel but I need to take back the rental car. There will be a location downtown somewhere."

With that, they hopped into the X5 and headed back to Sacramento.

9

Asian Docklands

Cross and Dunhill checked into the Holiday Inn on J Street and then called the office. He confirmed with Brandy that he would be there Monday and would do the presentation at the city council meeting the following morning. He needed to stay calm for fear of alerting her. He couldn't drag the company into this. They then ventured across the street to Macys and purchased some clothing and other essentials for a few days. The hotel had toothpaste and toothbrush.

Verenich met them both at Yard House across from the Holiday Inn around 7pm.

"What have you found Igor?"

"I did some research on Mr. Wu. He is a big player in Kaohsiung and operates a huge shipping business. During the height of the tech boom, Kaohsiung was the largest port in Asia and he had most of the control."

"I have a client there," Cross added. "I have been there four times. The first time was 2004 by invitation from a client who later worked for me. The second day I was there we were heading south from Hsinchu City on Highway 1. I was sleeping from jet lag in the passenger front seat and I was still in physical recovery from my accident. Suddenly my body jerks forward and I wake up. Within seconds we got rear-ended by a truck. My client swears in English, he is a funny man, and then we see the truck immediately exit the highway. We start chasing him through the streets of Taichung City. The truck driver eventually stops, the cops come and I am standing in the middle of the street wondering what the hell is going on. Eventually the cops leave and my client gets into the car and follows the truck driver back to his residence. He hands him some cash to pay for the damage. So, that is how car insurance claims are handled over there. It was hilarious," he said laughing. "I have another client there who treats me like a brother. It is incredible."

"That is a funny story," Verenich replied. "This may be your first CIA reconnaissance mission but I am only speculating. Mr. Wu wants into Russia and to control some strategic alliances which conflicts with what Mr. Romanov has in mind. Taiwan transports a lot of electronics around the world and they want to expand into Russia. He is also ruthless."

"I agreed to only test a diamond. What the fuck? However, I admit I am finding this fascinating."

"You will until the next bullet is aimed at you and not the person next to you," Dunhill said in a tone that expressed sincere concern.

Cross took her hand and squeezed without looking at her. He was engrossed in what Verenich was revealing.

"Mr. Romanov wants to disturb the oil and gas distribution out of Russia. Billions of dollars evidently weren't enough for him. A lot of Russians didn't like the breakup of Soviet Russia into 15 independent Republics, or States. He was allegedly involved in both Georgia and Chechnya unrests. CIA and FBI are concerned he was involved in the Boston Marathon bombing and part of any assignment to Russia might be to prove that." He looked at Dunhill and proceeded, "Your ex-husband may have also played a part in that. It is something the Feds are looking into.

"I want to ask you a personal question Chantelle," and she nodded her approval. "He is married in Russia. You knew this right?"

"I didn't at the time but later found out. Apparently this seems normal behaviour for rich Russians. He controlled my life, and to some extent still does. He wanted children but I made sure I couldn't have any with him. Divorce was inevitable but he allowed me to still make a good living. He isn't all bad and gave me several million dollars as part of the divorce settlement. I was doing high end real estate transactions in Miami Beach when we met. He was looking for an ocean view apartment and eventually bought one. I now own that. It was evident Romanov is in charge of their organisations and pulls all the strings."

This is good to know, thought Cross.

"Well, Chantelle and Daniel, I am done for the day. It has been quite eventful and entertaining to say the least. Let us catch up tomorrow after you spend your first day being trained. I am not sure you can be at your age," he looked at his friend and burst out laughing. "Some have tried and failed," still laughing.

"Some even walked away," Cross laughed too, with a reference about his ex-fiancée. "Perhaps she knew something."

"I read about that in your CIA dossier, Daniel," Chantelle now joining the topic. "What happened?"

"I have 'Crazy Lover' indelibly stamped on my forehead. I attract them, present company excluded of course," now he had tears from laughing.

"That goes without saying," now laughing with him.

"Good night boys and girls. Enjoy your evening and we will chat tomorrow."

Verenich hugged and then left.

"By the way, are you involved in this training also Chantelle?"

"No, but I will go with you, at least for the first day. I must head home this weekend. We can spend a few days together," she said with a contagious smile. "I can do some work from the FBI office."

With that, they left the bar, walked across the street into the hotel and headed upstairs to their room.

10

CIA Operative Training, Roseville, California

Three days in the FBI office wasn't really training. Cross was being educated and versed on the people involved. He needed to see their profiles and photos to get an idea of who they are. They went over the organisations and what they did, where they were located, key personnel. It was intense and Cross' head was hurting. This was all aided by a constant pot of fresh coffee and some Advil.

Lunch was sandwiches brought in from an outside source. They kept on working through the artificial lunch hour. He helped himself to the energy version of Glaceau Vitamin Water. He hoped it had energy.

The afternoon was spent watching more presentations to the point it was affecting his mind and needed a break. He walked outside with Dunhill and they stretched their legs.

"Wow, you were married into this? What were you thinking?"

"He was a handsome and charming man. He knew how to treat me right, something I hadn't experienced before. He dressed impeccably and he was different. You know, men with those accents, good looks and charm!"

"No idea what you are talking about," he said smiling. "I was married twenty years to a beautiful Asian. I could just never satisfy her enough financially. She always wanted more and more. We met in Hong Kong on one of my excursions to meet a client there. Interestingly, the client we met was English and took me to the Hong Kong Rugby Club. I played rugby in England to a high level. I was fast, kind of still am if the knee doesn't collapse that is. I hope I don't get chased on one of these assignments," he said chuckling to himself, but really he was being serious.

She held his hand as they walked around the building.

"Your history is fascinating, Daniel. Igor was right. You were a perfect choice for this. The way your mind thinks is interesting. It isn't normal. People don't think this way."

"Thinking this way gets me into trouble," he calmly added, being truthful, with a wry smile.

"I read that about you too."

"I was married twenty years but faithful only for the first ten," Cross added and continued. "She chased the attention of everybody. I grew tired of it so stopped giving a damn after a while. She wanted a child immediately. I said no so we waited. After four years we had one and that was all she wanted. I protested and we had two more. I came from a big family so wanted one too. Asians don't age and she is still beautiful. She filed soon after my left knee was irreparably trashed. I went through hell and wasn't prepared for divorce papers. I had damaged it playing sports in England but the car blind-sided me one night in Tahoe. She was young and drunk. A female, unfortunately, which just compounded my fear of women. I never saw her until the driver's door crumpled and I knew I was in trouble. I kind of looked at the knee and muttered something about it not supposed to bend that way. The rest is history as they say."

He let go of her hand and walked off to the side. He had tears.

"I am sorry. I don't usually do this in front of people. I have three very close male friends I can talk openly about most things. Certain topics set me off. I have no control. The surgical onslaught changed the body chemistry."

She followed him and then took both hands as she stood in front of him.

"Please don't apologize. You are an incredible man. I haven't known you long but I feel like I have, having read about you. Fuck your ex-wife. It is her loss. Thank you for trusting me to open up. Not many men can openly shed tears and still remain strong. They feel it is a weakness of some sort when in fact it breeds strength and humility. There is nothing wrong with those traits."

"I saw what people do. Some crack under pressure and stress of it all. Someone close to me committed suicide. All she had to do was call me. I would have flown anywhere to save her life."

He was composing himself again. It was true, some subjects set Cross off. Some topics he couldn't openly talk about without emotion so tried to avoid them.

"We should head back to the conference room. I have a few more hours to digest as much as I can. Thank you for listening to me."

Dunhill felt honoured for what he was telling her, perhaps because he didn't know her. Making love all night doesn't make someone know that person. He was a gentleman for sure. His presence, his aura and the way he dressed. She saw how women looked at him. He knew it too but he had this underlying insecurity thing which was very sexy.

The following day Cross dropped Dunhill off at Mather Airport in Rancho Cordova. Granfield had kindly requested the CIA's Gulfstream take her back to LA. They kissed before he watched her climb up the stairs onto the plane. His heart was heavy but he needed to focus. Namibia and escaping Africa will be nothing, he suspected, compared to what he is about to face.

The third day of training he was given his final lessons. Some of those were how to survive and don't get caught. Obviously, he mused. He had been provided with some useful tools, a secure satellite mobile phone being one.

"Will this one work in the US?" he had asked but they didn't find that one amusing for some reason.

A special pen with cable, night goggles, a small handheld with holster and strap with ammo, a silencer, an electronic scanner were all provided as part of his kit. Fuck, he had never carried a gun in his life. He was assured he could get through airport security even carrying the weapon. It was identifiable as Special Production but it was made of advanced material no one outside of some departments of the federal government knew about. Black rim glasses without eye correction, a special wallet and business card holder added to the extensive list of items he was given.

The final exercise at the FBI office was a physical. Perhaps this should have been the first thing, Cross thought. He had physical limitations although incredibly fit.

He was sent to an examination room and waited. A few minutes later a young attractive nurse walks in. She wore a blue nurse's dress, slightly below the knees and a white lab coat which was unbuttoned.

"Hello Mr. Cross, I am Monique. I am here to examine you," she said smiling. "You look fine to me so why are you here?"

"Please, call me Daniel. I have no idea. They may have read my history but I am physically fit. It is the mind that is screwed up and presume you are not testing that today?" he laughed.

"No, fortuitously. The mind isn't on the list," laughing along with him.

He liked her already and there was a palpable relaxing calmness in the room.

"Can you remove your sweater, undershirt and pants please?"

"Just like that? No dinner date and a movie?" he joked.

Monique smiled and took his blood pressure, heart rate and temperature before proceeding to look at his scars. His body was littered with them. She had a file in one hand and asked questions as she visually scanned various parts of his anatomy.

"I need to take some blood samples also."

"I can assure you it was red last time I checked."

"Haha. Left or right handed?"

"Left."

She tied on a rubber band around his right arm to enhance the vanes, then inserted a needle and drew blood into three vials.

"Leave some for me," he joked.

Monique's smile was infectious and Cross was captivated. Moving to his left side, with her back to him, she took a look at his knee.

"I read your file. Incredible what you went through, Mr. Cross. Interesting scars you have. They can design a railway with these."

Damn she was funny.

"It is a part of my life I will never recover from, Monique."

She loved his gentleness but the body of a man in his fifties was amazing, Monique thought. Men she dates half his age don't look like that and was in awe. His masculinity was transmitting tingles through her entire body.

She lifted his left leg and bent it. It was physically impossible to bend it further than about 110 degrees.

"You have physical limitations, Daniel. This may affect my report. You are going to be on assignments for the CIA."

Cross felt Monique liked him. He took a risk and moved his left hand onto her bare right leg as she stood next to him holding his. She didn't move and was frozen in time.

"I cannot have a negative report, Monique. This assignment might be critical for the human race," exaggerating a little but his voice was soft and provocative.

He squeezed her right calf and she didn't move. She couldn't, being mentally glued to the floor. He felt her shaking a little and moved his hand further up her leg. He was now above the knee and was squeezing the soft inner thigh as his hand moved higher. Cross started to hear light moans as the sensuality of the moment began to take over.

"Please help me," he gently asked.

His hand reached her panties and she was moist already. By now her shaking was magnified and her moans grew more intense. He massaged her softly and knew Monique was about to orgasm. When she did there was a gasp, her legs trembling in the process.

"Oh God. Oh my God," dropping his leg on the table.

"As you can see, I am physically fit and have no limitations."

Monique was spent and had to sit on the examination table. She was breathing hard and convulsing.

"Mr. Cross, I cannot believe what I allowed you to do," without looking at him. "I will see to it your file and records are in suitable order."

She got up, retrieved his file and left the room.

Tuesday morning came around and he went into his office to pick up the memory stick with presentations for the council meeting. He then headed over to the Tahoe airport where the local government offices presided.

"Good morning Mr. Cross. How are you?" asked the city mayor.

"I am fine Mr. Mayor. How about you?"

"We are looking forward to hearing your presentation. Proposition 64 has presented a lot of opportunity for our local community."

"I have been addicted to opioids, Mr. Mayor. I know one of your council member's son overdosed on drugs. There has to be a viable alternative to this madness that is killing our society, in particular the youth."

Statistics Cross uses in his talks include America occupies 4% of the world's population and yet it consumes 70% of the pharmaceutical drugs and 90% of the opioids. It is the only country Cross knows of that advertises drugs on TV. He finds it hilarious actually, in a sadistic way, because during any 30 second ad, they spend about 10 seconds talking about the drug and 20 seconds explaining the side-effects that could kill you. Fascinating country is America.

He walks into the room and surveys its occupants. He is familiar with most locals but there is a group of four people he hasn't seen before. All attendees have to wear name tags written on a sticky piece of paper. Cross has his embossed onto a plastic plate pinned to his suit lapel under the name Emerald Laboratories, Inc. He walks past the group and takes a cursory glance at their names. They are all Jewish. As he prepares to sit down, he sees his office landlord enter the civic room and head over to greet the four men. His landlord was Jewish also and a known asshole. Cross turns his head to face the front platform. It was a typical council room with a curved front bench behind which were sitting the prominent council members, the city's manager and legal councilor, the fire and police chiefs, the city clerk. He knew them all.

It was Cross' turn to give his presentation. He was being allowed more time because the city viewed the technical aspect of what he was discussing to be highly interesting and important. He plugged in the memory stick and rolled through it with some confidence. He knew the material and didn't need a cheat-sheet. He could do public talks ad-lib with some guidance from Power-Point slides. His back was to the audience because he was essentially talking to the council members. There were cameras on him and it was broadcast on various TV monitors throughout the venue. He threw in a few comedic references for levity which aided his presentation.

Once finished he returned to his seat. He observed the four men with the landlord and they had taken notes and were in deep discussion between themselves. Cross wondered about what. He remembers the discussions at the FBI building about a new Jewish entity that was entering the fray. He wondered and stepped outside the room before dialing Verenich' number. He doesn't believe in coincidences.

"Igor, good morning. I have names for you," and proceeded to pass them on, with emphasis on his landlord. "Can you do some research on these guys please?"

"Why?"

"I will explain later. I don't want to bias your search. Just call me with what you find out please."

"Ok."

With that, the line went dead. He called Dunhill. He hadn't spoken to her for a few days.

"Good morning honey, how are you?"

"I am feeling good now that you called me. How did the presentation go?"

"It went very well and was well received too. The building landlord is here with four other Jewish men whom I had not seen before. They evidently were making notes as I talked. I have asked Igor to research their names and get back to me. I walked past them as I went to my seat and took a mental note. Two had the same last name so perhaps may be related. I will call you later when I have that information and before I reach out to Granfield. I want to keep some of this private before going to the CIA."

"Good idea. Call me later honey."

"Wait, are you ok?"

"Yes. Romanov is trying to get me to finish my research and pay the insurance premium."

"Doesn't that premium get paid to Robert?"

"Technically, in the real world. We are not dealing with the real world honey, nor real world people."

She had a point. They said goodbye and will catch up later.

Cross drove over to his office and went upstairs. Brandy was waiting for him. She was so happy to see him and gave him a hug. She was different. Mid 20's, born and raised in California and hadn't been anywhere. She had married her high school sweetheart which Cross had always thought can never work. Never experiencing anyone else seems like something missed. He had been traveling on his own for work since age 22 but traveling the world with family years before then. Brandy was 5'9", long brown hair, brown eyes, around 110 lbs but he never liked guessing women's weight or age. She loved the scientific world and wanted to be part of the new cannabis laboratory.

"So nice to see you, boss," she always called him boss. He didn't much care for it but it is the way she is so didn't push it.

"Anything new going on, Brandy?"

"The landlord has been around here. He didn't come to see us but he has been around. The other tenants think he is a prick also," she said giggling, using the British vernacular for asshole.

"Well, he is," he said smiling. "Ok, he was at the city council meeting this morning too. He met four other Jewish men there. Please be careful. We should lock the front door and install a bell for visitors to ring. Can you take care of that please? Call Steve and he will take care of it for you. How is the lab doing downstairs?"

"We have two big analytical projects coming in. Two of our three engineers have been on site working. I emailed a list of things you need to take care of. Some clients have questions."

"I am being asked to do some work for the federal government. I am not at liberty to say what but it is important. It will likely include overseas assignments. I will let you know when these materialise, if they even do," purposely trying to sound vague.

"Ok, boss. I hope everything is ok."

"Yes, Brandy, thank you."

"I will be back in tomorrow."

Cross left the office and headed to Bert's, a local family restaurant with home-style cooking and friendly waitresses. He was in desperate need of coffee and a bacon sandwich.

Around 11:30 his phone buzzed.

"Igor, how is life treating you?"

"Like a baby treats a diaper," he responded. "I think you should come down to Sacramento again. We can go through what I am looking at with my laptop on hand. Mr. Horowitz is the name of your landlord. His lineage dates back some years. His family is Czechoslovakian and lived there when it was occupied by the Germans during World War II and then when it became a communist country until the Velvet Revolution in 1989. His family had ties, has ties, to the communists, those who survived the death camps that is, and knew people high up. He is connected and is a dangerous man. Mr. Horowitz is American and was born in the LA area but people with that background tend to think the world owes them something.

"You seem to be lining them up in bucket loads. What did you do in a previous life, Daniel? There are three crime warlords in the mix. Take your pick. I think you will need surgery," he hesitated before the punchline, "To have eyes installed in the back of your head," he was laughing now.

"Damn, you should be on stage, sweeping it," joining in the banter. "You recommended me. I wish I hadn't said anything about the veracity of the diamond now. So which one do we go after first?"

"The four individuals at the council meeting are likely part of his crime syndicate. I wanted to talk to you first before I got into their backgrounds."

With that, Dunhill was calling.

"Igor, I need to answer this. It is Chantelle. Let me put you on hold mate"

"Yes, Chantelle, missed me already?"

"Daniel, you need to get on the next flight to LA. No one has heard from Robert and I need you with me. I don't want to call authorities yet," she sounded scared.

"Hold on."

"Igor, I need to get the next flight to LA. Robert is missing and presumed dead at this point. I will call as I am heading south."

"Ok mate."

"Chantelle, are you still there?"

"Yes, Daniel. Please let me know flight details asap. I sense something is wrong. I will meet you at the airport."

Dunhill waited outside the LAX terminal for the Alaskan Airlines arrival. Her flight app told her it had landed.

"I am outside the terminal at arrivals, Daniel." as she answered the call.

"There in ten minutes."

He flung open the passenger side door of her orange and black Porsche 911 GT3 and climbed in. Jesus, a woman of impeccable taste. She looked scared.

"This is a good low-profile automobile for investigative work," he said sarcastically. "Nearly as good as my yellow Range Rover was," he chuckled.

"My other two cars are in the shop. I had no choice."

She sped along W. Century Boulevard racing through the manual gears to the 405 and headed north. They pulled up next door to Mitrovic's residence. His black limited edition Range Rover Sport Supercharged was parked on the driveway. It all seemed very quiet. Crossed reached for his small caliber handgun and climbed out of the GT3. He looked around scouring the neighborhood and vantage points where watchers could be. No cars were in the immediate vicinity, parked or otherwise. He asked Dunhill to wait and headed towards the front door. He tried the handle. It wasn't locked. Ok, now his heart rate was skyrocketing. CIA didn't teach him this shit. He clicked the huge door handle down and he felt the heavy door extract itself from the tight fitting seals and it slowly fell open.

He pushed the door more, keeping his head down as he peeped inside. There was a radio playing but low volume. He looked around and inched forwards into the home. Now he could see some broken sculptures on the floor, ones he had marveled a week or so before. A chair was lying broken. Moving further inside the home, he took cursory glances everywhere with his eyes darting all over the place. Now there was a pungent smell he wasn't familiar with. What the hell is that? As he creeped further into the home, down the short hallway, he was now approaching the kitchen area. Then he saw what the smell was. Mitrovic was dead on the kitchen floor. He had blood on his hands but what killed him was an unmistakable single shot to the heart. The blood was dry and he had been dead for perhaps a few days. No wonder Cross didn't recognise the smell. He hadn't been around someone who had been dead a while.

Feeling safe, since the killer wasn't going to hang around waiting all week, he got up and went over to Mitrovic. Poor guy. He had no idea what he was up against, Cross speculated. He moved outside and motioned Dunhill to come. It was safe now.

"Robert is dead. A single shot to the heart, the same method used on Ms. Mikhailov, or whoever she was."

Dunhill was shaking. Cross tried to console her.

"Are you ok?"

"I am scared now. This is getting too close to home. I know Vladimir was into some unethical things, shall I say, but rule of thumb is not to bring them home."

Cross dialed from his secure phone the CIA had given him.

"David, this is Daniel. I am down in Santa Monica. Mr. Mitrovic is dead and has been I am speculating, because I am no expert, for at least a day. A single shot to the heart but there was a struggle. Some artwork and a chair were broken and his hands have blood on them. Perhaps his own blood or the shooters," he added, trying to play cop. "It could have been staged also."

"Great observations. Is the area secure?"

"I believe so. No cars around. It is extremely quiet."

"I will take care of it and make the calls. Don't involve the local authorities. I will handle it from here. Close the front door and avoid tainting the scene," Granfield said matter-of-factly.

"Ok."

"Take Ms. Dunhill with you and head back to Tahoe. I fear for her safety. I will contact you later. I need to get some plans together for what I want you to do. We need to speed this up."

Before the conversation ended, Cross filled him in on the events of the morning and the people he saw at the council meeting. Granfield took notes and thanked him for being diligent.

Click, signaled the abrupt end of the call, and now the next one.

"Robert was shot a day or so ago Igor. He is dead."

"You need to get out of there now. This is becoming really serious, if it wasn't before. You don't know who you are dealing with anymore. These people don't give a damn about people's lives, including yours."

Click, another call ended, and turning to Dunhill.

"We need to get out of here."

He walked back inside and came out a few minutes later with the keys to Mitrovic' Range Rover Sport.

"People might be watching the airports. No one will suspect Robert's car being driven. He is dead. We can be back in Tahoe in seven hours in this thing.

She didn't question him.

"I live not far from here. I can leave the GT3 in my garage, hidden, and get some things for the trip north."

"I will follow you."

11

Red Herring

Brandy called as they drove north.

"I heard the council approved a cannabis testing laboratory license for Emerald Labs. That is fantastic news. Well done, boss."

"That is great news, thank you for letting me know. Text if you see the prick again."

"Be more specific, there a lot of them around here," she said laughing.

Cross couldn't curtail her jokes and laughter. He had to behave normal, at least normal for how she perceives his behaviour.

"That is bloody funny, Brandy. You get what I am saying now?"

"Yes, boss."

Click. He chuckled.

"My office manager is funny."

They shared the driving and made it home before midnight. A taxi had driven Cross to Reno Airport for the flight to LAX which was fortunate. He must have sensed something was wrong.

He was exhausted. They parked the Range Rover Sport in the one space left in his big four-car garage and made their way indoors.

"The bedroom is upstairs honey, if you want to freshen up. I know I do but want a drink first."

She disappeared upstairs whilst Cross headed to the custom-made bar in the lounge. He poured Glenfiddich 21 into two triangular Glenfiddich tumblers. This particular bottle was purchased from a bar in Taiwan. A beautiful Asian friend was a saleslady for Balvenie and she worked in the bar that evening. He felt obliged to buy the best bottle they had and she signed it for him. He reached around the bar and found the container of exotic mixed nuts and some crackers. The Russian caviar he found in the small bar fridge.

Dunhill came down after a quick shower and joined him on the large leather sofa. She had slipped into a night shirt and matching pink shorts with slippers. Damn, she was stunning. She picked up her drink on the coffee table.

"What a spectacular bedroom suite."

"Very few women are invited up there. It is my sanctuary. My escape from a world not so long ago was closing in around me. This home was rebuilt after the forest fire in 2007. I designed it to meet certain criteria."

She knew that already. It was a bad year for Cross.

They went over the events of the afternoon and both felt awful for Mitrovic.

"Was he really naïve or did he know something we don't know yet?" Cross broke the few minutes of silence.

Dunhill lifted her head from his shoulder to face him.

"Serbians are smart. He didn't strike me as stupid. He knew what he was doing with the contract. He knew the legal language and made changes where he deemed necessary. My guess he made contact with someone who didn't want him to have the diamond, one, or who didn't want him getting into the Cannabis grow business, two, or he found out something we aren't aware of, three. I don't believe in coincidences."

"No, me neither. It does happen in my engineering work but it is incredibly rare. Someone wanted him to keep quiet, which of course is what he will do now. I believe I saw a photo of him and a son from a previous relationship in his home. That is the real travesty."

"What now?"

"We drink our whiskey, perhaps a few more," he adds smiling, "And then call Granfield in the morning. I will be heading to Taiwan and Russia for sure. And who knows where else those excursions will take me. I need more information on Mr. Horowitz here in Tahoe. I sense something is going on with him too. Now I have the cannabis testing license, he will be upset."

"Oh, Daniel, be careful won't you, please? I worry about you. You are such a special, rare gentleman," reaching over and kissing him, "And so handsome too."

He was beginning to love the attention. Familiar with only cold, oddly narcissistic relationships, he needed to learn and adjust to Dunhill's newfound affection and intimacy. He loved holding hands, cuddling, kissing and her affection and intimacy were scintillating. It wasn't the love making per se, but the need for affirmation brought on by neglect and psychological abuse administered by the previous women in his life. It is possibly the reason why he signed the contract with Granfield last week. He wanted to feel worthy, to feel needed, to be on the edge, to be gratified.

"Thank you Chantelle. I have never met a lady like you before. I went for external beauty without even looking at what is inside. Without heart and soul, a body is just lifeless and has eyes like sharks. One stares at them and there is nothing there, just a deep black oasis of emptiness."

12

Medicinal Cannabis

The clock visually announced 7:05am the following morning when his secure mobile buzzed in the kitchen.

"Good Morning David."

"Good morning Daniel. Have you had your coffee this morning?"

"Yes. I made some fresh Kopi Luwak coffee, just as I like it. Chantelle is still asleep."

"I am working on some things here but we are looking at sending you to Kaohsiung tomorrow. I will confirm in an hour. There are things coming up on our radar that suggests something is happening. I will explain later."

Click.

Cross poured some more coffee and headed upstairs with some donuts. He had ventured out early to buy fresh-baked from a local bakery. Dunhill was stirring and he gently kissed her on the lips.

"Good morning beautiful."

"What time is it? It feels early. Come back to bed," as she reached for him

"Granfield called already. They are sending me to Taiwan, possibly tomorrow. There is something going on. I did a little research myself this morning and I have been watching overseas news.

People appear to be dying over there. I don't know how this relates but the shipping port and Mr. Wu were mentioned. Granfield will call back in an hour."

Now she sat upright.

"That is interesting. Robert mentioned once about a possible viral outbreak. I didn't know what he was talking about. He was referencing the need for cannabis research and specifically discussed the medicinal aspects."

"Oh, I am fully aware of the medicinal aspects. The pharmaceutical industry has been pushing to ban cannabis for obvious reasons. They didn't want Prop 64 to pass and lobbied heavily against it. I researched it four years ago when a friend came to my office and told me I need to get into testing. I didn't understand him so I did my research. He was right. Many articles and conferences later, I know enough to appreciate that this is opening up a whole new world."

"I wonder if Robert wanted to get into cannabis grow for that very reason."

"It would make sense, as would any person wishing to get into that field. It is speculated to grow exponentially and be a thirty to forty billion dollar industry in five years. The analytical testing field alone is expected to top one billion. People kill for a dollar on the streets. What would people succumb to, what level would the dredges of society drop to for billions of dollars? The mind boggles."

Dunhill sipped her coffee and he looked at her.

"The best coffee in the world ma'am," he smiled.

Granfield called and laid it out. 6am flight from Reno through San Francisco and Hong Kong on United and then Dragonair to Kaohsiung, all First Class, arriving around 11pm the following evening. Someone would meet him at the airport. He has reservations at Lees Hotel, which Cross is familiar with, and will be traveling as himself. His profile meant they didn't need any clandestine operations that would raise flags. He has already been there and his passport will adequately support a normal business trip. He will have meetings under the auspices of general analytical work with people speculated to be part of Wu's enterprises.

13

GreenSea Enterprises, Taiwan

With only a carry-on, Cross moved quickly through Kaohsiung Airport. Immigration is easy. The officer looks at the passport, scans it into the computer and hands it back to him. He is waved on. He walks through the baggage claim area, through Customs and out into the main airport lobby.

He isn't sure who is greeting him until a gorgeous young Asian lady approached him.

"Hello Mr. Cross," extending her arm to greet him, "My name is Ms. Huang but please call me Lin. I am here to be your chaperone for the short visit."

Her voice was soft and her spoken English very presentable.

"Please call me Daniel," and accepted the invitation to shake hands.

"Please follow me. How was your long trip?"

"Very pleasant. I managed to sleep so feel pretty fresh."

"I will take you to your hotel and then perhaps we can share a beer at the bar next door."

Her white Audi R8 was illegally parked outside the terminal

building but no one seemed to care because a special Diplomat's Pass was on the dashboard. They stepped inside and he placed his bag on the floor.

"I have driven one of these. A friend told me to buy a V8 manual but what is the point when they make a V10 version?" he chuckled. "I do love the transmission along with the metallic clicks as one is shifting gears."

"This is my boss' car. He lets me drive it once in a while, if I am nice to him. He too works for the American Consulate based here in Kaohsiung." She smiled.

What is it with these low-profile inconspicuous automobiles, he asked himself, grinning. He was somewhat familiar with the city. She took the main boulevard from the airport and then navigated through some side streets before she pulled up to the entrance of Lees Hotel. She parked in front and they entered the grand lobby adorned in marble and hand-carved Chinese rosewood furnishings with a large chandelier hanging in the centre.

"I will wait in the lobby for you to freshen up."

He walked up to reception and recognised two ladies there.

"晚上好，女士们." Good evening ladies.

He knew a little Mandarin, enough to get him into trouble but likely not enough to escape it.

"Hello Mr. Cross. Good to see you again. Your room is ready," and handed him the key.

"谢谢," thank you.

He moved over to the elevators and took one to the 14th floor. He stepped off and walked along the corridor to the room. Off to his right were glass windows which looked down onto the lobby area. Lees Hotel was five-star and being here gave Cross some level of comfort and control which Granfield knew.

He turned the key in the lock and walked into the living room area, placing his bag on a chair. The marble bathroom was off to the right and he took ten minutes to freshen himself after the long flights. He put on his favourite Chanel cologne. Now using the secure mobile exclusively, he messaged Dunhill and Granfield to let them know he had arrived safe.

Back downstairs Ms. Huang was sitting in the lobby waiting for him. She was around 5'4" and very slender. Red lipstick gave way to a beautiful, natural face and soft skin. She wore a short red dress with an open black coat over it. He would guess her age at mid-30's, but he could be off by years.

Without saying a word, they exited and walked across the side street next to the hotel and entered the bar. The outside winter night air was warm for Cross but not for Ms. Huang. The bar was quiet this time of night but a few patrons persisted. This establishment is known for live music upstairs but that stopped over an hour ago. Bars tend to stay open until the last person leaves. The bar was U-shaped and he took a table away from ear-shot. Cross ordered two Taiwan Beers before taking his seat. He handed one to Ms. Huang. She removed her coat and thanked him for the beer. He shuffled closer.

"Nice to meet you Daniel. I have heard a lot about you."

"Don't believe everything you hear, Lin," he smiled at her. She was sweet, and lovely. "People like to make stuff up."

"I am sure they do," and smiled at him. "The hotel has a breakfast buffet as you know so I will pick you up after that, say 10am?"

Cross nodded.

"We will head over to the huge port area of Kaohsiung. Mr. Wu has operations over there. You will meet with his right-hand man, Mr. Tsai. They are investing into a new product line and are very interested in hearing about the analytical needs. They want you to supply the scientific instrumentation and expertise. Be assured they will be vague about what it is they are doing. You are on a trip to garner information you can compile to help them. We have set this up for you. Don't get too deep with questions. They are serious people. By that I mean dangerous," her English was excellent if not for a few words she cannot pronounce properly.

"Ok. Do you have any idea what it is they are doing?"

"Some agricultural product we feel but not 100% sure."

Cross emptied the bottle of beer and nodded to the bar tender for two more. It was light, refreshing with low alcoholic content.

"What do you know about a group of people in a rural town dying from some ailment?"

"We are looking into this. It could be a localised virus and don't suspect anything yet. People are paranoid generally after the last big outbreak a few years ago. Mr. Wu does have a research facility but we haven't connected the two yet."

"What would be his interest in a Namibia diamond?"

"He and Mr. Romanov met last year in Moscow. Mr. Wu wants to expand into Russia by supplying essential materials using his transportation network. As you know, Mr. Romanov controls that through Russia's ports-of-entry. We understand the meeting didn't go too well partly because Mr. Wu didn't want to use a middle-man. We don't have a direct connection with the diamond but the monetary value lends itself to be an item of interest. Mr. Wu doesn't like using his own money and has been looking into funding for his new venture. He prefers cash."

"It will be interesting to see his operation tomorrow."

"You must be tired, Daniel. Let us finish our beers so you can go to sleep. You need to be alert for the meetings." She smiled.

They left the bar. Cross headed to his room and Huang took the Audi key from the doorman and took off. Cross filled Granfield in on what he had learnt and then called Dunhill. She was happy to hear his voice.

The morning came too early and his body clock was way off. He sometimes had a hard time adjusting after long flights. He took a shower and then put on a light blue Italian suit. On the second floor was probably the best breakfast buffet he has ever experienced. The food was exceptional and always fresh and plentiful. He pressed the cappuccino button on the coffee maker and watched it drip into the cup. He walked over and sat quietly in the small bar area off the main dining room. CNN International was on the TV monitor. I hate politics, he told himself, but wishing to operate a cannabis testing lab meant he was thrust into it whether he wanted to or not.

9:50am rolled around so he walked down the stairs into the hotel lobby. Huang was already waiting for him. This time she was dressed professionally in a white blouse, black skirt still above the knees, pantyhose and a yellow silk jacket. She wore little makeup except lipstick. She looked lovely.

"Good morning, Mr. Cross. Are you ready?"

"As I will ever be."

He was happy to see the R8 again and they climbed in and headed into the chaotic streets. Motorised scooters are everywhere in Taiwan and Kaohsiung is no exception. The owners have their own rules and are hilarious to watch. Accidents occur on a daily basis and it is common to see an ambulance next to a damaged scooter lying on its' side. He never finds out the disposition of the victims. The way they handle those things with little regards to traffic laws, he suspects they must actively contribute to the fatality statistics on a daily basis.

Huang headed to an area Cross knew. He had been to the docks on previous visits. The R8 purred through the streets, the manual gears ratcheting through the now-famous gates but vast traffic prohibited any advanced driving, except to avoid the said scooters.

Cross could see huge sea-going vessels and the truck traffic increased as they approached the dock areas. This was a madhouse. Taiwan was famous for its seafood being an island so large areas of the docks housed huge fishing fleets. As they approached, Cross could see how dilapidated some of them were. The perpetual erosion of steel from the chemical reaction with salt water caused vast decay.

Huang navigated around the docks and finally came up to a gate that looked new. A posted sign displayed 'GreenSea Enterprises' with Mandarin graphics underneath. An armed sentry stood by a guardhouse purposely erected. As they approached, he came forwards.

Huang put her window down and spoke in Mandarin to the guard. She requested Cross' passport and he removed it from his jacket pocket and obliged. The guard walked away and into the hut. Cross could see he had picked up a phone and was talking into the mouth piece. A minute or two later, he came out and spoke to Huang. He handed her two visitor passes along with their ID's and pointed to where they need to go. On the right were the docks. Two large container ships where docked and it was a hive of activity. People were everywhere.

She continued driving until eventually approaching a brand new warehouse. They exited the car and walked through a door that said 'Reception Area'. A receptionist greeted them and then she had them sign a register.

They sat and waited for five minutes before a big Chinese man came through the door off to the right.

"He asked that we follow him," as Huang stood.

He led them through a corridor with doors and offices on both sides. Eventually they reached a conference room and the big man gestured for them to enter. The large window brought in an abundance of natural light. An array of modern electronic gadgets were displayed on the table including a projector, conference phones, internet lines and USB ports. The projector screen was scrolled up mounted on the ceiling. In front of that was another big projector. At the far end of the table was a large lazy-Susan used during business lunches. It was common to share food during such occasions, along with Taiwan Beer. They sat down with Cross facing the door. A few minutes later a Chinese gentleman walked in with two big men either side of him and Cross and Huang stood up to greet them.

"Hello Mr. Cross and Ms. Huang. I am Mr. Tsai, Chief Financial Officer of this establishment. Thank you for flying out Mr. Cross. I hope you had a pleasant journey and appropriate accommodations welcomed you last night," he said looking at Huang.

She smiled. Chinese culture is very different to anyone else's in the Western hemisphere.

They all shook hands. It was a warm but hard shake and Cross relaxed. Tsai sat down opposite Cross but his two big guards didn't. They stayed vigilant and kept an eye on him.

"I will show you the premises shortly but let us go through what we are trying to do here. First, Mr. Cross, we researched your background and it is quite extensive. You are well respected in your field and we admire that here. We find it is better to be head of a field rather than trying to play catchup all the time. We were pleasantly surprised you are familiar with Taiwan."

"Yes, I love it here, Mr. Tsai," Cross said, wishing to keep it formal. "I always get treated really well and I have made friends here. I nearly moved to Kaohsiung after my divorce but I have three children in the US."

"We are sorry about what happened. You have published a remarkable book on your accident, the cycling heroics and the pile of shit life has thrown at you."

Cross hid his shock. They have done their research and he suspects Tsai was trying to show him who they are.

"Thank you. I felt my experiences could help others."

Moving on from formalities and small talk, Tsai opened up.

"GreenSea Enterprises is a new company. I say new but it has been in development for two years. This is 100% agricultural. We are looking to develop some new food products with medicinal applications. As you likely know already, Asia is big on natural remedies for common ailments. This is why we don't age, live so long and eat everything," he said laughing.

"Yes, I see that," adding to the jovial nature. He was beginning to like Tsai. "It is impossible to estimate Asians' ages," he said laughing and looked over at Huang. "I once watched a documentary on the two oldest twins in the world. They lived in rural china and the reporter was asking what they did with their lives. They didn't do anything. Were born and raised in the same house even. A wonder they didn't die from boredom," he added laughing. "They did eat healthy, locally grown foods which I am sure aided their longevity. They also used natural remedies from plant matter. Americans eat too much processed food and like to be prescribed pharmaceutical drugs."

"I cannot divulge too much but we are looking into exporting to America some naturally-engineered medicinal products. You were invited here because it is important for us to make sure the analytical testing is sufficient and suitable for your laws. I will show you the facilities we have built for such a laboratory shortly."

Tsai went into more details and talked for some time about what it is they are doing, or want to do.

Cross began his scientific monologue about what the laws were, the analytical tests they would need to perform and the instrumentation required to accurately accommodate those tests. Tsai sat and took notes but Cross brought with him some documents he would leave behind. He was well versed having built an agricultural testing facility in Ukraine for a client and he talked unbroken for around thirty minutes. Tsai was impressed and smiled. He sat back in his chair.

"I am sorry. I didn't ask if you wanted some coffee or tea. Please accept my poor manners."

"I would like some coffee please." Cross answered.

"Me too." replied Huang.

Tsai picked up the phone and dialed a number. They chit-chatted for five minutes and then a young lady brought in three cups of coffee. Cross must have made her nervous because she nearly spilt it as she leaned over and placed it on the table in front of him. He winked at her, said thank you and I love you in perfect Mandarin before she blushed and left the room. A second lady had brought in some famous Taiwanese pineapple cake.

"You have quite a reputation, Mr. Cross."

"I work hard and I am good at what I do, Mr. Tsai."

"You know that isn't what I am referencing here," he said laughing. "You said 'I love you' in perfect Mandarin?"

Cross just smiled at him but his command of English was remarkable.

"I like to surprise adversaries once in a while. The first time I entered Taiwan in 2004 I picked up a translation sheet at the airport. It translated the top ten most important phrases. I thought that one would be useful to know." He smiled.

"You view us as adversaries?"

"Not anymore," he responded.

Cross was in his element now. He was brilliant at international relations and the real reason Granfield wanted him to work with them. Adding humour changes every international predicament. He washes away the cultural differences and historical mountains that some people see as impossible. He doesn't see them as obstacles, or sees them and looks for ways to navigate around them. There is always a way over or around an invisible wall. If one has the perception it cannot be done, then they will not fight to prove it cannot. Cross never sees that.

"Mr. Cross, I would like to show you what we do here. Let us head over to the warehouse."

Tsai left with Huang and Cross following. The two big men took up the rear. There was security everywhere and Tsai was using his security pass to open and close several doors. Finally, the key card opens up a door into a large warehouse. It wasn't full but it has space to expand into something huge, with what looked like fifty foot ceilings. Cross' eyes opened. Many pallets were piled into one area of the warehouse, an area they were walking towards.

"This is where we package and transport some of the agricultural products for export. We are working on several patentable medicinal items which I cannot divulge, of course. You will respect that I am sure."

Cross and Huang nodded.

"The grow facilities are located in various places around Taiwan. These are private surrounded by high fences with additional security measures. The plants are harvested and brought here. We extract material from each batch and then send them to our research facility. Our PhD chemists, some from overseas, know what they are looking for and are in full development mode. The facility is compliant and ISO certified."

Tsai began to walk away and Cross saw his guards were focused elsewhere. He seized the opportunity to take his pen out that Granfield had given him and took a photo of one of the tags on the pallet closest to him. Still with pen in hand, he snapped a few more shots. To avoid any appearance that would alarm his hosts, he pointed the pen to some stairs that were leading up to what looked like office spaces suspended from the ceiling. Behind the stairs were two elevators.

"Those finished offices look empty, Mr. Tsai. May I be permitted to ask what those are for?"

"Of course, Mr. Cross. You are very observant. I am taking you over there now."

Tsai walked over and started mounting the stairs up into the suspended office area. The two guards were now behind Cross and Huang.

Using a different key card, he opened the door and walked in. They then entered through an air-lock security area.

"This is a 7,000 sq.ft. facility," as he proceeded to walk through it. "This is the reception and office areas, a conference room, small kitchen and break area, and then this is the key to this part, Mr. Cross," he opened up two double doors into a spectacular laboratory area.

This was expensive and some serious money had been invested into it already. The outer edge of the main room was lined with high-end laboratory cabinets top to bottom along with considerable work counters separating the floor cabinets with the wall-mounted ones. Disbursed among them where various fume hoods ducted in series to an outside vent through the roof. The space in the middle were floor-mounted cabinets, back to back, with marble counter tops, perhaps thirty feet long and fifteen feet wide. The power lines, internet and USB ports hung from the ceiling in conduits. Various stainless steel gas lines, regulators and valves were everywhere.

"This was built to be our testing laboratory. No expense spared. The cabinets in the middle will house the scientific equipment required, per your instructions."

"When was this built?" as he was trying to decipher how such a short-notice visit was made to incorporate all this. He was only told a few days ago to come to Taiwan.

"About six months ago. We weren't ready at the time and then a call came in requesting approval of your visit. We wanted you here anyway and we thought we would use your time appropriately."

Cross was finally speechless. He looked at his watch. They had been there almost three hours.

"We wish to continue this discussion, Mr. Cross, but our time today has limitations. Perhaps we can arrange another visit later in the week, before you fly home?"

"Yes, I would like to do that. I will ask Ms. Huang to make the necessary arrangements through her staff and coordinate that with your people. She will then inform me of those details, Mr. Tsai."

"That sounds agreeable. My men will lead you out."

They shook hands and found their way outside finally. That was intense and Cross was exhausted mentally. They climbed into the R8 and sat and pondered what they learnt.

"I know a good sushi restaurant near here for lunch, by the fishing docks," Huang added. "We can talk there."

Cross knew where she meant. His client and close friend wasn't far from here and he really wanted to contact him. He was afraid to though and will mull that idea over later.

Huang parked by the decaying fishing boats and they walked up the steep stairs into the famous blue-collar sushi house. It was buffet-style but they paid for what they took. Selecting what they wanted, the servers placed them on their plates and handed them their choice of drinks. They sourced an empty table, walked over and sat down.

"You were excellent in there. I believe Mr. Tsai trusts you."

"Thank you, Lin. I believe we made considerable progress. He didn't show the whole lab area though. They are hiding something."

He removed his pen from the suit jacket he had hung on the back of the chair and plugged a small cable in. The other end fed into his phone. He downloaded the photos. Once it had signaled completion, he took a look.

The tag on the pallet had an address on it. It was an address in the middle of Taiwan, up at higher elevations. Taiwan had famous tea plantations here at the higher altitudes. He showed it to Huang.

"I know roughly where that is. Are you suggesting we go take a look, Daniel?"

"I wasn't suggesting anything but that sounds like a viable idea," he said smiling.

Huang rolled her eyes.

"Don't fall into a false level of security. These people are dangerous."

"I can take a taxi, if you wish. I don't believe we need to be driving around in an R8 though. I do suggest we trade that in for something more obscure, especially for this next part of my trip which will fall into an uninvited guest category," he said smirking.

"That isn't funny, Daniel. They will be suspicious why you wanted to visit with such short notice. We provided a reason they may not have trusted but you handled yourself well today."

He was beginning to like Huang. No wedding ring either.

"What do you do for the American consulate here in Taiwan?"

"I have to work with weird foreigners like you," she said laughing.

He leaned over and put his hand on her leg.

"Lucky you," and they both laughed.

Finishing lunch it was now 2:50pm. Huang called her boss at the consulate wishing to exchange the R8 for something more appropriate, although the loss of power and speed could be a detriment. The bland Toyota arrived at the hotel and the driver waited for them to appear. He took off in the R8.

They had a few hours to kill before leaving. It needed to be dark and the address was two hours away. They went upstairs to Cross' room and went over a few things. Cross changed into black jeans and sweater. Huang was prepared also and had brought a change of clothes in a bag. She stepped into the bedroom to remove her business attire and then put on dark blue jeans and a sweater. Huang explained where the location was. It had security according to Mr. Tsai this morning. Huang showed Cross a map and they left the hotel.

14

Genetically Modified Cannabis

Highway 1 took them out of the city and then to Highway 10 and onto 3 north. An hour and half later they were getting close. Huang took a right turn and started to climb up a winding road. She found a place to pull over and stopped.

"I will park away from the location. If you need me, just contact me. I will be ready to come and get you if you need a rapid escape. This has security and is guarded. Please be careful."

They saw lights in the area so other places were close by. This helped camouflage their intentions if they were spotted. They were a mile away now.

"I will walk from here, Lin. Park at that 7 Eleven," pointing to the store across the street.

She pulled into the lot and he exited the Toyota. Cross put on his night vision goggles and started up the road. He carried a small flashlight but the moon even partially obscured was providing sufficient light with aid from the goggles. The handheld had the silencer mounted already. He approached the farm with trepidation.

Cross finally made it and saw signs posted 'Private Property, Do

Not Trespass'. It was obvious why they were out here. This was a fairly big farm but what were they growing? He walked around for a while and then saw lights from a car approaching so hid behind some growth. As it got closer, it slowed down. The entrance to the farm had double doors wide enough for a truck. One of them had a smaller size door for humans. It opened as the car approached. The guard recognised the vehicle and occupant, bowed to him before going back in to open one of the bigger doors. The car slid through and disappeared. The guard became a little distracted and Cross carefully ran into the farm before he closed the door. The field was large. He removed his goggles and he knew immediately what the plants were. The aroma was mitigated somehow but had no idea how. Cannabis stinks, and it is illegal in Taiwan. Authorities impose hefty fines and jail time if caught growing. He was silent now as he walked crouched down towards one of the rows of plants at one end of the field closest to the wall. He extracted a few leaves from the plant and put them in a sealed bag and into his jacket pocket. His pen came out and he snapped more photos.

Some distance away the guard shack was lit up and next to that what looked like an office space and living quarters. It wasn't fully clear at night but looked like a small home. Some windows glowed light but that was also mitigated by dark drapes. He imagined the farmers and guards living there. Cross looked around for security but saw so little of it. Where is it? He walked towards the vehicle and house and then saw one possible reason. The car that had rolled through the front gate belonged to a security system repair company. How fortuitous. Luck is on my side, he said to himself. He heard noises inside the home as he approached.

To the right and away from the property was a garbage can. He walked over and lifted the lid. He briefly turned on the flashlight and peeked inside. He saw some papers that looked interesting so he grabbed a few and pulled them out. They were from some research facility here in Taiwan so he stuffed them in his jacket pockets.

He needed to get out of here. He walked towards the gate and the small door was unlocked so he pulled back the locking mechanism, opened the door and walked through the doorway. He was ten feet away when the security lights came back on. That must have triggered the cameras also because now he could hear other noises behind the farm wall. He started to run as one of the big doors began to open up. His knee was killing him. He moved off the road and behind bushes as the security repair man departed the area. He watched as the door closed behind the car.

Cross made his way down the dark road wearing the night goggles and headed towards Huang who was still parked outside the 7 Eleven. He climbed in.

"They are growing cannabis but it doesn't smell. Cannabis is illegal in Taiwan with severe penalties.

"I found these papers in a garbage can but I have no idea what they are. Can you please drive us out of here? That was too easy." He finally finished. His heart rate was off the charts.

"Ok, Daniel. Let me get you back to Kaohsiung."

She parked the Toyota in the underground parking lot and they took the parking elevator to the lobby floor. As they stepped out the café and small bar were right there. They ordered some sandwiches, cakes and cocktails and asked if they could be brought to the room.

They walked across the reception area and took the elevator to the 14th floor.

Cross took his shower first. The sandwiches arrived whilst he was lavishing soap on his now aching and tired body. He dried off and adorned a soft luxurious hotel robe.

He entered the living area and saw Huang arranging the food. It was her turn so off she jumped into the shower. She also wore a hotel robe as she exited the bathroom. Cross had taken the liberty of calling Dunhill when Huang was in the bathroom. He knew she would be longer anyway. He filled her in on what he could. They spoke about missing each other and put the phone down.

Huang came and sat on the sofa next to Cross and ate the food and drank the whiskey. There was a mini bar and Cross opened it and brought out two bottles of beer and two tiny bottles of whiskey. He had ordered extra alcohol before he left the room that morning. He called down to the bar once he realised it wasn't going to be enough. He hadn't been expecting Huang to be with him.

"Can you bring a full bottle of Glenfiddich please? What vintage do you have? Great, that will do. Thank you."

That taken care of, he sat back and relaxed for a while. They went over today's events in detail and then he called Granfield.

"Great work, Daniel. You are impressive so far but be careful. Oh, by the way, a senator from Illinois left for Kaohsiung today with his entourage on a private flight. They will arrive tomorrow evening. We suggest you organise another meeting with Mr. Tsai for the day after. He has no idea the information I have just given you. It could work in our favour. Find out what their research facility is doing tomorrow, if you can. Good work but play it safe.

"Mr. Romanov is also moving on something. We are contemplating flying you to Moscow from Taiwan. Take care."

Cross called Verenich.

"Hello Igor, how are you?"

"I am great, how about you?"

"Tired, but ok."

He filled him in on today's developments and Verenich had some updates on the people at the council meeting. He informed him about Romanov in Moscow. They finished and he put the phone down.

Huang's robe was now partially open and her beautiful legs were showing. He could see her white panties.

The doorbell rang and he walked over and opened it. It was the Glenfiddich and two glasses. He tipped the busboy and then walked into the bedroom and placed them at the side of the bed. He came back into the living room and kissed Huang on the cheek. He gently picked her up, carried her into the bedroom and placed her on the bed. He then untied her robe. He poured two glasses of whiskey, climbed onto the bed and handed her one. His free hand was now at liberty to do whatever it needed to please her.

The research facility can wait…

15

The Research Facility, Outside Taipei

They had brought down the papers he had scrounged from the garbage last night and sat at breakfast with cappuccinos in hand. How stupid not to shred them, he thought.

The unmistakable logo of GreenSea was printed on the official papers. An address was printed underneath, which was farther north and closer to Taipei. A 300km drive, three or more hours from Kaohsiung.

The paperwork was mostly purchase orders for chemical compounds from pharmaceutical companies in China and some receipts for cannabis plants. Mr. Tsai had mentioned his chemists were working on patentable products. Cross looked them over and then saw a separate sheet that was written from the Official Office of the State Senator of Illinois. It had the Illinois state seal on it. He was now reflecting on what Granfield had told him. There was nothing illegal in the letter except that it was confirming an appointment tomorrow at Mr. Wu's office by the docks, 11am.

He showed Huang and told her she needs to work on a meeting tomorrow, perhaps at 9:30am. She immediately called her office, where ever that was, thought Cross. He had already been in contact with a very close PhD chemist he has known for decades and sent him the chemical information. He wanted to know what they could be used for.

"We need to get ready and head north, Lin. I want to visit the research facility. Now how can we get an appointment there?"

She pondered this for a few minutes whilst enjoying her coffee.

"Let me make a call."

Finishing their breakfast, they headed back upstairs. Cross saw the half empty bottle of Glenfiddich next to the king bed. Damn that was good, both the whiskey and the bed. He smiled.

Huang was in the bathroom getting ready. Her phone pinged. She came out half-dressed and looked at it. It was now 9:30.

"We have an appointment at 1pm at GreenSea Research Centre. You will go as yourself because we cannot raise more flags than we have already. Mr. Tsai will know anyway."

Cross had brought with him all the fake ID's Granfield had given him but he didn't need them, thankfully.

"Excellent," but he felt nervous. "Last night getting in and out of the grow facility was too easy and Mr. Tsai knew we were meeting up again. Don't forget Mr. Tsai tomorrow at his warehouse," he smiled.

"Got it," she messaged back whoever had just pinged her.

She went back into the bathroom and finished getting dressed. She came out wearing a beautiful blue silk dress, above the knee with pantyhose and a black jacket. She was beautiful. Low-heel white shoes complemented her outfit.

Cross put on a pinstripe grey suit, white shirt and a lavender tie that he had had delivered to his room when they were having breakfast. He knew people in the city. Huang stared at him.

North on Highway 1, they were two hours into the drive. Traffic was good. Huang's phone went off.

"Yes. Ok. Great. I will tell Mr. Cross. Thank you."

She turned to face him.

"9:45am tomorrow with Mr. Tsai. You might be running out of favours," she laughed.

"Yes, I am sure I am. They know it is a short visit and they will know we will be at their research facility in about one hour. I will gauge his reaction tomorrow. The exercise is to hang around long enough to see the Illinois senator show up."

They pulled up outside the research facility. It was a new 20,000 sq.ft. building with 20 employees, Huang was told. He noticed a second paved entrance with double glass doors on the side of the building.

They walked in and presented their ID's. The register was filled in and signed and then they waited. Dr. Lee eventually showed up and they followed her to a special room. They put on laboratory coats, face masks, replaced their shoes with linen slippers. They were ready for the tour.

They went through a vent-lock air system which required going through two glass doors. Cross could hear the first door close, then the rush of air as they walked through, and then the second door opened for them to exit. After the second door was shut behind them, their host used a key-card to enter another door and into the laboratory. There were similar laboratory cabinets and fume hoods to those at the warehouse. Cross noticed bottles of chemicals from the Chinese company he had seen listed on the order sheets as he walked through. There were small laboratory tools, glassware, pipettes, rotovacs, freezers, hot baths, etc as they transitioned from one lab to the other. Lee was explaining some of their work but skipped over big portions. Cross looked through a small window in the door going to another room and saw scientists in full protective body suits working in there.

"A biological lab," he whispered to Huang.

They did have a standalone LC and small LCMS for basic data analysis in a separate room but nothing substantial. The tour was forty minutes long. Cross asked some questions but they exited the research facility armed with more information.

They returned to the Toyota and Cross sent a message to his friend in the US and he immediately replied. 'Check your email', came the response. Cross sent a thank you.

Opening his emails he had several hundred unanswered. He scrolled through and found the one of interest. It was brief. He read it and paraphrased.

"The chemicals we are seeing are used in some vaccination medications. They can be dangerous to humans if they are mixed up and concentrations altered, apparently anyway," he said to Huang. "It is possible GreenSea Enterprises and the US senator are involved in some vaccination program. But for who?"

It was 2:20.

"Can we go get the R8 back please?" he said chuckling.

"Oh I agree. I don't like driving my Toyota," she said smiling.

Huang headed back to Kaohsiung and Cross called Granfield. He again filled him in. The chemicals and the research facility shed new light on what is going on here. He explained the full protective suits which points to a biological lab of some sort. He told him he had a meeting with Mr. Tsai at 9:45 tomorrow and the Illinois senator was showing up at 11:00. He didn't tell him about the illegal excursion into the grow facility up in the hills. He also didn't shed any light on a potential link between Taiwan and the diamond, because he hadn't found one.

"You are being looked after, Daniel?"

"Yes, David. The hospitality has been exemplary," turning and tossing a wink at Huang. "We are heading back to Kaohsiung now. What is the update on Russia?"

"I will tell you in the morning. However, Mitrovic was killed with a bullet to the chest but he had drugs in his system. There was a needle mark in the arm but we found no needle. The blood on his hands wasn't his. That is the update."

Cross called Verenich.

"Igor, how is the weather?"

"It is raining here and snowing in the mountains."

Cross updated his information including the senator's pending visit.

"That is interesting. Let me research him," Verenich said. "I will follow up. How is the hospitality my friend?"

"Exemplary, Igor. First rate."

They were now back in Kaohsiung's rush-hour traffic.

"We didn't time that right. Where are we going?"

"To the hotel. The R8 is waiting," she turned and smiled, and put her hand on his leg.

"Fantastic."

As they pulled up, the R8 was waiting at the front. Huang exchanged keys and the young Asian jumped into the Toyota and departed.

"Let us go a little casual and head on out. I feel like going to a nice restaurant. There are some really good places in Building 85. We can get a taxi there. Perhaps we hide the R8 down in the basement parking lot."

The food was an excellent local cuisine and Huang looked happy. She had taken off the silk dress and replaced it with a casual summer one and an evening jacket. Cross had adopted nice pants and a wool sweater. She knew of a nice bar to finish the evening so she sourced a taxi using a phone app and headed over there. It was upscale and they found a table and sat at it. The conversation was flowing and they had gone through perhaps three rounds. But Huang looked drunk and something was wrong. Her eyes portrayed the vision of a woman in trouble.

"Are you ok?" with a concerned voice.

"I think someone has been spiking or mixing my drinks. I feel terrible and want to throw up," she said slurring.

He moved her off to the bathroom and stuck his fingers down her throat. She vomited into the sink. Jesus.

"I cannot mix cocktails."

Cross couldn't either. He blanks out when mixing. He once tried Ukraine moonshine and then blanked for two hours. He took her back to the table and then noticed someone looking at them from the bar. It was unnerving him. Huang was semiconscious now and was not looking good.

He held her up and walked outside. A taxi was waiting so he manoeuvred Huang into it and then climbed in next to her. He knew of a local motel not far from here and found it on his phone. He showed the website to the taxi driver. Cross looked behind as the taxi took off and saw two men come outside. They did not follow but one of them was talking on the phone. He couldn't risk going back to his hotel. Ten minutes later the taxi pulled up to a security booth at a local pay-by-the-hour motel. He had been here before, once. These are common in Taiwan. Business men bring mistresses or girlfriends to these places for a night of debauchery, adulterous behaviour or immense pleasure, presumably anyway. Cross paid the lady at the entrance and she told the driver which apartment to go to. This was an interesting place. Garages were on the ground floor so people could drive into them and go inside unnoticed. The living quarters were a single bedroom apartment with a kitchen. It was decked out in marble and high end appointments and furnishings. The taxi driver dropped them off and Cross used Google Translate to ask him to wait ten minutes. He opened the garage door and carried Huang upstairs. She wasn't in a good state. He took her to the bathroom and tried to get her to throw up again. She needed to get whatever they spiked in her drink out. She did throw up a second time. He took her to the bed and removed her jacket and dress. He placed the bed covers over the top and let her sleep. Now she was safe he went back downstairs, closed the garage door and jumped into the taxi. He showed him a business card of the bar they just left.

The taxi pulled up outside and Cross climbed out. He paid the driver some extra money and gestured that he wait. He walked into the bar and it had a hand-carved decorative panel that separated the entrance from the main bar. He peeped around the side and saw the men had their backs to him but sitting at the bar. They weren't expecting him back for sure. Cross had learnt some martial arts in his past and knew he could kill with a swift strike. He didn't want to do that, at least not yet. He had to disable the first man and question the one who made the phone call. He walked up silently and struck the first man in the temple. He collapsed to the floor. Before the other could react he had him in a choke hold with one arm and the silencer of his handheld jabbed in his side with the free hand. He couldn't move.

Cross led him outside and then sat him in the back of the taxi. He motioned for the driver to move. Go, he said in Mandarin. A few turns later he asked him to stop, in Mandarin. The driver pulled over. Cross led the man out and walked over to an alley. He was young but wasn't strong. It was very strange. He punched him in the stomach and the man dropped like a stone. Holding the gun to his head, he managed to pry out some information he needed, deciphering the man's broken English. He had a Russian accent. One more punch to the stomach and then left enough marks on his face to let people know he had been roughed up. Foam started coming out of his mouth as the Russian bit into a cyanide pill. Cross stepped back into the taxi and asked he head back to the motel.

Huang was asleep but breathing normally. He sat on the bed and looked at her as she slept. He was afraid to sleep and stayed awake for some time. Eventually the exercise became futile and he needed some shuteye. He made sure she was comfortable and then sleep took a hold.

16

A US Senator's Arrival

The following morning Cross awoke early. Huang was still passed out but she seemed to be stirring as he was drinking his Asian tea. There wasn't much in the apartment but tea and sugar with small pouches of soy milk were available. Cross carried a mug of tea for Huang.

She gently came around but had a huge headache. Cross wondered if making her throw up saved her life last night.

She took a shower to try and wake up and put on the same clothes.

"Let us get a taxi back to the hotel. It is 7:30 and we have a meeting in a little over two hours."

They returned to the Lees hotel but someone had been in his room. The violators tried to leave everything normal but Cross left some notification features, as he dubs them, in various locations. He had delicately superglued some hairs across the dresser draws and the closet doors, hidden from normal view. Those are difficult to see for any perpetrator and they had been interfered with. They were all broken. Luckily the GreenSea papers and the letter from the senator had been left in the Toyota, a request Cross had made to Huang which she didn't understand. There was nothing of significance for anybody looking to find in the room.

There was no collateral damage to speak of except someone knows something and they are being followed.

He called Granfield and gave some specific instructions. He assured him it would be taken care of. Cross felt better already.

"Where was the viral outbreak in Taiwan?"

Granfield told him.

They took a shower together but only because Huang was still weakened by the chemical intoxication and had to be helped. Cross was trying to get her ready for the meeting with Tsai. They got dressed and left for the parking garage, taking their bags with them.

Cross removed another toy Granfield had given him and scanned the R8. He found what he was looking for, climbed on the floor and removed a tracking device. Brushing himself off, they climbed into the car and left, arriving at GreenSea Enterprises' security gate five minutes late. They were motioned through without the guard even checking ID's.

"Did you enjoy the laboratory tour with Dr. Lee, Mr. Cross?" said Tsai, at the same conference table, with his same bodyguards.

"Yes. I always enjoy visiting other laboratories around the world. The lab is very impressive and I certainly appreciated being allowed to visit it, especially with such short notice."

"We are optimistic of success with our research," he continued. "We have genetically modified a specific strain of an agricultural plant and we have expectations of it being commercially successful. Our scientists are working hard."

Avoiding that discussion, Tsai moved on. "I looked over the document you left two days ago. We are impressed with what you are suggesting we purchase for the laboratory to aid our endeavours."

"I have contacts deep within the instrument manufacturing world. I assure you we can put this together."

Cross had a good relationship with Tsai but he had to be careful.

Someone sent two men to the bar last night but they weren't Asian. Cross was confused. It is possible Tsai knows nothing about what happened and may be genuinely interested in what Cross can do for them. However, from Cross' perspective, it looks like GreenSea is entering into some clandestine and potentially dangerous operation. Genetically modifying anything is fraught with unforeseen complications and then tossing in the vaccine chemicals and one is entering the unknown. He needed to get to Virginia.

Cross purposely prolonged the conversation and insisted on seeing the suspended laboratory again. It was getting very close to 11am and Tsai was getting anxious, he could see. Cross made suggestions and added comments to the electrical and gas lines to extend discussions.

"I have another meeting scheduled, Mr. Cross. Can we wrap this up? I will have my people contact your office and we can work on the financial arrangements for the requisitions, perhaps as early as next week."

"That sounds great, Mr Tsai. Thank you so much for the exceptional hospitality on such short notice."

With that, Cross and Huang were shown to the reception area where they departed.

"Please let me drive, Lin."

As they were about to leave, two black Mercedes S-Class' pulled up. Cross waited until the occupants exited and then he recognised the senator from Illinois. He had several men in suits and a young lady who likely was his personal assistant in his entourage. The senator wore an expensive dark suit and looked the part, observed Cross. His eyes were shifting and then looked at the R8. Cross took some photos and then sped off before anyone wanted to ask questions. He looked in the mirror to see the senator turn around. The windows had been darkened to keep the heat out in summer, luckily. He also noticed just before they left the building the two big brutes guarding

Tsai were nowhere to be seen. Cross exited the dock area and took a right, then left. He saw the BMW come up to the rear right. He floored it but the BMW kept up. Then he heard gunfire and his heart jumped. They pierced the Audi. He kept going and turned right onto the road taking him to the airport. The airport wasn't far from the dock areas as Cross weaved in and out of traffic and avoided traffic signals. The damn scooters were everywhere. Per instructions he was given, he headed for the private entrance for the corporate jet pad. Someone at the gate saw him and opened it. The BMW fired more shots but kept on going as Cross turned left into the airport. He saw the plane Granfield had arranged dead ahead and didn't bother following the designated road system. He went right over a grassy area and onto the tarmac, pulling up just in front of the stairs.

"Let's go, Lin, we need to run."

No answer. She was slumped in the passenger seat. He saw blood. They must have thought Huang was driving. He quickly checked her pulse but it was faint. Exiting the car he started shouting to the attendants at the bottom of the ramp.

"Please get a doctor. Ms. Huang has been shot."

He ran around the other side of the car and pulled open the door. He knelt in and looked at her. The eyes were shut and she wasn't moving. Blood was running down her dress. He kissed her on the lips and felt for a pulse a second time. The pulse had terminated, as had Huang's life. Cross was now devastated but needed to get going. He grabbed his bag, kissed her one more time and ran up the stairs and onto the plane. The door shut and started taxiing before Cross was even strapped in. Tears were rolling down his face.

17

CIA Headquarters, Langley, Virginia

Cross arrived at a Virginian private airport and a black Chevy Suburban was at the bottom of the ramp when he exited. He climbed in and it whisked him off to CIA Headquarters.

"Good morning, Daniel," said Granfield. "Welcome to CIA headquarters. How was the flight?" They were in his office.

"Good morning, David. I am exhausted and still in shock I guess. Women I keep meeting are dying in front of me."

"Well, let us not make that a continuing habitual concern shall we?'" trying to console him. "We heard about Ms. Huang.

"My secretary will bring you some coffee and breakfast in a few minutes. Take your time and relax, before we go over details. Great work, by the way. We can train you all we want but how you are controlling the situation is remarkable. You have skills that cannot be taught. No one can teach you that and no idea where they came from," complimenting him was the best way to keep him from going into shock, thought Granfield.

"I am sure I was the target. Poor Ms. Huang, she was so nice and treated me so well. I am just in shock, again.

"I called Chantelle on the flight. She seems to be enjoying Tahoe and the fresh snow. It is very quiet over there but I got approval for the cannabis testing license."

"Yes, I heard that. Now we will find out what happens after that," he smiled.

A tall, slender older lady walked in with a tray of food and a pot of coffee with two mugs. Brown sugar and cream were on the side.

"There you go, Mr. Cross," she said with a nice smile.

"Thank you ma'am. I am hungry."

He picked up the bacon and egg sandwich and chewed into it. Granfield poured the coffee and added the requisite condiments. He knew Cross' taste but didn't go further than pre-ground Peet's French Roast coffee.

"I will let you finish the sandwich and drink the coffee. I have some slides made up from the information you have provided us. We will head over to the conference room shortly and then you can fill us in on what we don't have."

With that he left the office to let Cross relax and contemplate what just happened. Field Operatives are trained men and women. They go through psychological re-programming as part of any assignment. Cross was not an operative, knew Granfield. He is a scientist. He will need counseling after this but there isn't time for that yet.

Granfield returned after twenty minutes and Cross was done. Cross needed to put the facts together as he has found them. They left the office and walked over to a conference room. There were CIA personnel seated both sides of the table.

Granfield gave his presentation and ended with addressing his desire to convene again in the morning, same time, same place. Everyone nodded their heads. Then it was Cross' turn.

"GreenSea Enterprises is engaged in some agricultural business that involves genetically modifying plants. Their warehouse in Kaohsiung had some packaged already and they came from a grow farm in the hills two hours north of the city. Huang drove me there and we saw the farm."

"Wait," Granfield interrupted, "You went to the farm?"

"Yes. I am sorry but I kept this quiet because I knew you would be upset. I risked Huang and myself to find samples of the plants being grown," he reached into a pocket, pulled out a plastic bag with some green leaves in it and placed it on the table.

Granfield was exasperated. "You went into a very secure facility to get some samples?"

"Yes. It was important, but didn't seem that secure oddly enough. The thing of interest is they are growing cannabis but it doesn't smell of cannabis. It is illegal to grow pot in Taiwan with severe punishment if found guilty. This was a large farm, but out of the way. At higher elevations the soil is very fertile. Taiwan is famous for its tea plantations up there and this place was surrounded by those tea farms. However, someone has to know, I suspect. One cannot hide something like this unless they like to dispose of people who do find out."

"Please continue, Daniel," his opinions weren't warranted, thought Granfield.

"During my reconnaissance mission," he looked over at Granfield, "I found some papers in a trash can. I extracted those and found them to be purchase orders from GreenSea's lab just south east of Taipei to chemical companies in China. The chemicals they are ordering were confirmed to be ones used in vaccines. Along with the purchase orders, I found an official letter from the Office of the Senator of Illinois, complete with a seal," the room was totally silent. "He had a meeting with Mr. Tsai at their warehouse facility in Kaohsiung. I had Huang arrange a second meeting with Mr. Tsai so that our departure would coincide with the senator's arrival. We saw him. That was the senator Mr. Brownsville. It was him. I have evidence.

"The visit to the research facility wasn't too productive but it confirmed the chemicals they ordered have been shipped and are being used. There is also a biological component in that building. There was a part of the facility we were not allowed to venture into, or a part Dr. Lee neglected to show us. Interpret how you wish. Furthermore, a week or so ago there was some pertinent news related to our case that wasn't very well broadcast or printed. A virus had hit a small town in Taiwan that just happened to coincide with the area the research facility is located in. It appears they are genetically modifying plants to harm people so they can create a vaccine for it. I don't have an informed opinion on Mr. Brownsville's involvement yet. I cannot even begin to speculate why a top US senator would want to visit a company half way around the world developing viruses and then vaccines to combat them. I will leave that with you esteemed educated people," he added, looking concerned.

"Unfortunately, I am left with no connection to the stolen Namibian diamond. It seems Mr. Wu's operation is being well funded.

"This information risked my life and got Ms. Huang killed. Something is going on here. Oh, by the way, Ms. Huang and I were followed for the latter part of our visit. They drugged or mixed Ms. Huang's drinks, perhaps both, and then we were followed out of the bar. I did later return to find out they were Russian.

"I cannot connect the dots. They could have been sent by Romanov or they worked for Mr Tsai. I didn't get much information and one of them bit into a cyanide pill before I could extract anything material. All I could get from him was 'he was sent from Moscow'."

"That same night my hotel room was entered. I had set markers and they were all broken. Huang was killed as we left GreenSea but I suspect I was the target, or they were sending a message. Perhaps Mr. Tsai thought I knew too much or he found out about the break-in at his grow farm. Perhaps he knew I recognised the senator but how would he know that? I can only speculate," he was rambling now, a side-effect of jetlag, confusion and fear.

Granfield sensed this and reached over and put a hand on his arm. Cross stopped talking and took a seat. He was exhausted. The long-distance intercontinental flights beat him up at his age, especially under this stress. Granfield's second-in-command Dr. Harris Winwood took over the discussions.

"We now know a US senator is involved. Mr. Cross has photographic evidence that a meeting took place." Winwood pointed at an agent sitting across the table and told him to find out more. The guy left the room.

"We know two Russians were sent to Taiwan. Where did they come from?" He pointed to another agent and told her to find out.

"Mr. Cross is confirming some of what we already knew. Modified cannabis we didn't know. A research facility we knew but not biologically-specific. It appears the virus release has only killed two dozen or so Taiwanese and it was localised. It didn't even make the evening news. Given the information we now have, perhaps GreenSea is developing a vaccine to be distributed in the US. Why would a prominent US senator be involved if it had nothing to do with this country? When we connect the dots, perhaps there is a wider global disbursement for the virus and vaccine.

"Mr. Cross couldn't find information linking Mr. Tsai with the diamond. That connection was being elusive. It appears they have vast resources for what they are doing. This is an unknown. If the senator is involved, their operation may have some US funding attached," he pointed to another agent. "Go and find anything related to government funding, either through special interest or donors, that pertains to GreenSea or any of Mr. Wu's entities. Let us follow the money trail. The trail of money usually ends at the rainbow." The agent departed the room.

Winwood took his seat whilst Granfield finished by thanking everyone for their good work and asked they leave. "See you all same time tomorrow." He looked at Cross and motioned him to follow. They went back to his office.

"I know you are tired but we need some information out of Russia. There is a flight tomorrow morning leaving Dulles, through Frankfurt to Domodedovo. I had my secretary get some clothes prepared and there will be more waiting in the Hotel Metropol when you check in. I believe you have stayed there before, Daniel."

"A very historic hotel adjacent to Red Square, yes."

"You will be met in the airport lobby. Bear in mind this is a fact-finding mission. Attempt to avoid being killed, Daniel, or getting someone else killed please," as he adopted a more serious tone. "In the meantime, go get some sleep. We have a reservation at a local hotel. I will have someone drive you there and pick you up at 5am tomorrow. They will bring you back. We will go over details before the flights to Russia. Great work Daniel. We are making progress I feel."

Cross gathered his own bag and the one the secretary had brought him and made his way to the lobby. He staggered onto the bag seat of a black Suburban waiting outside and collapsed.

Later that evening he filled Verenich in on what he had found.

"Sorry to hear of Ms. Huang's death."

"Thank you. Any further news on the Jewish contingent?"

"Not yet. I am finding pieces and starting to create a picture. Be careful in Russia, my friend."

"Thank you. I will."

18

Russian Hospitality, Hotel Metropol

'It's easy to see what really matters. Welcome to Moscow' was the mural at Domodedovo Airport as Cross headed towards immigration.

"Привет, как дела?" hello, how are you, Cross said in perfect Russian.

The immigration officer said nothing and just focused on his passport as he scanned it into the system. He looked at the picture and then him. The visa was a vacation visa and had multiple-entry status for another two years. He was good. The officer gave Cross his passport back along with the entry paper and sent him on his way. Cross had seven days to register with a local police station and have the entry paper stamped, normal for any non-Russian national, but he didn't intend on staying that long.

"Спасибо. до свидания." Thank you, good bye. Cross smiled.

He was tired and didn't even know what day it was anymore. Now through Customs with his carry-on he entered the vast main terminal foyer. It would be cold in Russia and Granfield's secretary must have been acutely aware and got him scarfs, a long black cashmere coat, leather gloves and a hat.

As he walked into the main terminal a young brunette approached him.

"Hello Mr. Cross. I have been waiting for you. Is this your only luggage? My name is Alexandria."

"Привет, как дела? Приятно познакомиться, Александрия. Меня зовут Даниил." Hi, how are you? Nice to meet you too, Alexandria. My name is Daniel.

The perfect Russian impressed Alexandria as she smiled. Russians typically are when one tries to speak their language. Cross knew this already.

"Please follow me. It is 1pm here so the traffic is light getting into the city," she said, in a strong Russian accent. "I am a liaison for the American Embassy in Moscow."

They stepped outside into the subzero Moscow winter. Snow and ice were everywhere and Cross would have frozen in his tracks, had he not been dressed for the occasion.

An hour or so later she pulled up outside the front of Hotel Metropol. Cross snatched his bag and climbed out of the Mercedes. Before he shut the door Alexandria gave him her contact information and said she would call him later. Go and get some rest, she said. He looked at her card: Alexandria Fedorova, American Embassy Foreign Liaison Officer.

Cross walked up the steps into the main lobby. The last time he was here the entranceway was being renovated. He stepped through a metal detector manned by two relaxed hotel security guards and then proceeded up to the counter off on the right. He presented his passport and entry document.

"Hello Mr. Cross and welcome to the Metropol. Mrs. Cross checked into your suite already," as the receptionist handed him the wallet with the keys in it. "Let me retrieve a package left for you this morning." She turned and went into a room behind her. "Here are your suits and accessories, Mr. Cross. We had a bottle of champagne and two glasses sent to your room, along with crackers and black caviar, as a courtesy. Oh, and a bottle of the finest Onegin vodka, sir."

"Большое спасибо, Это так щедро, для вашего здоровья." A big thank you, you are so generous, to your health, he said smiling.

He picked his bag up and headed towards the elevator. Mrs. Cross? Who the hell is Mrs. Cross? He stepped into the elevator and pressed the button for the top floor.

He opened the room door with some trepidation and tried to be quiet. He looked inside the living room area and saw a lady's coat draped over the couch. The champagne, vodka and glasses where on the coffee table. The bedroom door was ajar and he could see a robed lady lying on the bed. She had the TV playing. He knew who she was as he entered the bedroom.

"Hello Katie," he said, rather surprised.

He met her two years ago. Katie is an absolutely stunning and radiant local Moscovite with an exotic look complemented by long black curly hair, a 5'8" voluptuous frame at around 115 lbs. She was educated, an MBA if he remembers correctly, and had a small command of English. He was sitting at a bar one evening down the street from Gum Mall minding his own business when she came over and sat next to him. They had quite an interesting evening of discussion, punctuated by an occasional use of Google Translate, before walking back together to the Moscow Savoy. Cross mentioned her to Verenich at the time and he must have researched her picture. He was good at that, damn him.

She got up and walked over to hug him. He kissed her on the cheek.

"Igor called me and said you were coming."

"He does tend to care about my wellbeing, Katie. I have a lot of work to do here and trying to keep a low-profile."

"You need to relax after your long flights. Let me take care of you for a few hours."

She slipped off his coat and removed the hat and scarf, placing them on the couch. She then handed Cross the champagne and opened the caviar. She had released the tie holding the bath robe already and Cross could see her black lingerie. He didn't feel tired anymore. She then removed his clothing with the exception of his white undershirt and briefs. He carried the champagne into the bedroom and she brought the flute glasses and snacks as she followed him.

The house phone jingled.

"Is everything to your liking, Mr. Cross?" said the chambermaid. At least that is who she said she was.

"Да, спасибо." Yes, thank you, he said and replaced the receiver.

19

Romanov, the Oligarch

Cross picked up his secure mobile. It was 5:15pm. He had been up for an hour and Katie had already left.

"Hello Mr. Cross, this is Alexandria. Did you get some sleep?"

"Yes, I did, thank you." He didn't get any.

"We meet with Mr. Romanov at 7pm. Russians like to work late hours. The premise of your visit is to figure out his analytical needs with regards to the changing import environment. He has an office building in Moscow City. I will pick you up at 6:15. He doesn't like people being late."

Cross took a shower and put on a dark woolen double-breasted suit. It is cold outside. 6:15 arrived and so did Alexandria.

Moscow City was a city within a city and could easily be viewed from anywhere around Moscow. The cluster of tall buildings close together set it apart and it was Moscow's financial district. Fedorova pulled up outside one of them and parked in the lower-level visitor's spot in the multi-storey parking structure. As they stepped out and walked towards the building, Cross saw Russian graphics on a sign posted above the entrance. Underneath was written 'Romanov Plaza'. Cross looked up and was immediately in awe. It had been dark for several hours but the low glow of neon lights elevated the building to a different stature.

Entering through a metal detector, a security guard greeted them behind a large desk highlighted by a whole bank of camera screens. On one of them sat the Mercedes they had just pulled up in.

"Я Александрия Федорова, а это мистер Даниил Кросс," I am Alexandria Fedorova and this is Daniel Cross.

The guard took their ID's and went and looked in a guest registry. He picked up the receiver and pressed a button. He spoke some words, nodded his head and placed the receiver in its cradle. He spoke to Fedorova.

"We are in his guest book so we can head to the elevator as soon as he processes our passes. Someone will come down to escort us to the 20th floor."

"This is very impressive."

He wasn't immediately understanding the diamond situation either. This is a substantial building with vast monetary investment required, which someone evidently had. Cross wasn't seeing a connection yet.

The elevator doors slid open and an elegant lady stepped out to greet them. She was flanked by two large Russian gentlemen dressed in suits.

"Good evening, Mr. Cross and Ms. Fedorova. I am Ms. Sorokin, Mr. Romanov's personal assistant."

What is it with the Russians? She is also beautiful and elegant, thought Cross. The harsh winters must really do something over here.

The pleasantries and introductions over with, they proceeded up to the 20th floor.

They walked off the elevator and Cross looked around. The lobby area was rich with expensive construction materials, artworks and furnishings. They were invited to dispense with their winter wear which they did, courtesy of a coat stand and shelves. As they proceeded towards a conference room surrounded by opulent glass walls, he took mental notes. Pictures lined the walls of construction projects and major structural developments. Rossiya Hotel had been demolished years ago. When Cross first visited Soviet Russia in the 80's, he stayed there. At the time it was the largest hotel in the world but occupied prime real estate.

The football World Cup was only last year and Putin wanted to create an image of an affluent and friendly Russia which, for the most part, he succeeded in doing. Rossiya Hotel was replaced with a park over time and recently a pedestrian bridge was erected that went out over the Moskva River and looped back in. Cross saw the project displayed pictorially on the walls in various stages of construction.

They were led past extensive glass and into the ostentatious, lavish conference room. The windows overlooked Red Square, The Kremlin and St. Basil's Cathedral off in the distance, lit up with a spectacular display of lighting.

"Hello Mr. Cross and Ms. Fedorova. Welcome to Moscow."

Romanov was a large, imposing human specimen. He was in his early 60's and incredibly handsome. He must have breathed fear into any man he did business with. His strong handshake confirmed this. His chiseled and hardened face was a picture of experience, a man who had seen a lot in his life. His head was shaved but the hair was beginning to grow back. This fierce portrayal was enforced by a few days of facial growth. His body was muscular and contoured underneath expensive black European clothing. Cross took the lead, to show strength in the Russian tradition.

"Здравствуйте, господин Романов. Приятно наконец встретиться с вами. Я много слышал о ваших предприятиях. Должен сказать, очень впечатляет." Hello Mr. Romanov. It is a privilege to finally meet you. I have heard a lot about your enterprises. I must say very impressive, he said.

"Вы красноречиво говорите по-русски мистер Кросс." You speak eloquent Russian, Mr. Cross, he replied. He was clearly impressed.

"Спасибо." Thank you.

"This is my corporate president Mr. Kuznetsov."

Cross shook hands but wasn't sure what else to say. He was sleeping with his ex-wife and Kuznetsov was another imposing Being whom he didn't want to piss of. Cross and Fedorova were introduced to several others in the room. The two big men who stepped off the elevator were standing by the wall next to Romanov, paying special attention to their surroundings and guests.

Coffee, tea and Russian pastries were available so Cross poured himself a tea and reached over to take a piece of cake. Everyone took a seat. Fedorova sat next to Cross. The formalities over with, Romanov continued.

"Welcome to my corporate offices. As you may know, we import a number of essential materials for construction within the Russian Empire."

For a lot of Russians, they don't perceive the fall of Soviet Russia as reality. It was a huge embarrassment to many. Cross thought about the words Romanov was purposely using. It would explain his military and political incursions into former Russian Republics. Cross had met several, mostly the older generation, who wanted the old Soviet Russia back.

Romanov had a laptop hooked to a large screen on the wall. Someone dimmed the lights and he went into what seemed a choreographed presentation. Who knows how many people he does this to. Romanov obviously took centre stage and was used to the attention. He was a narcissistic megalomaniacal psycho who was incredibly ruthless and dangerous. He was a formidable figure in the room.

Fifty five minutes later he was done. Cross posed a few questions and then continued.

"I understand imported materials into Russia have to be tested. You must have a facility that does that, Mr. Romanov?"

"Yes. We have a big laboratory built specifically for this purpose north east of Moscow. We have arranged for you to visit this location tomorrow morning. It was built some time ago but we are required to expand it as we legally require additional scientific research and development. As you know, the rules for analytical testing keep changing and Russia must also comply with those rules, despite the western world's skepticism. It may surprise you but our facility is certified to numerous ISO standards. We have no choice."

"I am very impressed. This is remarkable progress since the fall of Soviet Russia."

Cross wanted to gauge his reaction, but Romanov didn't flinch, or take the bait.

"We had no choice. The collapse was unfortunate but it actually was predicated on President Gorbachev creating an environment that wasn't financially or politically sustainable. The end was inevitable, Mr. Cross."

"I understand. I have read the history and followed it. I was actually here before the collapse. It is completely different now and Moscow is a world class city."

"It is, within the inner two circular roadways surrounding it. I assure you things change beyond an unmarked boundary," he gave him a dark look, perhaps a warning. "Rural Russia is very different."

"Thank you for accommodating Mr. Cross' short visit, Mr. Romanov. We are truly grateful and appreciate your time is precious and expensive," said Fedorova, breaking in to salvage the decorum.

"I did some research on Mr. Cross and he is well respected. He has a client in Russia which I actually admired. I am honoured to have met him, Ms. Fedorova.

"Sorry for being so abrupt but now I must finish because I have other appointments. My time never stops. There will be a car waiting for you at 10:30am tomorrow morning outside the Hotel Metropol. It will be a black Range Rover and unmarked. However, the driver will recognise you."

Interesting, Cross never mentioned which hotel he was staying at. Perhaps Fedorova did.

"Thank you Mr. Romanov for your time. I am looking forward to visiting your facility tomorrow."

They all shook hands and then taken downstairs. Outside the building Cross turned to Fedorova.

"A very interesting presentation, Alexandria. I am curious why they require more advanced scientific instrumentation. We will find out."

"Sorry, I had to step in. You were purposely, I guess, testing the boundaries," she said.

Cross just smiled at her. Fedorova dropped him off in front of the Metropol and disappeared into the cold, dark Moscow evening. Cross looked at his watch. It was approaching 11pm. Across Revolution Square was the Four Seasons Hotel, so he proceeded in that direction.

20

The Identical Twin Sister, Four Seasons Hotel

Cross sat at the bar in the Four Seasons. He knew they had some local beer so ordered a glass, along with a shot of Russian Standard vodka. He knew the Colombian bartender, Sebastian, and they sat and chatted. The guy was funny, married to a Russian, who had traveled and worked a few cities in Russia. He had some interesting stories to tell so they connected. Cross always marveled at how people are just people wherever he went.

Half way into his beer and engrossed in another story with the bartender, he felt a lady's presence as she sits next to him. He swivels the chair to face her and turned white.

"Hello Mr. Cross. Do you mind if I sit next to you?" she said in broken English.

He tried to form some sort of dialect, tried to massage some words together but couldn't muster anything. He just stared. The memories of recent events slapping him in the face.

"I am Ms. Natalie Mikhailov."

He couldn't move, couldn't get his mouth to operate. He was momentarily taken over with fear. He somehow took the shot glass and emptied the contents into his mouth. He turned to his friend and asked he get the lady a drink.

"Cassandra was my twin sister."

Cross couldn't control his emotions anymore. His eyes welled up and a tear started to roll down his cheek.

"She died in my arms. That day keeps me awake at night. The site of her taking her last breath leaves me petrified," he said mildly shaking.

Sebastian brought the lady an aged whiskey, neat. She took a sip.

"Are you ok, Mr. Cross?" he asked.

"Yes, thank you, Sebastian. Ms. Mikhailov is an old friend I haven't seen in years."

Mikhailov wiped the tear from Cross' face. He was visibly disturbed and haunted.

"Cassandra was Romanov's mistress. I work for Romanov as a liaison and in a secretarial capacity. He moved on from her and then Cassandra met Robert. That part is real," her Russian accent was strong.

"But you left LA using your sister's name."

"Yes, I had to. Romanov told me to. You met him tonight and can appreciate I had no choice. We had to hide her death in Namibia."

"She was murdered, Natalie. I was there remember," clearly agitated.

Now Mikhailov was upset.

"Thank you for clarifying that, Mr. Cross. I know she was."

"What happened to Cassandra's body after I left her?" showing he cared.

"She was flown back to Russia on a private charter. Our family was told to keep quiet and we gave her a private funeral."

"What capacity are you here acting on, Romanov's behalf or voluntarily? How did you know I was here?"

"I was in the building when you arrived with Ms. Fedorova. I knew you were coming. Romanov cannot know I am here. I know you like this bar so took a chance.

"I am in trouble. There is something big going on. I don't have the details yet but I am expendable as they say. I know things I am not supposed to know. I may need your help."

"I have one question. Why Cassandra? Why did she have to die?" he was emotional again posing this question.

"Romanov had deemed her redundant and was expendable as a consequence. She was terminated because she outgrew her usefulness and knew too much. This is how Romanov operates."

"What about the diamond?"

They left the bar area and walked over to be more private and comfortable on one of the quarter-moon shaped luxury-cushioned sofas. Luckily the DJ was on a break. He couldn't believe how matched the twins were in physical appearance. They even had an identical voice.

Cross spent the next hour or so listening to Mikhailov, if she really was Cassandra's sister. He knew she must be. It was impossible to mistake that but which twin was she? He had no idea. This was heading into a dangerous territory, one he wasn't qualified to understand nor languish in.

"You know Mr. Mitrovic is dead?"

"Yes, I heard. I am sure he wasn't aware of anything going on. He just wanted to sell the diamond to make some money so he could invest in the cannabis grow in California and purchase Cassandra a nice home. All his assets were leveraged to purchase the diamond."

"How did he know about it?"

Mikhailov filled him in on that too. He had begun to relax a little with all the information she was divulging. He also knew she must surely be expendable.

Cross ordered some more drinks as they continued their discussions, and his friend brought them over. Mikhailov gave him some insight into the facility they will be visiting, he looked at his watch, in eight hours from now. She told him what to look for.

Armed with that, Cross decided it was time to head back to his hotel.

"Please tell me you can help me?"

Cross knew she is in trouble. She was trembling a little and held out her hand so he grasped it to comfort her. Dammit.

"Do you have a safe place to go?"

"I have to be in Romanov's office in the morning. We have things to go over. I cannot give the impression I know something and we must keep your excursion to Sergiyev Posad as planned. If I don't show up, he will suspect something."

"I will leave now and exit through a different door. Give it half hour before you leave."

Cross kissed her on the cheek and she departed. He ordered another drink.

Back in his room he called Granfield and they filled each other in on newly garnered facts.

"Her twin sister?" he asked shocked. "Please be careful now. This is becoming very delicate."

Granfield always had an articulate way of stating the obvious.

"She might need protection but will let you know. I promised her we would but I don't have the authority to promise her anything."

"Yes you do," Granfield assured him.

They were beginning to build a picture of something big. They had found government-funded transfers to Taiwan via a web of offshore accounts. GreenSea Enterprises was being partly funded by a special-interest account in the US. No connection with the two Russians in Kaohsiung, as of yet.

He called Dunhill next. It was nice to hear her voice again, and Cross was happy to be doing so. It was still snowing in Tahoe but an upper-atmospheric Hawaiian hot air pocket was heading California's way. It was going to rapidly melt the vast snow, Dunhill told him.

He then dialed Verenich's number.

"Was Katie happy to see you?" laughed Verenich.

"You had me scared as hell, Igor. That wasn't funny. But yes, she is as beautiful as I remember her to be."

"Just presenting you with nice Russian customs," he said still laughing.

Cross filled him in on the recent findings. The trip to Moscow City, Cassandra's twin sister Natalie's visit to the bar and…

Verenich cut him short.

"You met Cassandra's twin sister? There is nothing about her having a twin."

"One of the twin sisters. I don't know yet who is who but the spitting image. I nearly had a coronary when she sat next to me."

Cross went over what she had discussed.

"This is getting very dangerous, Daniel. I don't know if you should proceed with this. Get Granfield to get you out of there."

"No. I need to visit their facility in a few hours. Alexandria meets me at the hotel. I need a witness for protection but I hope I am not endangering her life. She works for the US Embassy which leverages some defense. We get picked up at 10:30. I will keep my head down."

With that, he clicked off and tried to grab a few hours of sleep before breakfast.

21

Trouble in Sergiyev Posad

Fedorova calls at 7:30am. Unusual for Russians to be working so early, thought Cross. He was awake anyway having had little sleep.

"I will be down in the lobby around 9:30. Perhaps we can partake in some breakfast."

"That would be great."

He took a shower and slipped into a suit and tie. He applied some Chanel, reached for the winter outerwear and headed downstairs early. He was enjoying a coffee at the bar when Fedorova joined him. They headed off to the hotel's famous restaurant for breakfast.

10:30 rolls around and they step outside. A black long wheelbase Range Rover Autobiography is already waiting. The driver sees them and walks around to open the rear door.

"Good morning Ms. Fedorova and Mr. Cross. I am Vladimir and I will be your driver to Sergiyev Posad. Drinks, coffee, pastries are available in the back. The ride will be approximately two hours, depending on traffic. Please relax." His English was sufficient to understand, if a little rehearsed. It was unlikely Cross could ask him any questions.

The driver navigated the dire Moscow traffic and headed out on

E115. He finally pulled off the main highway after some stop-go traffic most of the way. Dilapidated properties lined the highway and got worse the farther out from Moscow they traveled. There was road construction everywhere, which had stopped because of winter. They took a two lane country road off the main highway when they passed the city. Cross had been conversing with Fedorova and warming to her. They were obviously just north of Sergiyev Posad when Vladimir took a right. It was secluded with very few properties in the vicinity. Everywhere looked drab aided by the cold, harsh weather. Then Cross noticed a looming multi-storey complex off in the distance. The construction looked new but behind that was a mega-warehouse coming into view as they neared.

"This must be it," he said to Fedorova. "Keep your eyes open and stay close to me," he whispered.

The Range Rover crossed over some railroad tracks and then drove a little further before parking in front of the complex. The driver stepped out and opened the rear door. A lady came out to greet them and then escorted Fedorova and Cross into the building. The building had two external signs attached in Russian with the English translation underneath. The first larger one had 'Romanov Materials Testing' and the smaller one had 'Advanced Agricultural Engineering".

Through two security doors and a metal detector they entered the lobby. There they handed ID's to the security staff behind the thick bullet-proof glass window. Cross' eyebrows lifted. They were provided visitor badges to hang from their necks and then walked through another secured door before being shown into a conference room. Mr. Romanov was already there, along with Mr. Kuznetsov and their people.

"Welcome Ms. Fedorova and Mr. Cross. Please remove your winter jackets, gloves and hats. You don't need them in here," Romanov was courteous. "Please take a seat. There is some coffee or tea, with brown sugar and cream, Mr. Cross." They did their homework.

"Thank you. This is another impressive facility, Mr. Romanov," as they sat down and poured themselves a coffee. Russian chocolates were on the table.

It was new construction. It looked new. Security was everywhere with cameras, motion detectors and electro-magnetically-sealed doors. Cross guessed six storeys.

Romanov introduced the facility, production and office managers.

"I will have two scientists show you around and then they will bring you back here. The tour will be about ninety minutes. Then we can discuss our analytical needs, Mr. Cross."

Romanov left the room. After the coffee and some small talk, a young lady and gentleman, presumably the scientists Romanov alluded to, escorted them out.

The work here was staggering. Any goods imported into Russia had to be tested for toxins, rigidity, structural integrity and the like. This was especially valid for construction materials. Cross knew enough to know that most construction projects had money siphoned to pay off government officials, bankers, other bribes and so on. This meant not all money went into the construction so most ended up being sub-par, particularly residential tower blocks. He believed this was a front for the industry in general just to appease the populace perhaps, not that they had a choice.

They navigated each floor and some had large equipment to structurally test items the equipment was designed to test. Workers were everywhere. They don't see many foreigners because some of them gawked at Cross. Offices for the employees to work and hang out in were attached to each area of test and the various floors had their own break area and small kitchenette, bathrooms and shower facilities. He would help himself to a cookie as they walked through.

The third floor was vacant but had been designed to be an analytical facility. They entered through special key passes and it too had air-lock double-door access. Cross moved around and took visual notes and confirmations. It was large, perhaps 6,000 sq.ft. of laboratory space plus offices, another break area, conference room. It was all plumbed and electrically ready for scientific instruments and chemists. He also noticed a second set of air-lock doors into a separate area. Perhaps an area for biological compounds, Cross surmised.

The two people escorting them had a call so they walked out for a few minutes. Cross took advantage and quickly started opening cabinets looking for anything suspicious. Then he noticed some bottles of chemicals he was now familiar with. They had been supplied by the same Chinese companies as those found in GreenSea's research facility. His heart skipped a beat and he quickly closed the chemical storage cabinet just as the escorts walked back in.

"Let us move to the next floor," the lady said.

They walked through floors four, five and six (Cross was right about the number of floors) observing all the testing. There were a lot of people working here and it was a hive of activity. It really was very fascinating to see. Even Fedorova was interested in what she was observing. Likely not many Russians know of such a facility existing, especially when they live in the vast city of Moscow and don't venture anywhere. This one was certainly set off the beaten track.

After their time slot was up, they took the stairs back down to the conference room and waited. Ten minutes later Romanov shows up.

"How did you like the facility?"

"It is a nest of honey bees. Extraordinary, Mr. Romanov," answered Cross, stroking the ego narcissism demands.

Clearly Romanov was proud of the building and of the work that goes on. Cross had to remind himself of his ruthlessness but this was a show piece for someone, or some people, to see. It was meant as a selling point or perhaps just a front for his real enterprises. Likely the latter.

Cross was curious about the chemicals he saw and of the mega-warehouse out back. Mikhailov had been right about this place.

"Let us discuss the third floor and what we are looking for."

Romanov discussed his needs to test agricultural products. He didn't elaborate. Cross was stunned but didn't show it. He had the same conversation the other side of the planet only a few days ago.

"What kind of product, Mr. Romanov?"

"I cannot divulge proprietary information that will be patentable when finished, Mr. Cross. However, for centuries people have been relying on naturally occurring biological compounds for remedies. We don't need engineered pharmaceutical products."

That was an interesting comment from the array of chemicals Cross just saw in the laboratory cabinets.

Moving on, Cross removed some material from the folder he had been carrying and presented them to Romanov. It was identical to the brochures he had given Wu, only this time translated in Russian, instead of Mandarin.

He laid out what they needed based on the limited information he was being given. However, agriculture is similar throughout the world so he knew generally what they required. Anything special he could of course discuss that. His presentation lasted thirty minutes.

"Thank you, Mr. Cross," said Romanov, whilst attentively listening. "I will have you escorted out to visit the warehouse. We will meet back here in forty five minutes."

Romanov was strict, structured and regimented, probably from days in the Russian KGB.

The warehouse was vast. It comprised a lobby, more offices, a break area with kitchenette, bathroom and shower rooms and a high-tech conference room. They were shown the warehouse area and there were already some crates with product on. The loading dock area had rollup-doors exiting out to the railroad tracks they had crossed reaching the complex. He could see that through a side door that had a window. Cross was careful but needed to see the crates. The warehouse was split and had security doors leading to a huge isolated area. He needed to see this area too. He saw a lone warehouse worker standing near the doors and asked Fedorova to help him. He needed a distraction from their two male escorts.

"Security is in the front offices and facing external doors in the warehouse, I noticed. I need about three minutes."

She dropped the zipper on her dress a few inches and then pretended to fall on the floor, twisting her ankle. Her dress rode up her legs as the two Russians came over to console her. She wore black woolen stockings but the view of her black panties had them salivating.

"Please can you take me to the conference room so I can suppress the pain a little? Do you have any ice packs?"

The first carried her whilst the second ran off to the kitchen. Cross was now on his own. The distracted men had forgotten about him. He walked over to the warehouse worker and lashed out at his temple. Works every time, thought Cross. His eyes would have flashed just as the young Russian dropped to the floor and was out cold. He removed the security pass and quickly walked a few paces to the double doors. Knowing people would be working the other side he keyed the security pad and slowly pulled the door open. He peaked inside and was shocked. The grow area was vast, and multi-layered with suspended floor systems, but he could tell by the leaves what they were growing. Again, there was no characteristic aroma in the room. Looking to see any workers, he quickly pulled a few leaves from the nearest plant and then closed the security door. He stuffed them into his jacket pocket. He carefully moved the worker he had cracked across the head to an area that was isolated, placing the security badge back around his neck. He would be awake shortly.

Cross looked over at the pallets and took a few pictures with his pen. The packaging looked familiar also. He then quickly ran back to the conference room where he knew Fedorova was being attended. When he walked in she was sitting on the table with an ice pack on her ankle. The knees were bent and her dress was purposely pushed up revealing a very pleasant distraction, thought Cross. She smiled at him and winked. The young men were falling over themselves to console her. Fedorova was beautiful and Cross didn't question them at all.

"Are you ok honey?" he asked.

"I think I am going to be fine, Mr. Cross."

"Perhaps we should make our way back to the main building so we can say good bye to Mr. Romanov and Mr. Kuznetsov."

She brushed down her dress and climbed off the table. The two men then escorted them back to the main building.

"Are you hungry?" Romanov added.

Without providing an impression of needing to run and run is precisely what he wanted to do, Cross said yes and looked at Fedorova. She nodded in agreement.

"I cannot join you but my assistant will. I will have the driver take you to a fine restaurant in town. The food is excellent, the ambiance is impeccable and they have young cute waitresses," now looking at Cross. "It has already been taken care of. Order what you would like. The bill is paid for. Perhaps we can convene in Moscow City tomorrow morning, say 11?"

"Thank you. Tomorrow sounds excellent," and scary, he wanted to add but didn't. He wonders if the guy in the warehouse will remember his blow to the head.

It was late when they arrived at the Metropol and Cross already had messages on his phone. He invited Fedorova for a drink at the bar and she obliged. They needed to sit away from earshot of anyone and found a table with round luxurious chairs in a quiet area. Cross found out Fedorova's preference and ordered two Beluga Gold Line vodkas, neat. Why do Russian women always like expensive drinks?

He smiled to himself.

"You were really good back there in the warehouse."

"I know Russian men, Mr. Cross," she said smiling. "So what did you find out?"

"They are growing cannabis, perhaps the same strain as the plants in Taiwan. They had no aroma either. It was surreal. The grow area was huge. I did manage to pilfer a few leaves and will have those tested back in Langley.

"You notice the chemical bottles in their laboratory?" he asked.

"I saw you looking but I didn't get to see. I was worried about the two escorts coming back in."

"Thank you. They are the same chemicals from the same Chinese companies as those I found at GreenSea's research facility. They appear to be working on the same product and doing similar research. This could be colossal and very dangerous. It could imply they are collaborating in some form."

He paused and looked at Fedorova. They picked up the glasses and clinked.

"Thank you. It has been a pleasure working with you the past two days. We get to do it again tomorrow but I am worried," he continued.

"I wonder if the warehouse employee will remember," she said.

"My guess, being a Russian, he would be scared to bring it up to his supervisors. Mr. Romanov is ruthless. The guy would end up in a field and never seen again. He will find it best to keep his mouth shut. They built that facility away from the population for a reason."

He moved his chair closer so no one can hear anything or in case someone is lip reading. He covered his mouth.

"I suspect this is a collaborative effort to generate a virus. Can you do something for me please?"

"Of course," she smiled. She would do anything for Cross.

"When you get back to the office, or perhaps in the morning, can you do some research to see if anyone has been killed by a localised virus in Russia? Research the area immediately surrounding Sergiyev Posad."

"I can do better than that, Mr. Cross."

She purposely uncrossed her legs and slightly opened them to display her stockings. She reached for her phone and made a call to someone. He had no idea who. She spoke some Russian and then ended the call and placed the phone back on the table.

"We can have another drink while I have a friend I trust look into it. He owns a controversial paper so can find all sorts of things the average Russian has no access to."

Cross smiled.

"How about appetisers? I don't like drinking without some food," she said. "My friend will be a while."

They devoured the delightful food plates and then Cross invited her back to his suite. He had the bottle of Onegin he hadn't opened yet and some caviar left. They sat on the sofa and talked openly about her life in Russia. Cross wanted to listen. He poured two fresh glasses of vodka. They were both relaxed, which was surprising, considering what they had just done.

"Wait, I took some photos," and downloaded them onto his phone.

There was an address and he showed it to Fedorova.

"Know where this place is?" Cross asked.

Fedorova nodded just as her phone buzzed. She listened to her friend on the other end and then put the phone down. The journalist confirmed what Cross had suspected. Now he was beginning to piece things together.

"The address is close to where the warehouse is located."

Cross filled up the glasses again and, after some more conversation, she took his hand and headed into the bedroom.

It was early hours now. He walked Fedorova back downstairs and waited until she was picked up by an embassy car before heading back to his room. He called Granfield first.

"I am piecing this all together. There is something big going on here. Romanov was very hospitable and charming but he is a powerful, formidable character in a room. I was careful not to create any hassles or make gestures that would open more cans of worms. I think we have enough worms working overtime already. It is hard to say now because they aren't operational, but it looks like both the laboratories in Taiwan and Russia are biological labs. Both have air-lock access and both hosts hid access to certain areas. The air-systems in both were huge, required in biological labs for positive pressure."

"Great work, Daniel. I was worried about you today. We will now look into the money trail which sends money to Russia. Wow, hard to believe the US government is funding this."

"We have another meeting in Moscow City tomorrow at 11am. I am not sure about this. I am not even sure the Russian government knows about this but who knows. I doubt the Taiwan government does so why would the one here be any different? He may wish to proceed with requisitioning the scientific equipment. That would be my guess, and he wants it expedited with no cost concerns."

"Keep this going. Be relaxed, be yourself. Keep up the impression that is your mission. They may be freelancing. This conspiracy is staggering. Let me find the money trail into Russia and will get back to you. A bank in Grand Cayman is involved. You may be heading there next."

"Great," said Cross, but he was tired and too old for this shit. "Romanov has vast resources over here and there is a substantial investment in this already. Natalie provided me some information on the diamond but I cannot see it being for this project. $16M, the difference between what he paid and the insurance premium payout, isn't buying this. There is no indication at all it is funding any of this venture. I didn't see that today. I will see if I can reach her. She gave me a private number."

"Be careful," Granfield was genuine. "These people are vicious," he added before putting the phone down.

Verenich next.

"That is amazing. Something big is being developed, Daniel. How is rural Russia?"

"Same as before but just a different geographical location. Romanov's complex is vast and impressive. Natalie mentioned something last night I would like you to research." He provided the details and a name.

"Will do, komrad. Not to worry you but there is a tropical depression coming from Hawaii which will melt the vast snow being dumped over the course of the past week."

"Yes, I know. Chantelle told me and then I got on the internet to read about it. I will be ok, I think. 50% sure anyway," they both laughed.

"How is she anyway?"

"Doing well and relaxing in my home. She may head back to LA, she wants to anyway, but I advised against it. Her husband is a foreboding figure in Romanov's empire. He doesn't speak much. Perhaps Romanov does all the talking when he is around."

"Robert's murder spooked her and she is scared of Vladimir for obvious reasons," added Verenich. "That sounds about right for a Russian mafia figurehead. They control. The people underneath are all dispensable, all of them."

"The money trail goes across the globe. I may be heading to Grand Cayman after this."

"Are you happy I signed you up for this?" he laughed, but it was strained and not genuine.

"Thanks, mate. I will return the favour one day."

Click. One more call.

"Hello Mr. Cross."

"How are you, Natalie? Please, call me Daniel."

"Good. How was the trip to Sergiyev Posad?"

"The trip was very interesting. It is an impressive setup out there. We got to see the main complex with all the testing facilities and were invited into the warehouse. This is a secure line and I have scanned the room but I don't know what line you are using. This needs to be discussed in person."

"I am at my apartment and away from prying ears. I see you have a meeting this morning at 11."

Cross didn't know what time it was anymore. He was tired but wide awake. This was gaining momentum.

"Yes. I haven't made plans to leave Russia yet. Perhaps we can meet in the afternoon. I don't know what Romanov has in store. I believe he wants to discuss the analytical laboratory."

"Yes, he does. He is a gifted but sinister individual. He knew about Namibia because he arranged my sister's murder. He hasn't figured the rest out yet. However, keep vigilant. He usually knows more than he lets on. He must have heard about Huang's death in Taiwan, as a guess."

This put Cross on edge. He never divulged that information last night. How did she know? Time to end the call. Romanov is a clever man. He cannot dispose of someone with an American Embassy representative in his presence. That would be suicide, but then perhaps he can because he doesn't give a shit. Cross needs to keep Fedorova safe with him and he was nervous. He was becoming suspicious of everyone, yet Mikhailov was the one who approached him.

"Let us catch up after my meeting with Romanov. I need a few hours of sleep at least so chat later."

22

The Virus, the Vaccine and the One World Order

Now daylight hours, although cloudy and intermittently snowing, Cross could observe the stunning vista from the conference room in Romanov Plaza. He stood by the windows to take it all in. Who is paying for this, he wondered. The vast majority of Russians are poor but here, lay an opulent oasis of extravagance and corporate wealth.

The meeting wasn't too long but Romanov re-iterated his need for scientific equipment. In the material Cross had presented in Sergiyev Posad, was a breakdown of costs.

"I want to begin the formal process of purchasing equipment, Mr. Cross. Next week we will transfer money to an account that can be accessed by you. You tell me you have friends who can provide equipment both at a reduced cost and quickly. I don't much care about the reduced cost. When you return home fill me in on final prices, including installation. We will take care of shipping to Moscow. The quickly part of this equation is essential for the needs of my company. Be aware time is of the essence."

"Mr. Romanov, when I return to the hotel today, I assure you I will be asking my people to work on this. I will have final pricing within two days."

"Excellent. My assistant Ms. Sorokin will provide you with contact information. However, you perhaps have that already."

"That would be fine."

"Again, please accept my apologies but I have other urgent necessities requiring my immediate attention. I appreciate you flying half way around the world to meet me. What I researched doesn't do you justice. You are a fine gentleman, Mr. Cross. I will look forward to doing business with you."

With that they stood up and shook hands before Romanov departed the room with most of his entourage.

Ms. Sorokin presented Cross with pertinent contact information and then led Cross and Fedorova downstairs and into the lobby. They too shook hands and then walked past security, through thick glass double doors required to keep the bitter cold out and out into the freezing Moscow air. It was noon.

"I would not have known his history by just meeting him the past few days," Cross said as they walked towards the black Mercedes.

"You did very well, Daniel. I was impressed too. You can handle these international formalities. Some people struggle with cultural and language barriers. You excel."

"Thank you, Alexandria. It drains me though. I am trying to act normal whilst finding information I don't know exists.

"What are your plans for this afternoon?" he asked

"I am responsible for your wellbeing and safety," she said chuckling.

"God help me," Cross laughed. "I feel sorry for you."

"I have some things to find out this afternoon but we can do lunch if this is fine with you? We could meet up later too."

They went back to the Metropol and left the car there, walking over towards the Four Seasons Hotel.

"There is a restaurant just across the square here. I cannot remember the name now but it is next to McDonalds and across from the Tomb of the Unknown Soldier."

"I know where you mean."

They carried on walking past the hotel and across the square.

Inside the restaurant Cross selected a table with a bench seat. He wanted to be next to Alexandria. Just as they were seated, his mobile rang.

"This is my friend Igor in the US. Please excuse me, Alexandria, I need to take this."

He stepped outside and answered.

"Daniel, the name Hosseini has come up. Natalie gave you a name so I researched it per your instructions. Hosseini is a high profile Major General in the Iranian army. He is actually the head of the Iranian military, to be more precise. I got special permission from a friend and satellite images show a huge building being oc-cupied by an enterprise he owns on the outskirts of Varamin, which is forty miles or so south east of Tehran. It is an industrial city. This is highly privileged information, my friend. I am not even sure the CIA or FBI knows this. The building is surrounded by high walls and security. The complex could be as large as the one you describe in Sergiyev Posad. Electronic chatter detected some agricultural fa-cility. I will get back to you with further information when I have it."

Cross returned to the dining table, perplexed by how his friend found that information. There is something he doesn't know about Verenich, and perhaps doesn't need to know.

"We have found a contact in Iran perhaps doing the same thing as Wu and Romanov," he said to Alexandria. "I will have more in-formation soon but this is extremely privileged."

"Oh my God, what is going on, Daniel?" She held his hand.

"I am shocked. CIA needs to find the money trail on this too but they might not have Hosseini's name on their radar. If I reveal to them this contact, they will wonder about my intelligence sources. I don't want to reveal I have privileged information. People could get killed knowing this.

"As far as I can tell, we have three separate entities developing similar if not the same products in three different countries.

"I can trust you, Alexandria? Too late to ask now, I realise."

"I work for the American Embassy in Moscow. My job is to look after you and make your stay better. I am your liaison. I don't want to be involved in something like this because I could end up dead. You have my word."

"Sorry, I had to ask."

Cross ordered Borscht soup which Ukraine claims to be their recipe. He added breaded pork cutlets and fresh vegetables. Fedorova added a protein-based salad, "To protect my figure and allow me to run from any villains you encounter," she said chuckling, looking at Cross.

After lunch she left him at the Metropol and would contact him later. It was now 2:50pm. He picked up his phone and dialed.

"Hello, Natalie. How are you? Are you working?"

"No, I just got off." She sounded happy to hear from him.

"Want to meet me at Bosco restaurant in Gum Mall, say 4pm? I don't want to talk anywhere near the hotel."

They were seated in the restaurant and Cross ordered two vodkas.

"The name you gave me led us to a military commander high up in the Iranian army. He likely is head of the Iranian military."

"I couldn't tell you who he is because I didn't know but this makes sense. I told you I have heard his name discussed in secret meetings in Romanov Plaza."

"Knowing this could get you killed?" said Cross.

"Yes indeed, Daniel."

"It opens up a new chapter in this already insane challenge. We are searching for money being transferred to Romanov courtesy of the US federal government. We have found it for Wu's operation.

The senator from Illinois is involved."

Just then Granfield calls.

"I will keep this short. You need to watch CNN International, Daniel, where ever you are."

"I am with Natalie just off Red Square. She has information that will get her killed, David. She needs taking out of here."

"Find a TV, go back to your room or something, but go watch CNN. Let us continue this conversation after you have seen the news. Take Natalie with you."

Granfield sounded almost desperate.

"Can you come back to my hotel room, Natalie? There is something we need to watch."

Cross turned on the TV and found the channel. Now they had to wait as the news was repetitively circulated around various events going on in the world. Then there it was. He remembered his face.

"We need to pass this bill. The health of the nation, may be the world, depends on a suitable vaccine for the American people to combat the next virus. This is vital."

The words eloquently emanating from Senator Brownsville's mouth as he stood in front of the lectern inside the White House briefing room. He almost sounded plausible and credible, and would have had it not been for Cross seeing him outside Wu's building in Kaohsiung. He was a piece of shit, knew Cross. Politicians in their expensive suits full of crap.

"Brownsville is siphoning money under the guise of special interest in order to fund this. I imagine he will make substantial monies and may even have control of the US government," he said to Mikhailov.

With that he stopped talking and picked up the phone to do a little research. He found what he was looking: Upon the death of the president and vice president, the leader of the house would be the next US president. Cross' heart skipped at least one beat and he typed in more words. Found it. Senator Brownsville is the current Speaker of the House. He turned to face Mikhailov.

"The senator you see standing there would be the next president if the president and vice president both die."

Cross called Granfield.

"Did you watch it?" asked Granfield before Cross had said anything.

"Yes. Brownsville's involvement in the development of a vaccine is part of his takeover of the US government, it looks like. It is tantamount to biological deception. He is deceiving the public for his personal gain. I wonder if this all pertains to the One World Order rhetoric?" Cross added.

"Yes and possibly. It is important you get back to the US. The vote for the bill is in three weeks and it is already gaining momentum. They want to have enough vaccines to vaccinate everybody. The fact we are seeing development of this emerging in other countries suggests this is going to be worldwide, or at least in specific controlling countries," added Granfield. "It could be being developed here also."

"David, I cannot divulge sources because I promised I wouldn't, but this may be happening in Iran too. Did you find the money trail to Romanov yet?"

"We have made progress on this, yes. We see it being funneled through similar channels under the same guise of 'special interest' funding."

"I will get back to you with the Iranian information later today."

"What do you have left to do in Russia?"

"I have contacted my office in Tahoe and they are providing pricing and availability for Romanov's equipment going into his scientific testing laboratory. I promised this. I have to keep this illusion and pretense going. I should have that prepared tomorrow morning Moscow time."

"I suggest you get out of there as soon as you can. Find a flight tomorrow afternoon. You can always do an overnight stay somewhere but get out of Russia. This is developing rapidly and we need you safe. I will arrange to have someone talk to the American Ambassador in Iran. Perhaps your next trip will be there. Sit tight. Thanks for the update and I will respect your requirement to keep sources confidential, as long as they don't keep information that is vital or interfere with our ongoing activities and objectives, Daniel. You understand this?"

"Yes, David. Thank you. I think Natalie needs to get out of here also. I will arrange this too."

The call ended and Cross turned to Mikhailov.

"Go pack. Be prepared to leave the country tomorrow afternoon. I will have Alexandria make travel arrangements. I will contact you later."

She left his room.

Fedorova called.

"Are you hungry?"

"I am. We have things to talk about but not on the phone."

"I will pick you up in an hour. Wait for me downstairs."

It was now 7:10pm. Damn time flies, thought Cross. He took a quick shower and stepped into some Italian jeans and cashmere sweater, all black so he could blend in.

He called Verenich.

"Did you watch CNN?" asked Cross, knowing he detests CNN and it would irritate him.

"I saw the news, not necessarily CNN," he clarified. "So now we know what is being planned and more or less when. We have three weeks to stop the vote and get him arrested, or killed, whichever is more appropriate. Even if it passes, it would be months before any vaccine is ready for implementing."

"I don't advocate shooting people except perhaps in this case,

Igor. I wouldn't be too sure about the vaccine comment either. I could have been played to give the perception everything is kosha. They may have done the research already at facilities we don't know about. There was something about Romanov's complex that struck me as odd. It looked staged, like a show facility. It was too organised.

"I am planning on leaving Moscow tomorrow afternoon. I will have Alexandria make the arrangements when I see her in an hour. I will message later."

An hour later Cross was being driven by Alexandria over to a reclusive restaurant away from the madness of downtown, in the direction of Moscow State University, the grandest of the seven Stalinist architectural buildings in Moscow. There was no parking but she said it doesn't matter. The restaurant was situated on a major multi-lane boulevard so she parked in front of the restaurant and turned on her blinkers, just like several other motorists did.

"This is how we do it here," she said laughing.

Cross was mesmerised and amusingly wondered if that could catch on in the US. They entered the European style wine bistro but Fedorova assured him it had many facets of different foods from many places. They were seated in a quiet corner and Cross wanted to try Chechen. Not a wine drinker, they stayed with Baltika Russian beer, which he liked. They quickly ordered the food so they could talk.

"I need to leave tomorrow afternoon, Alexandria. We also need to get Natalie out of here. Have you seen the news today?"

"Yes, I saw it. It made the news on Russian networks also. We have been doing some research at the embassy and we don't believe the Russian government is involved. We feel it is a clandestine operation. If what you are saying is true, there are some select people wishing to hijack the planet."

"That is our feeling. I may be asked to head into Iran but that country is more dangerous than Russia. I have been here and have some familiarity. Iran is alien in more ways than one.

"We are trying to link the flow of cash. Usually all one has to do is track it to find the rainbow and the culprits. This is a massive operation. You have to admire it all from a distance."

"Iran is dangerous, Daniel. Please be careful."

She put her hand on his leg and he placed his on top of hers. They were becoming close in such a short period of time. She was beautiful inside and out, he now knew. The picture of her on the floor in the warehouse he couldn't purge and last night in his suite was perfect. She leaned forward and kissed him gently.

"Please be careful."

The beers arrived with the food and they picked at it as they talked.

"I will work on flight details tonight and have them to you by morning."

"Do you ever sleep?" he asked.

"Not since you have been here," she laughed. "I am not allowed to."

They talked and ate some more. The towering majestic university building all lit up was a spectacular backdrop. Fedorova dropped Cross off at the Four Seasons and disappeared. She would message him later and meet for breakfast at 10:30am.

Crossed walked into the bar and sat down. He was mentally exhausted. He made a call.

"Hello Katie, how are you?"

She recognised his voice. He had promised he would call her. Thirty minutes later she was sitting next to him enjoying a cocktail. An hour later they were heading back to his hotel room.

23

Another Assassination Attempt

Cross had all the information ready to send to Romanov's assistant before breakfast. Brandy had stayed late in the office in Tahoe to get it taken care of. The pretense was ongoing. He emailed it over.

Down in the lobby Fedorova arrived.

"Good morning honey."

"Good morning, Daniel. Breakfast in the usual place?"

"No, I have ordered room service. Let us go into my suite."

She trusted him so obliged. Breakfast arrived and was served. Cross poured some coffee and added cream and brown sugar to both cups.

"I have it taken care of. You need to be very careful with Natalie. I don't feel Romanov would like her to leave."

"That is an understatement of huge proportions," Cross interrupted.

"I imagine he has people watching her. The embassy has arranged a private plane and you will leave through the auspices of being a diplomat. Your names will not be on any flight manifesto. Be vigilant which I know you are already. The plane will head to a private airport north of London. I wasn't even given the airport name. The CIA will meet you and proceed to the US, is my guess. I don't honestly know that for sure. You may be heading elsewhere. Natalie will be safe.

"The transport company will pick you up from here at 2pm. It will not be a black Mercedes S-Class, since they know the embassy fleet by now. It will be a Toyota Camry with a reinforced frame for added protection. I will message the color and license plate when the time comes. I will not be with you. We are using a special service. We may switch cars numerous times on the way. You will be departing from Vnukovo Airport. No one will suspect this departure point.

"We are working with the Russian government on this. At least people we know and trust.

"This may seem too much but we need to get you out of here safely."

They talked some more before they said goodbye, hugged and then she left.

He dialed a number.

"Where are you?" he asked. "You need to be at the Metropol by 2pm, Natalie."

"That is good. I can take my lunch at that time."

Whilst he waited for her, Cross took the extra time to view the route to the airport using GPS, and then planted it into his brain's memory cells.

The car arrived and they climbed in the back. The windows were darkened. Cross scoured the surroundings and saw nothing. It left the hotel area and moved into afternoon traffic. The driver was young but a strong man. He gently weaved in and out of traffic and then they exited the mayhem as he drove underneath Moscow's inner ring road. They now approached open spaces as they headed south west. They stopped at a light and a car pulled up next to them.

One bullet penetrated the window hitting the driver and he slumped over. Cross pulled his handheld out and fired through the window and into the car sitting next to them. He had already mounted the silencer on it before leaving the hotel. He aimed at the passenger and got him. Cross jumped out and opened the front driver's door of the Camry and pushed the driver over. He looked over and saw the driver of the other vehicle. It was one of the warehouse escorts in Sergiyev Posad. He pointed his gun, pulled the trigger and saw blood coming out of a hole in the guy's forehead as it dropped onto the steering wheel. Cross climbed into the car and started driving. He had prepared for this so knew where he was going. Now weaving with the gas pedal firmly planted, he had about seven miles to go.

He yelled at Mikhailov asking her to look for anyone else. Soon she saw another vehicle and yelled.

"Behind you on your right."

Cross looked and saw it. Another Audi. He asked Mikhailov to hold on. He went faster, pulled to the right and slammed hard on his brakes. The Audi didn't react fast enough and slammed into the back of Cross. The driver went flying out of the windshield. Some Russians outside of the inner ring roads rarely wore seatbelts. The car was now damaged but Cross could still drive it. A mile or so to go.

Up front he could see a car behaving erratically on the opposite side of the highway. As it came closer it worked its' way towards Cross. Before they had time to react, he fired two shots into the driver's side of the windshield. It swerved right and the car next to it t-boned it, rolling it over and over.

Cross saw the entrance to the private jet compound and as he approached someone opened it. They were expecting him. He looked ahead and found the embassy's Learjet waiting. He pulled up, got out and ran around to help Mikhailov. She was crying in the back as he grabbed her. Someone came over and hauled their bags before they climbed the stairs and into the plane. A few minutes later the door slammed shut and it started to taxi.

Mikhailov was a wreck. Memories of her sister poured through Cross' head. He consoled her, or tried to, as the plane headed down the runway and took off. He too had tears.

24

The Stolen Hydrocarbon

They transferred corporate planes at an airport near Birmingham, Cross heard. Langley was next. Mikhailov had relaxed and slept during the four hour flight to England. Cross had been on the phone.

"We left Russia but we were followed and chased. One of the men I killed we met in Sergiyev Posad. He was an escort at Romanov's facility."

"Good you are out. Get some rest. Call when you are on the flight to Langley."

Next call.

"Igor, we are out of Russia and on the way to England where we transfer to a CIA plane for Langley. We were chased."

"That is good you are out. Who is 'we'?"

"Oh, Natalie is with me. She had too much information and likely scheduled for execution just like her twin. The people chasing were from Romanov's enterprise. I wonder if he knew Natalie was with me."

"He knows everything, Daniel. You put yourself in danger. Get back to me when you land in Virginia."

Dunhill was next.

"Hi honey, how are you?"

She filled him in on the events in Tahoe. It was beginning to rain hard and flooding was anticipated from the melting snow. She was staying indoors. Cross told her he had now left Russian airspace and was heading back to Virginia via England. He explained, but didn't elaborate, on potential trips to Iran and Grand Cayman. She had seen the news about the senator and was scared.

"This bill is worrying. It sounds like they want to vaccinate the whole world."

"At least just the important and dangerous countries do. They may have developed the virus and vaccine already. The labs I have been seeing might be hiding the fact they are doing this already."

They said their goodbyes and Cross fell asleep.

They transferred planes and a few hours into the Langley flight, Cross called Granfield.

"Daniel, this is becoming very dangerous and I may elect to take you off this project. We are getting a few others up to speed on facts."

"No way. I am here now. Let's keep this going. We are making progress here. When do we tell the president about all this?"

"We have had that discussion already within the CIA confines. Not yet seems to be the general consensus. When you get here we will lay out the money trail. It is quite extensive.

"We are looking into Hosseini's activities also. It seems to us we have at least three countries all doing the exact same thing.

"The rain is now hitting Tahoe areas really hard. It will be like that for the next two to three days, they say. I hope everything will be ok.

"And Mitrovic was killed using a different gun. That didn't surprise us of course. However, the type of gun used did. It doesn't link his death to any Russian entity. They don't use that make and model of gun. His death we feel is domestic rather than an international syndicate. Just FYI, Daniel. Enjoy your flight and will see you in a few hours."

Cross called Dunhill.

"Robert's death they believe to be a domestic issue rather than an international syndicate. Type of weapon used I guess."

"That is interesting. This lends itself more to the cannabis field he wanted to get into, unless there are things we haven't uncovered yet."

"I agree with you. I also have no further information on the diamond he wanted to buy. There are already vast resources being spent in the countries of interest. The extra ten or so million makes no sense to me."

They talked a little more and then hung up the phones.

Mikhailov was now waking up. She had been asleep for long periods and Cross didn't want to disturb her. She went to the bathroom and cleaned herself up, applied some makeup and came out. Cross knew Russian women are elegant and she was still impeccably dressed, even after this ordeal. At least she wasn't on a United Airlines international flight in sweats, he laughed to himself. She sat across from him.

"Thank you for rescuing me, Daniel. I was sure yesterday was my last day alive."

"I cared about Cassandra. You even have her emerald green eyes. It is remarkable really. I didn't wish the same happen to you. I do have a question though. From our research, no one could find twin sisters. What happened?"

"We were orphaned when our parents died in a car accident early in our lives. Mr. Romanov's family took us in because my father worked for them. He isn't all bad, Daniel. Our family history was scrubbed and we were kept separated presumably because he had plans for our futures. As Romanov profited from the collapse of Soviet Russia and expanded his empire, he needed people to work for him. Beautiful Russian girls were required in certain capacities, usually in business settings such as assistants, secretaries, liaison officers. In the Russian culture a beautiful woman is the forefront of any business. It sets the reputation for the company. Cassandra became one of his mistresses for several years but he doesn't usually keep them around for long. She would travel with him from time to time, which is how she ended up in LA."

"That is quite a story. We complain in the west over stupid things not realising of course how people in the rest of the world truly have it."

"Are you at liberty to discuss things here? How private is this environment?" asked Mikhailov. "I have something important to share. But first promise me I will have protection."

"Come and sit closer to me. I am not 100% sure of our privacy level but it should be ok. Just keep your voice down. Mr. Granfield at CIA granted me the authority to do whatever I feel is required. I promise protection. I understand a little Russian also so we can use that dialect if need be."

"I had a feeling we would be void of Customs and Immigration problems, once you told me the exit strategy, so I brought something of value with me. Let me show you."

She removed her bag from the overhead and looked around the cabin. They were the only two with the exception of the flight attendant supposedly attending their needs. She was preoccupied reading a book. She opened the zipper to reveal a mahogany box.

Cross sat upright. His mouth dropped. The last time he saw a box like this was in a jewelry store in Windhoek.

"What have you brought us, Natalie?"

"Please promise me again I will have immunity and protection. This could get me killed like Cassandra. She knew too much also."

"Mr. Granfield at CIA has already confirmed this with me and I trust him. You will have immediate protection once you reach

Langley. This I assure you. I will protect you if he doesn't," he was being serious.

"Romanov already arranged to buy the diamond through contacts in the Namibian mining industry. Cassandra found out about it and knew Robert needed money to fund his cannabis grow operation. Actually he didn't need it. He had enough money but he wanted to buy control of the grow market. That was his downfall that likely lead to his death."

Cross was impressed because the evidence was supporting her claims and she was spot on there.

"Cassandra was dating Robert so she gave him privileged and confidential information which made Mr. Romanov angry, to be polite. He doesn't like being double-crossed. It was convenient for him to arrange a dummy purchase in Windhoek and to dispose of my sister."

"He knows people everywhere which is why you need to be very careful also. He didn't need Robert to be the middleman and he certainly didn't appreciate him knowing his transactional details."

"How the hell did you get the diamond out? You know he is going to come after it?"

"I have special access to certain areas of his building that others aren't allowed to go in. Those areas are reserved for people close to him. He didn't understand how upset I would be with Cassandra's death. She was my twin sister even though we spent many years separated. We still had a bond. He was beginning to suspect which is why I took the risk of coming to see you in the Four Seasons. You do need to change your habits by the way," she said laughing. "But yes, he will want it back."

"Yes I do, evidently. However, in my defense, I am not doing covert operations looking for information on behalf of the CIA. Usually, anyway," he said laughing along with her. "Well he isn't going to ring the door bell and politely ask for his diamond back, Natalie."

He was beginning to like her. She had this wit and effervescent charm which was immensely seductive.

"So, am I allowed to see it?"

She carefully brought out the box and released the latch. The lid opened to reveal a stunning example of one of the finest diamonds recently found. Now he could observe the magical colors and its perfection.

"Oh my God," carefully observing the specimen. "Please, close it up and keep this very quiet. Place the bag back in the overhead," and looked around as he was telling her this.

She did as he instructed.

"What was Romanov going to do with it?"

"He paid $9M which was far under value. Even Robert was going to pay more. It was insured for $25M which could be the end payout so he already is winning. But, from what I can gather, it was allegedly going to be a gift."

Cross' eyebrows were raised and he swiveled and leaned closer to her.

"When you told me to watch CNN yesterday, I went cold and my body froze. The gift was for a Mr. Brownsville. I didn't know who he was until I saw the news. I couldn't research names because I may be caught and I didn't want to know too much."

Now it was Cross' turn to freeze. He couldn't move. His facial expression just encapsulated the horror and shock of what he just heard. He had to unfreeze himself and gather his thoughts.

"Things are slowly beginning to make sense. It must be a gift for the senator funding his agricultural enterprise, shall we say. Can you confirm if Putin is in on this, Natalie?"

"The Russian government, at least the people controlling the country, know nothing of what is going on. I suspect Romanov has someone high up who would become president if Putin and his cronies were killed. If he made his contact President of Russia, he would be Romanov's puppet. He hated the collapse of Soviet Russia. It was insulting and humiliating for the Russian people. By that I mean the government. Some have never recovered psychologically.

"They are building a park that incorporates 15 statues representing the 15 previous Russian Republics. I mean it is a remarkable construction project but it keeps the memory in people's heads."

"Yes, I have been there. It is very impressive. It is also the largest outdoor ice skating rink in the world in winter."

The flight attendant appeared and brought them coffee.

"We will be landing in seventy minutes or so. I am going to be serving a prime rib dinner if this is agreeable. Would you like another cocktail?"

Cross motioned for Mikhailov to answer first. Prime rib it is and they both ordered another aged single malt whiskey.

Cross was very tired. His head was moving around all these chess pieces but things were beginning to build a structure, an organised structure that looked to be coordinating the demise of the world as they know it today. This plane needed to land.

They sipped the cocktail and ate the prime rib. Then Mikhailov put her head on his shoulder and went to sleep. Cross followed suit, not that he had a choice.

25

Game Changer

The Learjet landed and it was escorted to the terminal building by two Suburbans. Stairs were brought up and the main door was opened. Cross stepped out first and then Mikhailov. He had already given her instructions about her bags.

Security was all around them and Cross then saw Granfield waving towards one of the Chevys. They climbed in and exited at high speed away from the airport.

They were now in Granfield's office and someone had brought them fresh coffee. Cross introduced Mikhailov and Granfield was gracious.

"Nice to meet you, Ms. Mikhailov. I am David Granfield. Please call me David. I am sorry about the loss of your twin sister Cassandra. Mr. Cross was deeply distressed about the whole event."

"Thank you Mr. Granfield. I loved my sister, but she knew too much in the end."

"Get yourselves relaxed. I suggest you both take your time and recover a little from the long flights. It is very late. We have special bedroom suites for such circumstances in this building. Under pending adversity and imperiled potential threats, I have already made arrangements for you to occupy two of them tonight. This building is obviously very secure. We can convene in the morning at an hour which would be suitable for both of you."

"Thank you David," Cross responded but looking rather disheveled.

"Impressive work again. You are getting good at this," he said trying to relax him and give him confidence.

"I have some information we need to discuss in the morning. This is moving fast. I can be up at 7 for an 8am meeting. Ms. Mikhailov can wake up whenever she feels like it."

"Yes, this is gaining momentum now that Senator Brownsville has opened Pandora's box. There are two security guards with guns outside my office. They will take you to your rooms, which are adjacent. See you around 8am, Daniel. Good night Natalie." He then departed. When did he ever sleep, thought Cross.

The suites were separate but Mikhailov didn't want to be alone. She moved her bags into Cross's suite and he offered to take the sofa. They talked for a while whilst they took showers and drank some tea. Cocktails were made available in the room. Totally void of energy, Mikhailov adjourned to the bedroom but left the door open. He saw her remove her robe and climb into bed. Cross arranged a blanket and pillow then mounted the sofa and collapsed.

Morning rolled around but way too fast. Cross was up and had made coffee provided in the room. Mikhailov was still asleep. She didn't need to be part of the discussions so he left her alone. She is in enough trouble, he surmised. Romanov will be after her to retrieve his property.

He walked over to the conference room which was already busy.

"Good morning, Daniel," said Winwood and they shook hands.

"I don't know what day or time it is anymore. It feels like a morning," he laughed, but it was strained.

Winwood continued, with Granfield next to him.

"We will ask you to fill us in but take your time. I am going to present some findings so you will have time to wake up."

Another half hour presentation revealed a large money scheme. It was been wired all over the place, finally ending at a bank in Grand Cayman. The starting point, however, was the US Treasury. The room was dead silent. One could hear a pin drop. The occupants in the room were focused.

Cross leaned over to Granfield.

"I have some more information from very secure sources. Please allow me to talk openly, discussing what I know, without revealing those sources yet. I will fill you in later, David."

Granfield trusted him. He had to. He was doing a job he wasn't trained to do but doing it with professionalism and courage. This man had nerves of steel and was getting results, thought Granfield.

"Of course I trust you, Daniel," and he smiled and winked.

It was Cross' turn to get to the podium, per se. There wasn't one, except an imaginary one.

He discussed his findings in Russia and how those compared to findings in Taiwan. He went into revealing a contact in Iran who seems to be doing the same thing. He discussed Brownsville's press conference and how this relates to the case they are following. Cross mentioned the virus deaths in Taiwan and Russia. The Russian virus was not known by the CIA even. This is all related, he felt.

Then came the kicker. He was about to toss a lion into the chicken pen.

"I have information that Romanov bought the Namibian diamond for Senator Brownsville as a gift."

The room was now a cacophony of noise and bedlam. Granfield tried to step in but Cross stopped him. Cross has earned it. He risked his life on several occasions to get this information no one else had.

"Can we please restore some calm? I haven't finished yet."

Silence transcended once again and order was restored. Damn, Cross liked this.

"Romanov purchased the diamond for $9M through contacts he already had. Cassandra Mikhailov was killed because she knew too much of Romanov's plans. He orchestrated the purchase and then had her shot. The contract and arrangement through Robert Mitrovic were fraudulent. Romanov had no intention of purchasing the diamond from him. As far as I know, the insurance policy on the diamond is still valid and the company is required to pay out $25M. I will confirm this today but that looks like fraud also.

"I know where the diamond is," he finally added.

Now the room erupted again.

"Please, I haven't finished," and waited for silence. "My conclusions are that three elicit countries that we know about, four if we include the US which I presume we must, are conspiring to create a deadly virus. In order to combat this virus, the same countries, actually the same companies not countries, are developing a vaccine. It is my theory that the vaccine will also kill people or create a medical condition. I have seen the chemicals they are using. We have a list of them on our spread sheets. These are specific for human vaccines but they have to be mixed correctly and in controlled amounts.

"I am well informed that the Russian government isn't part of this. At least those in control. It is likely Romanov has someone he would make president if Putin and his people were killed or impaired. I have also looked into the US' position and Brownsville would become president if our current president and his vice president should be killed, or become impaired."

He wasn't convinced they wanted to kill people with the vaccine, but surely they would die from the virus. Perhaps the vaccine would be given to only a select few, he realised now in horror.

"The alternative theory I have is that the vaccine will only be for a select few and the virus will actually kill the rest.

"I have not pursued leads to determine Taiwan's political position but I believe the virus and vaccine are for mainland China, and not Taiwan. Being in Taiwan is a distraction that worked.

"I believe this is all being funded by the US government to control the world. Those are my conclusions ladies and gentlemen."

Granfield was on the phone. He ended the call and stood up, commanding silence.

"Which high ranking senators can we trust? Who do we have on our side, ones in our pockets?"

He was given a short list of names.

"People, let us get some of them in here this afternoon. Can we coordinate this?"

He looked at Cross.

"You need to head to Iran. I share your conclusions. We highly doubt the Iranian government is involved with this either, not with Hosseini being a top military chief. I want you in the meeting this afternoon with some senators and then leave for Iran tonight. We have contacted the government in Tehran who has contacted an English diplomat they like, for some reason," he added trying to inject some levity.

"There is no accounting for taste."

"No, seriously, Iranians do like the Brits. The White House screwed our diplomacy with repeated sanctions so it is hard for them to trust us anymore. At least they have to portray the image of not liking us. Their economy is in disarray and they will not be prepared for this virus."

"What information have you released?"

"We haven't told them much for fear of retribution despite the fact we are trying to help them. They know about Hosseini and his desire to bring about change. They are not aware of his progress so far. It is possible they can arrange to have him out in the open, if you get my meaning."

"What, you want me to take him down?" he said with an elevated voice.

"I am not going to rule out anything, nor am I going to advocate taking out a top military official in a foreign country. That is tantamount to a war congress has not authorised us to start or fight. However, the meeting with senators this afternoon should open the door to include plenty of leeway should something happen that wasn't authorised, Daniel."

Damn, Granfield was so eloquent in his bullshit, laughed Cross.

"What?" said Granfield.

"Nothing. I was just thinking of something that wasn't important."

"You will be met in Tehran by the British Ambassador, James Butler. He may also have someone else meet you and then head to the British Embassy, we were told. We will be using low-profile flights so nothing commercial or with US livery. The British have volunteered to fly you in from London on one of their diplomatic planes. We have recommended a commercial flight to London from Dulles. You leave tonight with a First Class ticket. Sorry this is short notice and your body clock will be switched off by now."

"Yes, I am tired but this is important. We need to keep going."

"Oh, by the way, you will tell me one day how you got some of the information you presented, won't you? I will not ask about the diamond yet. I will leave the details with you for now. I trust your judgment, Daniel. You have earned it. Excellent work," and with that Granfield shook his hand again.

"I will head back to the suite and see where Natalie is. She should be awake now. She will be safe, right? She risked her life to be here but her execution will be on top of a short list for sure. Romanov doesn't play games. He likely doesn't even give a damn about the diamond."

"Yes, she will go into a witness-protection program. I will message you with details pertaining to the senators. I hope we can do this today, before you leave. Also, the next trip will likely be to Grand Cayman. We need their cooperation in shutting off the money. This will be key to how we control the events. It is still raining in Tahoe. Please call home."

"I might need to head home for a few days if I can, before Grand Cayman."

Cross walked off in the direction of the suite.

Mikhailov was awake and drinking coffee. Someone had brought her food so she was being taken care of.

"Good morning, Natalie. How are you feeling?"

"I am good. I had a nice sleep, finally. That is a comfy bed. Perhaps I will live here. There are some American hunks walking around and they seem to like Russian ladies," she said laughing.

"I don't think you would survive here. They are mostly nerds in suits. It would be more dangerous than outside," laughing his head off.

"You could be right."

"I am leaving tonight. They are trying to organise a meeting this afternoon with some senators they trust. David has asked me to participate. I then head to Iran."

"Oh, please be careful. I am worried now."

"It is ok. I will be safe. I am meeting the British Ambassador so things are kosher with regards to the Iranian government letting me in. It is all arranged."

"I never thanked you for taking care of Cassandra the way you did. You cared about her and that means an awful lot to me and our family. We were orphaned but we still had relatives we later learned in life. They miss her. I miss her," tears rolled down her face.

Cross went over and hugged her. He had to control himself too.

"It was devastating but I had to take care of her after she passed away. I couldn't just leave her there."

Granfield pinged him: 'Meeting with senators in two hours.'

The two hours quickly rolled around and Cross entered the conference room and recognised some of them. Granfield introduced him and they looked at him funny because of his accent.

"He is a Brit but we don't hold it against him, much," said Granfield.

It added humour to an otherwise disturbing meeting. Granfield explained what they are working on and what they have found. He gave a presentation and someone had taken the time to add to slides what Cross had discussed earlier that day. The senators were silent. Almost stunned.

One of them opened up after Granfield had stopped talking.

"You realise what you are suggesting, Mr. Granfield?"

"Well aware of it, senator. We have the proof. We have pictures of Senator Brownsville outside the office in Kaohsiung. We have the paper trail." Finally he added, "We have a witness in protective custody whom can corroborate Brownsville's involvement.

"Mr. Cross has risked his life numerous times to get this information. People have died. This all merges into one big cluster-fuck orchestrated and paid for by the US government. We have the bank trail, or money trail as we call it.

"There are things we still need to work on. Mr. Cross is heading to Iran this evening. We are collaborating with the UK and Iranian governments to organise this trip. This is adversaries working together and is unprecedented. Now we want your support."

"What do you need from us, Mr. Granfield?"

"We don't know what will happen in Tehran yet. Then Mr. Cross will head to Grand Cayman. When the time comes we want to shut down the money flowing into Grand Cayman. It has to stop. However, the timing has to be right otherwise many people will die.

"We will need the cooperation of the Taiwanese and Russian governments. We fully believe they have no idea this is going on. They are not part of this. We want you to see who else is involved with Senator Brownsville. Who is close to him? Who belongs in his inner circle, his entourage? This is an active investigation and we need help, senator. We cannot call Putin and ask him how things are going. We don't believe the US president and vice president are involved.

"Mr. Cross has pictures of the senator in Taiwan. There are others in that photo. Are they part of the government? Tell us what help you need, what information, and we will get it. Sometimes even the CIA doesn't have access to everything it should. We keep requesting improved technology but some people think we have too much access already. We require the Senate's approval for war, for killings on foreign soil, if it comes to that, senator."

The meeting came to an end but discussions were rampant, noise elevated. Some peeled out of the room.

Granfield asked Cross to follow him to his office.

"Do you have what you need? Go get some sleep in your suite. Natalie is still there I think. My assistant got you more clothes and will deliver them shortly.

"You will be picked up from here around 7:30. Your flight is at 10:10pm and you get to avoid security as before. Please update me as needed.

He called Dunhill and filled her in. She was still in Tahoe but was desperate to leave for LA. He couldn't control her so she needed to do what she needed to do. He didn't believe Kuznetsov would be after her now. They have too much else to worry about. He imagined she wasn't a priority so likely safe for her to go home. He asked she message him often when she gets to LA and he would do the same thing on his travels.

He called the office and talked with Brandy. The rain was still falling but was due to end tomorrow, she said. Flooding everywhere and she was concerned about the building. Cross was too. It had low points and when he and his wife owned it, they had built a drainage system for the water to drain around the building. Who knows what the landlord had done since Cross' divorce had forced him to sell it. He was concerned. He told her he was going overseas again but will be back in a few days. He clicked off.

He headed back to the suite for a few hours of sleep.

"Granfield will be taking care of you when I am gone. I don't know what plans he has yet but you are in a protection program. People will be around at all times. You have my number so please use it."

She wore a beautiful wraparound dress, makeup, high heel shoes and a European wool jacket. She was stunning, thought Cross. Those green eyes were entrancing.

She sat on the sofa and asked Cross to sit next to her. The lower part of her dress had come open revealing stunning legs. She talked about life in Russia growing up. It was tough after their parents died. She was emotional and just needed someone to listen to her so he did just that. Sometimes that is all people want, admitted Cross. They talked for an hour before he succumbed to needing sleep before his long trip.

She obliged and thanked him for being there, and for caring. He walked into the bedroom and she watched him remove his clothes. She saw his toned body and then shuddered at the scars he had. She didn't know. He entered the shower. A few minutes later she followed him.

26

British Embassy, Tehran

Cross was met in Heathrow's Terminal 2 and whisked away through side doors and hidden passageways. They took a government vehicle across the tarmac to another private terminal where a grey Royal Air Force VIP Airbus A321neo was idling, waiting for him. He climbed the stairs, entered the cabin and selected one of the lounge seats before strapping himself in, tossing his bag on the floor. Two embassy personnel followed him and then the front door immediately closed. The engines ramped up and they began taxiing.

Six and half hours later the Airbus touched down at an air base some distance from Tehran. It was a military base and kept the pretense that this was a normal flight. A British military plane flying into an international airport would have stirred some waters. The waters were already stirred and murky, Cross thought. It taxied up to the terminal and then stairs were brought to the front door. Cross picked his bag up and exited the plane per instructions. Down at the bottom of the ramp he saw two white Supercharged Range Rovers waiting. Their windows were blacked out. Presumably one was for him and the 518hp supercharged V8 might be useful when the time comes, he thought nervously. The two British embassy personnel headed for the rear Rover. The drivers remained inside but a young

Iranian lady approached Cross and introduced herself.

"Hello Mr. Cross. Welcome to Iran. I am Parisa Sadeghi, but please call me Parisa. I am Ambassador Butler's Personal Assistant and I have been asked to ensure your stay goes as planned," she held out her hand.

We have a plan, thought Cross.

It was winter in Northern Iran so she wore a full length tan cashmere coat, what looked like brown woolen stockings and expensive heeled shoes. On her head was a full Islamic light brown cashmere Hijab that continued to wrap around her neck underneath the coat collar. Her face was perfection behind dark brown eyes and an exotic-looking darker skin. She wore black eye-liner, mascara and skin-coloured lipstick. He put her age at early 40's, height around 5'8" and weight at 120 lbs. Cross was smitten, almost to the point of being speechless. Her Chanel perfume was almost an anesthetic.

"Hello Parisa, please call me Daniel," as he obliged and shook her hand.

"Please, it is cold. Let us proceed into the car so we can continue our discussion," she had this adorable accent.

Cross opened the door and Sadeghi stepped inside. He went around the other side and climbed in. The car left the airport tarmac and exited onto a main highway. As they headed towards the capital Cross saw the snow-capped mountains north of the sprawling mega metropolis and the Milad Tower overlooking the city, like a praying mantis watches for its' pray. It was a vast city.

"Ambassador Butler is looking forward to meeting you," she continued. "He has read about you and has heard a lot about your recent trips. We will be there in two hours or so, depending on traffic which can be horrendous at times."

Over three hours later they arrived at 172 Ferdowsi Avenue. It was surrounded by a brick wall and the entrance way housed a thick blue iron gate attached to two square brick columns. The columns supported iron castings of a lion on top of one side and a horse on the other. On top of the 12 foot wall and gate were coils and coils of razor-edged barbed wire. Added to that were metal spikes.

"Well, this place looks interesting," he smiled, kind of. "The British Embassy was attacked in 2011 so they had to take precautionary measures I presume after that."

"Yes, and Iran is likely different to any other place you have been to, Mr. Cross."

"I have not been to an Islamic country before. This is new to me and fascinating already."

As the Range Rovers approached, the gate swung inwards and they entered the complex. The red brick building was large and multi-storey. Along the top of each portion were ornate concrete railings.

They came to a halt outside what looked like the main entrance, with an arched brick column alcove, and then stepped out. A tall, eloquent, medium build gentleman stepped forward to greet them. As Cross got out, the gentleman obviously knew who he was.

"Hello Mr. Cross. Welcome to the British Embassy. I am Ambassador Butler but please call me James."

"Nice to meet you finally, James. Please call me Daniel and thank you for accommodating me. This was short notice but so important."

"Yes, we understood the urgency and the necessary requirements to get you into the country. Please step inside where we can talk. Ms. Sadeghi will be your personal liaison, interpreter and assistant during your stay. She will make you welcome and comfortable, Daniel. You have never been here before, right?"

The ambassador behaves as if he gets to greet many visitors, thought Cross. This is going to be interesting.

"I have never been to Iran before but I have been invited. I wanted to come, but under different circumstances."

They walked into the lobby of the Embassy and then moved off into a private study area. They had inviting chairs and a coffee table.

"Let us have a Turkish coffee and some famous Iranian gratuities before we go to the conference room to discuss this visit. You need to relax first. We might even have some McVitie's chocolate biscuits to make you feel at home. Iranians like those."

Sadeghi and an assistant brought in coffee, pastries and indeed some biscuits on trays with plates and spoons, and placed them on the centre coffee table.

"Please don't be shy and help yourself, Daniel. We are English and know how this works," he laughed.

But before Cross could, Sadeghi was already pouring his coffee and placing various sundries on a plate. She handed them to Cross and smiled before sitting next to him. Cross thought she was the most captivating and beautiful lady he had ever seen. Perhaps it was her ethnicity that drew him. He had no real answer. Her winter coat had been discarded along with the Hijab head scarf, revealing an elegant and simple tan European wool dress. But her face now free from the scarf blinded Cross.

"Thank you, Parisa."

Cross and Butler chatted for a while and talked about England, the changes, why Cross moved to the US, his accident, his divorce, his work and world travels. Butler talked about his government roles, what he did before his ambassadorship in Iran, why he wanted this position. They sipped their coffee, poured more and devoured the delicious Iranian pastries.

"I love the Turkish coffee and pastries. Thank you so much."

They were warming to each other and Sadeghi added a comment here and there. Her English was very good, acknowledged Cross.

"I learnt English from when I was six and attended an English school here in the city, Mr. Cross," still trying to be formal and respectful which Cross didn't want to correct. "I did three years of college at an English university before returning to Tehran to work for the British Embassy."

Cross was impressed. Butler stirred and it was time to discuss their predicament before the night ended. He motioned them to follow him as he navigated the building corridors and ended up in the conference room. Other people had evidently been waiting, including the two personnel on the flight from London. Butler introduced them all, including his Deputy Head William Cartwright, and then they sat down around the table. On the end wall was a screen that had been dropped down and a laptop lay on the table. Parisa had sat next to Cross and helped him set up the computer. He inserted his memory stick and then proceeded with his presentation.

The room was silent as he went through in detail his findings. He now mentioned Hosseini, the military leader of Iran. Cross had satellite imagery of his compound south east of Tehran planted on the screen. This shocked Butler.

"How did you get these, Daniel?"

"I am sorry but I am not at liberty to divulge certain information. Not even the CIA knows some of my sources. All I will say is that I know people. This particular information is privileged, James."

He sat silent again as Cross continued finishing his monologue. The presentation left the room dead silent. Nobody moved. He ended with Senator Brownsville and his plans to take over the US government, and his collaboration with the entities he had been discussing.

No one spoke a word, not even Butler. Cross had to finally break the silence.

"That concludes what we know. Hosseini needs to be stopped and we need to find out what he is doing in his complex outside of Varamin. I wonder if people have been killed by a virus in the neighbourhood there. This will be something we need to find out.

"During times of a depressed economy and the impact severe US sanctions have, it is bizarre this guy was allowed to build his facility. I mean don't people watch for this sort of thing here?"

"Daniel, he is head of military and will know people. We have to be careful with this information. I mean he will know people high up in the government because the military is part of the government here. He might actually want to be President of Iran. He may even want to be the Supreme Leader. He may in fact have those aspirations. This is a dangerous game.

"Let us conclude this discussion tonight and get some rest, Daniel. You look tired and have flown a long way today, which we appreciate. We can start again bright and early in the morning, around 10am is ok? I have contacted someone I trust within the Iranian government and we meet him tomorrow morning."

"Yes, fine," Cross replied.

"Parisa will show you your accommodations. We have rooms in the compound for guests. Good night, Daniel," and he shook his hand and left.

"Follow me. Your bag is already in your room, Mr. Cross."

"Thank you, I will. I am very tired."

He followed her to a separate wing of the compound. They climbed some stairs to the second floor and walked a small corridor. She handed him a key. He took it and opened the door. She followed him in but only to show the suite and to explain certain things. There were snacks in the fridge should he need any and a stocked bar.

"Russian vodka and aged Scottish whiskey are your preferences, we heard. There is also some Iranian beer just in case," she smiled.

"You heard right, although the beer sounds interesting," he smiled and Sadeghi reciprocated.

"It is non-alcoholic. I was joking. Alcohol is prohibited in Iran but still is a $700M business here. We do have some British beer. I am staying here too whilst I am your liaison. I will be next door should you need anything else. This is my room number and here is my mobile number, if you need anything."

Cross was enamoured. It couldn't escape him how beautiful and elegant she is. So pleasant and nice also.

They both said good night and she exited his room, closing the door behind her.

Cross called Granfield to let him know he had arrived. He messaged Verenich but nothing new there either. He chatted with Dunhill but she was in LA already. Mikhailov was surviving Virginia and had been moved to a safe-house. Just out of curiosity he called Fedorova.

"Hello Alexandria, how are you?"

"I am fine," but surprised by his call. "Your exit from Russia caused a huge problem for Romanov. You killed three of his men."

"To be fair it was me or them. What choice is that? We found some more information linking Romanov to the US senator. It is the unequivocal final nail that we needed. Oh, we also found the diamond. Can I reach you later, perhaps tomorrow or the day after?"

"Of course. Where are you?"

"Iran."

They said goodbye and he put the phone down.

He walked over to the bar and found an aged whiskey. He unwrapped the top, pulled out the corked stopper and poured it into a glass. He needed something strong. This is becoming insane.

27

The Persian Hidden Agenda

It was 8am and Sadeghi called Cross' room but no answer. She headed downstairs where she found him in the kitchen.

"Good morning, Mr. Cross. You are up early. Did you sleep well?"

"I slept like a baby, thank you, but I was awake early. I walked around the compound and then was led to the kitchen. You look beautiful this morning, Parisa."

Cross had heard Iranian men are cold and not romantic. She did look beautiful.

"Thank you," she said, smiling.

Cross needs to concentrate today. He is going to get himself into trouble, he can tell.

"I see food is already prepared. Have you tried it yet?"

"No, I just walked in myself after getting fresh air into my head."

"Ok. Let me describe what we have. Black English tea is traditional but I see you have coffee already. The oval bread is barbari with accompaniments such as butter, jam which is sour cherry and carrot, and some honey. There are of course feta cheese, sliced cucumbers and tomatoes along with walnuts. Omelette, which will be made fresh, is scrambled eggs with onions and tomatoes. What else do I see? Oh, yes, Kaleh Pacheh which is a rare delicacy. It is sheep's head, hooves and everything else boiled in water, with onions and garlic. Being English you will like this. The Ambassador does but I don't recommend it with an omelette," she laughed.

"I am going to have an omelette with bread," he said, laughing too.

She asked the cook to prepare the food and then suggested they eat at the table.

The food was brought over and Cross was chatting away when Butler walked in.

"Good morning, Parisa and Daniel. I didn't think you would be up this early but nice you are feeling at home. Once you have finished eating, let us head to the conference room for an update. I have some details and information for you. Bring your coffee."

Cross finished his food and headed off to the conference room. Sadeghi followed.

"You asked about a potential virus being localised around Hosseini's facility, or close to it. His complex is on the outskirts of Varamin and recently around thirty people died from a mysterious virus. No one had seen it before. It was localised so the government's Department of Health brushed it off as an anomaly."

"We are seeing the same patterns here as we found near Taipei in Taiwan and Sergiyev Posad in Russia. This is a common thread. It is interesting they are limiting the viral deaths to between twenty and thirty people. It seems they don't want to draw media attention, for obvious reasons."

"We know someone high up in the Iranian government who we trust. We have worked with him for years. He is Farbod Karimi and is the president's Chief of Staff. He has a different Iranian title but we will stick with this one for clarity. He agreed to meet around 10:30am in a local tea house down the street, so it is convenient you didn't sleep in," he smiled. "He assured me the president and supreme leader are not versed on these developments. He will be alone.

"We are aided here because the media is primarily controlled by the Iranian government. They will restrict what can be published. This will be important tomorrow because we want to meet Hosseini at his complex outside Varamin. When I say we, you do realise it is the proverbial we, Daniel? You will meet him to discuss analytical requirements. Trade embargos have destroyed the economy here and it is very difficult, almost impossible, to get foreign goods into Iran. However, we have convinced the Major that you can get goods in through Russia. This is a private meeting. Parisa will be your interpreter but we will be close by. Mr. Karimi will confirm this morning the plans. Hosseini believes you are operating on your own through an Iranian government contact, who will also be present. Hosseini trusts Mr. Karimi.

"I do need to impress upon you the delicacy of all this, Daniel. People are putting their own lives at risk."

"I have seen two ladies die in my arms, James. I have also killed three people and incapacitated others. I understand the situation very well."

Sadeghi's eyes opened wide and Cross saw her reaction.

"I am sorry, Parisa. It was me or them," a statement he had repeated before.

Someone brought in more coffee and Cross filled his cup.

"We have a couple of hours before we meet Farbod. Let me go over the terrain in Varamin," said Butler.

They drove to the cafe in an old non-descript Land Cruiser. Cross would have preferred the Range Rover but he was out voted, based on common sense. Best to be indiscrete and incognito, as Butler put it. The need to escape wasn't part of his equation apparently, Cross mused.

The property was a mile or so away, on a wide avenue lined with private stores. It was located in the old part of the city which meant red brick buildings were standard. They were mostly two storey and the individual shops were shut at night using metal rollup doors. At this time of the morning, the owners had the doors open and the walkways were lined with goods and merchandise. The street had cars parked on either side. It was dusty but the area was bustling with activity, which worked to their advantage.

With parking difficult, the driver pulled up outside the Nabery Cafe and let out Butler, Cross and Sadeghi before he sped off, returning when needed. They all headed inside. There sat Karimi in a corner, well away from the window. Butler walked over and introduced Cross.

"Good morning Mr. Karimi. This is Mr. Daniel Cross from California and my assistant Ms. Parisa Sadeghi."

Once the pleasantries were over, they sat down and Karimi ordered tea and pastries. He was dressed in traditional Iranian business attire of dress pants and a shirt. He didn't want to stand out and look conspicuous. He was average build and had a beard, which seemed to be common for Iranian men. Butler and Cross wore black although expensive European clothing, as did Sadeghi who had to wear a Hijab.

Karimi was fluent in English which helped. Cross went through what he knew about the development of Hosseini's facility. He discussed the virus release and comparisons with other known entities around the world. He concluded the brief discussion by offering their opinions on what is being planned. Karimi was attentive but looked shocked. Butler jumped in.

"We need your assistance, Farbod. We discussed earlier a meeting between Mr. Cross and Major Hosseini tomorrow at his compound."

"Yes, I have talked with people in my government whom I also trust, James. These developments are deeply disturbing. Our economy is dire but the Major is attempting to control Iran by killing people, including perhaps the president and supreme leader. We are not at liberty to open discussions with the president yet. We feel it more important to eradicate the threat, or at least determine what the actual threat is before barfing all over the leaders, if you know what I mean."

Butler brought a folder and gave it to Karimi. He opened it up and looked at the pictures.

"This is the compound I discussed this morning with you."

"Where did you get these images, James?" in a surprised tone.

"Please excuse my frankness but that is classified information."

"I can respect that. Presumably Mr. Cross brought them with him," he smiled at Cross and continued, "I have arranged this for tomorrow. Major Hosseini doesn't suspect anything because he won't know what we know. How could he? I am just seeing the evidence now. I talked to him this morning and explained Mr. Cross' visit."

Karimi went through some details, although wasn't fully versed on specifics yet. He would educate them later that afternoon.

"Can we be assured of media discretion, Farbod? This cannot get out, not yet. We have to coordinate all this with other entities and governments. This truly is an international collaboration between governments who haven't cooperated before. This is setting standards no one has witnessed since World War II and the Yalta Conference, where Churchill, Roosevelt and Stalin met. It will take some days to set it in motion. We also have to get Senator Brownsville conspiring to commit espionage. This is delicate."

"Discretion is assured. We also have the power to shut down the internet in Iran. No one will know about the facility outside of Varamin."

They talked some more before it was time to depart. Karimi left first and disappeared into the mayhem.

"What do you think, Daniel?"

"I am not going to claim I am not scared and apprehensive. This is a dangerous country. Who can we trust fully?"

"I understand that. I have worked with Farbod for years and he is a loyal Iranian. He sounded awful on the phone this morning learning some of this. Did you see his facial reaction just now? He is a good man. Let us hope there are other good men so we can curtail this thing that has been set in motion, Daniel."

With that they left the Cafe and headed back to the embassy.

Cross needed some free time to research the area around Varamin and was provided a computer in a private study.

He started the research and found Varamin is a major industrial area. It would be convenient to hide such a facility amongst other developed buildings. Then he was pleasantly interrupted. Parisa asked if he wanted some tea or coffee and came back with coffee. She gave it to Cross and asked if she could hang around with him whilst he researched his new developments.

"Of course, please do," answered Cross, now delighted. "What do you know about this area?"

"I have never been there. I have lived a quiet life in Tehran. There were excursions and holiday trips with my parents, mostly overseas to Turkey and Dubai. I have been to Russia once and obviously in and out of England during my university years."

"Well you are no help then, although I do want to visit Turkey. Have any siblings? Ever been married?"

"Three siblings and married once to an Iranian man. It didn't last long and I stayed single. No children."

"But you are simply stunning. Why aren't men here falling all over you?"

"Thank you, Mr. Cross. You always flatter me with compliments. I had a boyfriend in England but it didn't work out in the end. The culture is different here, as you may know and the vast distances prohibited anything serious. He didn't want to move to Iran and I had reservations about him and his family in the UK. I wanted to behave anyway," as she winked at him.

"Oh, I see. Well don't behave on my account, Ms. Sadeghi," he was laughing so hard now. "Seriously, I find you captivating. There is something about you I cannot put my finger on."

"Oh, well. I do need to behave then," she was now laughing.

"Thank you for the coffee which was done right, too. Very impressed you remembered such things."

"It is my job."

"Looking after me is harder than you think."

"We shall see won't we?"

This was bordering on flirtation and he wasn't sure how to handle it. She was different and he wanted to be different. He wanted to be a gentleman.

Just then Butler entered the office.

"Daniel, are you finding anything useful?"

"Yes, but not sure it relates to this," he said smiling.

"Farbod will be calling in ten minutes. Can you and Parisa meet me in the conference room?"

They headed over as instructed. The phone rang and Butler pressed the conference button.

"Hello Farbod. What do you have?"

He filled them in on their plans for the morning. They would meet Hosseini around 11 at his facility outside Varamin. Mr. Cross, Ms. Sadeghi and another member of the embassy along with Karimi would be at the meeting. Karimi would pick them up from the same cafe. He couldn't come to the embassy. He assured the ambassador that the Iranian government would have trusted military people standing by in the area. Cross gulped. This is serious now.

Butler clicked the phone off and turned to Cross.

"Before you ask, this is a secure area and phones cannot be tapped. Farbod used his secure mobile line I noticed. We are entering dangerous territory. Ms. Sadeghi will be replaced with someone who looks like her from the military."

No one looks like her, thought Cross.

"Hosseini doesn't know who Ms. Sadeghi is so we will not raise any flags. His perception is that of a scientific and analytical nature in which you, Daniel, have options to help him. The brochures and quotations you provided Parisa earlier today have been printed in Persian. These you will take with you.

"Depending on how this goes, it should only be a diplomatic mission for reconnaissance only. We are looking for facts and information about what it is they are doing. You can carry your gun but expect to be frisked and they do have security as you pointed out. We are allowed guns in Iran, under specific conditions, being diplomats. Farbod will allow that but let us consider this option before you depart.

"I talked with David Granfield this morning at CIA in Langley, Daniel. He trusts and admires you and asks we take care of you. He is also worried about this mission because of who you are dealing with. However, he stressed this is reconnaissance. They are working with specific senators and have made contact with trusted government people in both Taiwan and Russia.

Cross' heart rate shot up.

"Mr. Granfield is a good man, James."

"I have also been talking with people at MI6. This is serious. No one wants you dead, Daniel."

Sadeghi reached over for his hand. She surprised him.

"Mr. Cross, no one wants you dead," she added. "People here like you."

Butler knew he had made a wise choice with Sadeghi to chaperone Cross. She was doing an impeccable job of trying to save his life. She was giving him a reason to because Cross didn't know what he was stepping into. These people were ruthless and vicious. They truly didn't give a damn.

"Listen to Parisa, Daniel. She knows what she is talking about."

Cross being an emotional man was stunned and hid the tears welling in his eyes.

Butler went further into details and outlined his expectations. Karimi would meet them at 9:30am and then head out of the city.

"Varamin was about 60km south east of downtown Tehran and about an hour drive, depending on time of day. We added half hour to compensate for the unknowns such as traffic, people, cattle, tanks, etc."

He was adding levity and looked over at Cross who wasn't moved.

"The facility we will be visiting is just on the outskirts of the city. That concludes our meeting this afternoon, Daniel."

"Parisa will show you the compound and immediate area, perhaps. Let us meet for dinner around 7:30pm," and then he left.

"Since alcohol is illegal in Iran, I know a friend close to here who has a nice place. I will take you there if you wish. He has alcohol."

28

Whiskey and Lingerie

Dinner was served at 7:30 and Cross was hungry. A delightful afternoon with Sadeghi had them talking for hours in the rear of her friend's restaurant. They seem to have this chemistry that he had never experienced before.

At the dining table she was pointing out the various dishes.

"Lamb Kebab, which I know you will have had before, sabzi khordan which is a herb and feta cheese plate, safron rice, Tahdig is a crunchy fried rice dish, gormeh sabzi is a green herb stew, baghali polo is rice with fava beans and vegetables with chicken, and khoresht bademjan which is eggplant and tomato stew. It is all delicious. To drink there is Persian tea, doogh which is Persian yoghurt drink and side dish, and non-alcoholic Iranian beer," she added laughing. "Dessert is Baklava."

"I will help myself to some of each. It all looks good."

"Of course we have alcohol but we can adjourn to the bar after dinner if you would like."

Cross filled up on the palette of food laid out in front of him. It was all delicious. Butler had finished with their assessment and arrangement for tomorrow morning so excused himself and disappeared to attend other urgent matters. Cross was left with Sadeghi.

Finishing up, she showed him to the compound bar area and it was quiet. I few people sat around and helped themselves to drinks. Cross found a quiet area with a comfy sofa by a table.

"What can I get you Parisa?"

"I will have a vodka martini please."

Cross poured himself a Balvenie from an open bottle and mixed a martini. He placed them on the table and sat next to Sadeghi. It seemed very intimate and the lights were dimmed. The Brits knew what they were doing despite being supplanted in an inhospitable environment. Iran wasn't exactly stable and Muslim countries are erratic and utter chaos. At least that is the perceptions to the outside world. Behind a walled compound topped with razor coiled wire and security cameras, nestled this bizarre and seemingly secluded setting that was surreal. It was all some fantasy land.

Cross and Sadeghi talked for a few more hours and they were sitting close, with legs touching. They held hands for a while and then placed hands on their legs as they laughed and seemed happy. Cross may die tomorrow but at this moment in time it wasn't on his mind. He was possibly spending his last moments alive with someone who sent his sensors into overdrive. He had never met a lady like Sadeghi before. Perhaps he was in fantasy land.

After their third or fourth drink, Cross was tired and needed sleep before his travels tomorrow. He was nervous and apprehensive but showed no outward signs of that. To Sadeghi he was a man calm, collected and confident. He exuded this charisma and aura that was exciting to her simple life.

Cross didn't want to let go of her hand and he held onto it as they left the bar area. They walked upstairs holding hands. He opened the door and was about to say good night when Sadeghi followed him into the room.

"Let us have a night cap, Daniel."

She had never called him Daniel before. It was genuine, sincere and erotic all at the same time. His heart was pounding.

He went over and poured two drinks and when he turned around, her silk dress had been removed. Underneath was expensive lingerie with stockings. His mouth nearly hit the floor. She headed to the bedroom and Cross followed carrying the two whiskies.

29

Orchestrated Death Count

There were three cars in convoy on the way heading to Varamin. They had met up with Karimi at the cafe and he had several staffers with him. Cross sat next to him in the front passenger seat of their government Toyota Land Cruiser. The lady representing Sadeghi was in the back and an embassy staffer was next to her. The two Land Cruisers following had government staff for Karimi. It had to look like a state visit had been authorised. This was genuine government business. Hosseini couldn't suspect anything was going on.

If this was a cannabis grow facility, Cross thought, Hosseini is going to have to handle this delicately. Not only alcohol was banned but also illicit drugs, period. This didn't stop creating a huge drug problem within the Iranian borders. Cross had seen documentaries on this very subject and the Iranian youth was being systematically destroyed by it. The youth has no hope, no jobs and no prospects. They had nothing to do but find refuge in drugs, similar to the US drug problem as Cross saw it. In fact, this is actually a world-wide dilemma.

The Tehran-Varamin Highway was a quality four lane road but very dusty. Winds in the mountains cascaded around the area as they drove through part desolation. Cross knew this from living in Tahoe.

Since Hosseini knew government officials, he didn't have to hide his facility. He could explain the development simply as an agricultural research centre, as the other two entities had, partly camouflaged by the industrial areas surrounding it. It wasn't difficult. The government wanted to help him secure some scientific instrumentation. That was also easy to explain. Cross knew this setup and government involvement would be easy to hide. He had no idea how Karimi had arranged this meeting though. Perhaps they were close friends and Karimi couldn't be trusted. Cross was becoming cynical but the Ambassador trusted him. He had to dispense with certain theories as they tracked south east from Tehran and through rural Iran.

He was the Military General, their chief, the leader. He had to have loyal soldiers supporting him. How much did they know? Was he going to annihilate them also? He would need an army once he took over the government. Their loyalty would be paramount. Perhaps Brownsville was going to fly in a battalion of American or Russian troops to help orchestrate the collapse and takeover of Iran. Cross' mind was racing and he was thinking too much.

Passing through Qarchak he needed to distract himself. Cross talked a little with Karimi about Iran and the makeup of the country. It all fascinated Cross but he couldn't get Sadeghi out of his head. She was controlling him somehow, in a good way. Her gentleness in bed and then the rawness of what came afterwards was incredible. He satisfied her satiable appetite for lust and desire in a way he had never experienced before. Her soft spoken words before they fell asleep in each other's arms swirling around his head. He wasn't in the real world. The drive through rural Iran was proving it. What was he doing here? He wanted to be back in Sadeghi's arms, not here perhaps counting the final minutes of his life.

They approached Varamin, drove through town and then took a right turn and headed to the outskirts. Cross saw the big complex, similar in scope and size to Romanov's facility, come into view as he remembered it from the satellite imagery. He didn't know how Hosseini was going to explain this to Karimi. Cross had his gun strapped to the ankle. He hoped they didn't pad him down there. It wouldn't set off metal detectors but their hands can certainly feel it. Fuck, he gasped as they approached.

They turned off the highway and meandered a little farther on a private road. Romanov had his facility rurally hidden. Hosseini didn't seem to care. Perhaps their strict society here precludes special circumstances. People talk they die. It also might not be up and running yet, something Cross had considered. It also could be that Taiwan and Russia supply the chemicals for Iran. The people are poor and generally controlled so they wouldn't need much.

"Hosseini has described some of what he is doing here, Mr. Cross. Cannabis is illegal, yes, but they have developed a strain that doesn't have THC. This is the information Hosseini has released to me."

He was reading Cross' mind, but clearly Karimi wasn't versed on cannabis and its chemistry.

"Ok, I was concerned about what you knew and what he had told you. I wasn't sure how he was going to hide what is going on inside."

"We are about to find out," he said smiling.

Cross was glad Karimi was relaxed. He did have this aura about him too.

They stopped at the gate and a security guard approached brandishing a Russian-made machine gun. The guard and Karimi spoke in Persian, Cross feeling his hidden gun as they did.

Karimi showed him his government credentials and handed him the other occupants' ID's. The guard went back to his booth and made a call. A few minutes later he stepped out with security badges.

"You are expected Mr. Karimi. Please proceed after I open the gate. The reception area is off to your right," he said in Persian.

Karimi proceeded and headed as directed. He parked and waited for the other two Land Cruisers.

It was new construction and Cross knew that. But he didn't remember the two smoke stacks at the back of the property in any of the satellite pictures. They entered the reception area and were met by another guard. He motioned them to follow.

Now seated in a conference room, in comes Hosseini draped in his military uniform. Another significantly imposing figure enters Cross' life. Accompanying him was a wimpy guy in a suit and three armed guards. Cross had seen Hosseini's picture and it was hard to imagine he was talking with the man who wanted to take over Iran, and who had zero empathy for the people he must sacrifice in order to achieve that.

Karimi greeted him and they shook hands. It was obvious they knew each other. Hosseini had a good command of English.

"Welcome, Mr. Cross. It is a pleasure meeting you. I understand you are in a position to possibly help our analytical needs," he said straight to the point.

Hosseini handed the meeting over to the guy in the suit after some introductions. He was their head scientist but came from Switzerland. He gave a formal presentation about the facility and what they wanted to accomplish.

Cross listened but he had heard this crap twice before. It was all the same stuff. Fifty minutes or so later the guy was done. Cross didn't have questions but made up some just for cosmetics. Karimi did. Cross wanted to see the analytical facilities for his proposed equipment and asked.

"That is part of our presentation, Mr. Cross," said Hosseini.

They drank Turkish coffee, had some informal chats and then headed through security doors. They went through the glass airlock system Cross was expecting to see and into the new laboratory facility. It was a little behind in their construction which piqued his attention. Perhaps the virus isn't ready to be released yet and they may have a little more time. The other horrific possibility immediately sprang to mind that the virus and vaccine will be supplied by someone else. This facility will be used as storage for the vials and containers. His body shuddered. The air-lock security system told him it was designed to be a biological laboratory.

The lab space was just a distraction, a way to hide the construction and get approval for it. It is perhaps likely the Iranian government approved this construction project and paid for it.

He looked around the new laboratory and had questions for Hosseini. He wasn't a scientist so the guy from Switzerland answered them. The fact he was a foreigner also raised another thought. Iran cannot find the scientists and people required to do the research and production processes necessary. Taiwan imported some of their people but who wants to move to Iran? Who would want to live out here?

Cross wanted to leave. He wasn't comfortable anymore. He was forming an image in his head about what is going on. That image conflicted with what they thought was happening. He had to keep the pretense going of his visit though.

"Can we see the warehouse area, Major Hosseini?"

"Yes, let me take you there."

Two more security doors requiring keyed access and they were in a vast open space. This was an agricultural research facility but nothing was growing. It was void of anything agricultural, at least that Cross could see. Part of the warehouse was walled off with keyed access doors to get in. There were a series of large steel containers off to one side. In the middle of the warehouse were wooden tables lined row upon row. Wiring was suspended from the ceiling in conduits for power, network and USB outlets and computers were attached to them.

"This is where we will be monitoring the plant life and ensuring the research is going as planned," said the scientist.

Cross just nodded his acceptance but noticed one of the doors wasn't shut properly on a metal container. He was so desperate to see inside. Over in that area there were bathrooms so he asked to be excused.

"Please create a distraction or head towards the conference room. I just need a couple of minutes," he whispered to Karimi.

He is a scientist so who is going to suspect anything. He knew what he was looking for but they didn't.

He came out of the bathroom and saw the group heading to the conference area. The thing about narcissistic arrogant people is they think they are better than everyone else. Cross had experienced this in his life. He quickly cracked the steel door open so he could look inside. He was stunned and almost motionless. His legs nearly buckled beneath him.

Pushing the door closed, he almost ran to catch up but he wanted to run out of the building. They entered the conference room and sat down. More Turkish coffee was offered and a few English chocolates were left on plates. Cross kept his cool and sipped the strong coffee and ate a chocolate. He tried to suppress his shaking as he presented Hosseini's package that included brochures and quotations for scientific instruments printed in Persian. Even Hosseini was impressed.

"I can have the instruments sent through a different country, Major Hosseini. I have contacts that would hide the shipments into Iran. Even the British Embassy would look the other way. This would all be confidential and legal, I assure you. I know people who will do this for you. We would include installation. I would come here myself."

He was trying to impress his host and get the hell out of there. They needed to leave now, but couldn't. An hour later Karimi closed the meeting and insisted they need to get back. They had a 60km drive back and will hit Tehran rush hour traffic, Karimi had said. He needed to be back in his government office before the evening.

They exited the complex and Cross saw the guard close the gate behind them as they left.

"Are you ok, Mr. Cross? You look shaken although you concealed it in there. I was impressed with your brief presentation and how you handled yourself but I sensed something was wrong. Something has rattled you."

"Do you know what I found in those steel containers, Farbod? May I call you Farbod, sir?"

"Of course, Daniel."

"Body bags. Tens of thousands of body bags."

Cross' face was almost ashen.

30

The Viral Scope

Butler called Karimi to ask how it went and then arranged a meeting point so he could get Cross and his embassy staff member.

"I need a drink, James." Cross said as Butler drove him back to the embassy compound.

Sadeghi met them as they arrived and the blue security gate closed behind them.

"Daniel, what is wrong? You look absolutely destroyed." She then turned to her boss. "I have some drinks waiting for you at the bar, Ambassador Butler."

Cross said nothing and seated himself at the bar. He reached for the whiskey Sadeghi had prepared for them and downed it in one shot. He had tears rolling down his face. The reality of what he had seen was sending him into shock. This was now more real than he had thought possible. Preparation is being made to kill millions of people.

Sadeghi tried to console him. Butler was clearly getting upset.

"James, that wasn't an agricultural facility. It has a lab space fabricated into the building but I don't think it was for instrumentation. There was no power for that. It was, however, a facility to handle biological samples. I know that. It was the same as the other two labs I have been to."

He took a breather, and Sadeghi poured him another drink, only filling the glass higher this time.

"Thank you, Parisa. I am sorry for my emotional behaviour now. I saw what looked like tens of thousands of body bags, James. Tens of thousands of bags in one metal storage container and the room housed many of them. They are preparing to annihilate a lot of people. They had examination tables lined up. Rows of them. I am not sure for what but to perhaps confirm certain deaths. Out back I noticed incinerators to presumably burn the dead bodies and remove the virus. There were two smoke stacks I hadn't seen before. I didn't say anything to anyone, not even Farbod. What is happening is real. Preparation is moving forwards."

He stopped to take another drink. Sadeghi had grabbed his hand and was squeezing it.

"Holy shit Daniel. No wonder you look ashen. I need to make some calls and come back to this discussion. You did incredible today. Not many people would handle this the way you are. Take a break. Go and lay down. Drink more," he added, trying to console him.

"What the fuck, James. What is wrong with people?"

Butler left and Sadeghi moved him over to the sofa they were sitting on last night. Clearly he was troubled by what he saw. Perhaps the shock of being so secluded, surrounded by the top military commander in Iran didn't help. Perhaps the pressure of trying to save the lives of millions on his shoulder didn't aid his savouring disposition either. It didn't matter in the end because he started crying and couldn't stop. Sadeghi put her arms around him and cried with him.

31

The Love Story

Cross had no idea what time it was or what day it was for that matter. Where was he anyway? He came around and found he was lying on the bed in his suite. He checked his watch. It was 8 something but who knows what day. How did he get here, was the next question. That was quickly answered because Sadeghi was lying next to him. Her eyes were open and staring at him. She had never met someone so handsome, so secure, so brave, so strong and yet so sensitive and fragile.

"My head hurts," he said. "Thank you for taking care of me Parisa. What happened this afternoon? What did I do? I feel like shit, honestly."

"Rest, Daniel. You have been through a lot lately. I cannot imagine what your head is processing. They called up for dinner but you were sleeping so I let you rest. I will let them know you will be down in half an hour."

"I have never had someone care the way you do. This is surreal. Thank you."

She kissed him on the lips.

"I need to take a shower before dinner. Is that ok?"

"Go ahead. I will head downstairs and help them prepare. The ambassador wants to talk to you."

"I am sure he does," he said trying to laugh.

She departed the room but not without Cross staring at her. God, she was gorgeous, he thought.

Half hour later he was dressed in linen pants and a Merino wool sweater. Granfield's assistant knew his taste in clothing, for sure. He headed downstairs.

Butler had waited and joined him for dinner.

"I am sorry for this afternoon, James."

"Forget it. We would be more worried if you hadn't broken down after what you are developing. This is becoming insanity." He carefully paused, "Mr. Granfield will want a chat and I called MI6. Everyone is stunned. We are arranging your flight back to the UK for tomorrow and then CIA will arrange the pickup in London. You have things going on at home you need to take care of. Apparently flooding is everywhere. We now see the events being orchestrated and others are taking care of this. Mr. Granfield will fill you in also. They are attempting to seek assistance from a bank in Grand Cayman but that will be something you will likely need to handle too."

"Thank you."

Sadeghi looked sad now. She will not see him again after tomorrow, she thought.

"We have time. The virus and vaccines will take weeks to produce in large enough quantities. We are working with the governments involved. The Iranian government has been shocked at what you have extracted so far and is extremely grateful. There will be international repercussions for what you are doing. The governments involved are formulating a plan to seek and stop the perpetrators. When that is implemented, it will be fast and swift. People will die.

"Please call Mr. Granfield. They are swinging into action but await your arrival. I will have someone make the travel plans and then will let you know. Likely midday tomorrow is my thought right now."

With that, Butler left the room.

Sadeghi moved closer and kissed him.

"I am proud of you but will miss you, Daniel. I have fallen in love so fast. I cannot believe myself."

"Come with me?" was his shocking reply.

He called Granfield and they chatted for half hour. His flight was arranged to leave Tehran around noon and he confirmed the pickup at Heathrow this time. They could not deviate flight paths or plans. They were still perpetrating the pretense of this visit. He filled him in on Mikhailov but Cross had momentarily forgotten about the other women in his life. She was in a safe house but Granfield really needed Cross to see her. Ok, he agreed. Butler had already filled him in on details in Iran. Granfield assured Cross that they were working with other governments to put a plan together. He would need to be part of it. They were keeping tabs on Brownsville and his activities.

They ended the call and Cross called his friend.

"Hey, Daniel, how are you?" was the cheery voice. "How is Iran?"

Cross went through what he had found which stunned Verenich.

"My oh my. That is crazy."

"Did I tell you we found the stolen diamond?"

"No, when?"

"I am telling you now," Cross needed a laugh.

"No, when did you find it, silly?"

"It was in Russia. Romanov had it and bought it as a gift for Senator Brownsville. I thought I told you?"

"I cannot remember with all the stuff going on. By the way, you will need to deal with the Jewish contingent when you get back to Tahoe. I reached out to Brandy knowing you were out of the country. They have flooding in your building. She emailed you but knew why you hadn't responded."

"Shit, I haven't read emails for many days. Thank you, my friend. That sounds really bad. I will call Brandy tonight. I head back to the US tomorrow through London. See you soon."

He clicked off and called Dunhill. He really didn't want to anymore but he needed to fill her in. The diamond is still insured and she is waiting for confirmation. Romanov wants his check but he isn't going to get one. Cross smiled. He told Dunhill he has seen the diamond but would not elaborate. She got irritated but understood. She will hold off paying Romanov another few days.

Just as Cross ended that call there was a knock on his door. He went and opened it.

"Well, who do we have here?" he smiled and hugged Sadeghi so tightly.

"This is your last night in Iran. I wanted to spend it with you."

"Have you thought about my suggestion, Parisa?"

"Yes."

With that she walked into Cross' room and the suite door was closed behind her.

Breakfast was served and Cross and Sadeghi looked so happy. Cross had packed his bag and was ready to leave. The Range Rover was pulled around and then they left for the air base.

"I will come back for you, Parisa. I promise."

They hugged and kissed for what seemed like eternity and then it was time for Cross to climb the stairs and onto the plane.

He was exhausted and finally sitting on the Royal Air Force Airbus heading to London. Yesterday was so mentally intensive and it was rather a subdued morning today. He was happy. He had asked for a favour and Granfield had assured him his request would be granted.

The Airbus throttled up its engines and headed down the runway. Within minutes it was in the air. He muttered to himself.

"God, I love you, Parisa."

32

Connecting Some Dots

Cross was in Granfield's office in Langley. The adrenaline was keeping him alive now but even that had its' limits. Granfield was filling him in on developments. Five governments were now collaborating and they were gathering evidence and compiling it all.

"Brilliant reconnaissance in Iran, Daniel. That was impressive work. The Iranian government has been in contact and our president is considering lifting some sanctions to help them deal with this crisis. The British government has agreed already but we cannot let others know.

"There is a small window for you to head back to Tahoe. I hear it is a mess back there. We have a few days before you need to depart for Grand Cayman. Sorry, the senators and the Brits insisted you go."

"I talked with Brandy on the flight. She is so upset and I confirmed that I am heading home. I need to see Natalie before I leave, David."

"We can arrange that. I will have someone take you to see her before we fly you back to Tahoe. I have requested one of our Gulfstreams fly you directly into Lake Tahoe. They will wait to then fly you elsewhere. It is at your disposal. Time is of the essence but be careful."

"There is something else, David. Whilst I was seeing body bags I saw a pallet between the steel containers. I have not mentioned this before to anyone. The pallet was loaded with cash, US hundred dollar bills to be precise. It had a US military emblem on the opaque plastic wrap. Remember during the Iraq war billions went missing? Perhaps I found where some of it went."

Granfield looked concerned.

"Let us continue this discussion at a more appropriate time, Daniel. This is useful evidentiary information that we can address later."

Cross left Granfield's office and climbed into the Suburban waiting outside. He was whisked off to see Mikhailov. Twenty minutes later they approached a non-descript apartment complex. He saw two agents standing watch and one was outside as he entered the apartment.

"It is so nice to see you, Daniel," she hugged him so hard.

"You too," he said smiling. "I will fill you in on some things but do you still have the diamond safe and secure?"

"Yes. David provided me a secure box in his office for me to hide some valuables. I was very careful and he left the room while I placed them there. I created my own security code and it also has a key. He kind of knew what I was doing, I suspected."

"I trust him, Natalie. He is on our side. He needs our help so he isn't going to interfere. He is one of the good guys and a brilliant man."

She hugged him again and then kissed him. Cross was different now. He was in love but not with Mikhailov. He had things to do.

"How are the accommodations?" as he scoured the living area.

"It could be worse. David told me it will be this way for a few months until they can resolve some things. I knew what he meant. It is better than working for Romanov. I took my sister's place when she was murdered. I had no choice."

Cross was angry as he saw Mikhailov's eyes tear up. He needed to finish this thing once and for all.

"I will be back shortly. I have some priorities to deal with."

They hugged again and he left.

The Gulfstream landed in Tahoe and Brandy was there to meet him. She took him home so he could drive his Range Rover.

Back in the office he was surveying the flood damage. It was bad and the laboratory had to be shut down. The water was percolating through new cracks in the foundation in different areas of the floor. The smell was horrendous and toxic.

He made a call.

"Frank, I need your help please. We need to drill some holes in my office and lab area so we can install sump pumps."

He trusted Frank and relied on him often. Cross then headed to the rear of the property and found the drainage system had been filled in. The melting snow and vast water had nowhere to go except under the building and up through the foundation that was now splintering. He was livid. Other areas and tenants were also affected. He called Horowitz.

"You removed the drainage ditch. The building is now flooding."

"I don't know what you mean," protested Horowitz.

God this guy is a professed moron. No wonder the rest of the city detested his very existence. Cross was warned before he sold the property. Verenich had educated him on this guy's family background and knew what he wanted. Horowitz wanted to control the Californian cannabis grow market and he was also ruthless and dangerous. Fuck him, thought Cross. I have been around the world and dealt with people worse than this idiot.

"I assure you this needs to be addressed. I suggest you come down to the building," he said with conviction and authority.

He then called the local property management company who

were just as useless.

Half hour later Horowitz shows up with a few of his entourage. Cross wanted to punch him out but now he remembers his associates' faces from the city council meeting. He wasn't scared of him or his people and he was still carrying, courtesy of CIA protection. Cross was curious now that he has a cannabis testing license from the city. Horowitz could not use the building to grow anymore since only one cannabis license per property was allowed in the ordinance. He had been thinking about all this on his many long flights as he tried to piece it all together. He possessed a burning desire to solve Mitrovic's murder. The Russians had no reason to kill him and he was beginning to throw suspicions in Horowitz' direction.

The management company shows up ten minutes after the landlord and they get into a heated argument. Cross was livid and didn't care anymore.

"The property has been tampered with. The drainage ditch has been filled in. I will assure you once more I have the authority to deal with this my way."

Horowitz had never seen Cross like this. They had been cycling together in the mountains. He saw it in Cross' eyes but he didn't give a damn.

"I know what is going on, Mr. Horowitz. Does the name Robert Mitrovic mean anything to you?"

The look on Horowitz face answered his question. Wow, Cross was shocked. How did this man become ruthless?

"No, I have no idea who he is."

Cross had asked Verenich to do some research. He wanted to keep this separate from Granfield for the time being. He wasn't convinced of any connection with Romanov anyway and killing Mitrovic served him no purpose. Horowitz owned some guns and they were licensed with the state. Verenich found that the type of gun he liked matched the gun that killed Mitrovic, although they couldn't actually match the one that had the bullet's imprint on it. Cross didn't believe in coincidences.

Cross saw that Horowitz was physically shaken and tried to hide it. Now he could piece more facts together and had the resources. It was obvious they wanted Cross out of the building. They wanted to control the cannabis-grow empire. His lease didn't allow him to be removed because it had extension options. Horowitz also wanted Mitrovic removed, it seems.

The owner of the property management company looked shocked too. That surprised him but he knew he was involved in cannabis. Cross stared at them.

"You have until tomorrow to get the water out of my laboratory, Mr. Horowitz. I suggest you do it," he wasn't scared anymore of anyone. Fuck these people.

With that he walked into his office and went upstairs.

"I don't recommend staying here, Brandy. Let the employees go home and I will still keep paying your salaries."

She hugged him.

"I cannot tell you what I am up to. I will when the time comes. Trust me," he already knew she did. "I was in Iran a few days ago. I have other places to visit but keep me up to date on details and happenings here. I told the dumbass to fix the flooding. I honestly doubt he will. I gave him some information that shocked him. This is going to get messy. Please go home and be safe. It isn't safe to be around here."

"We watched the senator give a speech about his support of a vaccine bill," Brandy added. "It is getting scary, Daniel. I am worried. Please be careful."

Brandy had never called him Daniel before. She looked scared.

"I cannot say anything, Brandy. Please trust me. Go home."

He called the pilot of the Gulfstream and asked that he be ready in two hours. Cross had to go home first.

"Hello Igor, how are you?"

"Back from Iran, Daniel?"

"Yes. I am home in Tahoe. I am 100% convinced Horowitz was involved in Mitrovic's murder. The look on his face when I asked if he knew him was priceless. How is he a ruthless, dangerous person?"

"I hope you don't find out but, trust me, he has his people. I have my resources working on the gun. You should let David know. Then CIA can get warrants to search his properties."

"It may be time to request that. I wanted to find out myself first. When he flooded the building by filling in the drainage system, I knew then. That was the red flag and a light went on."

"Great work, my friend."

"I am heading to LA next to see Chantelle. Why don't you join me? I can pick you up at Mather Field. I will call you when we leave Tahoe."

That taken care of, Cross called Dunhill.

"I am heading to LA, honey. I will be there in about three hours. I will message you when we leave Northern California."

He was very straightforward. There was something he needed to find out.

He downed a glass of Glenfiddich and went upstairs to pack and take a shower. He was once again alive on adrenaline and his head was working overtime.

He stepped out of the house and walked to the Range Rover. He heard the first bullet whistle past his head. He was familiar with that sound and dropped his bag. Three men approached him and he recognised Horowitz' people. The first tried to punch his head but Cross was ready, and quick. He grabbed his wrist, twisted the arm and thrust his free hand under the elbow with such ferocity he heard the crack as it snapped backwards. The first one dropped on the blacktop screaming in agony. He swung at the second one and hit him in his Adam's apple, crushing the larynx. A second bullet hit the ground and splintered. Another hit the stained redwood on his home. Cross quickly took hold of the third man and moved him into the path of the bullet. He was so quick the assailant had no chance. The fourth bullet nestled in his abdomen and he screamed. Two more bullets to go. Cross didn't let go of his attacker and used him as a defense shield. A fifth bullet hit Cross' right shoulder and he reeled in pain. Luckily he had a huge pain threshold.

Using his left hand, he reached for his small arms in the jacket pocket and aimed in the direction of the bullets' trajectories. He quickly released two bullets. He saw the shooter run between two trees but he was too slow and grossly underestimated Cross. The third bullet fired hit his head and Cross watched it explode. The shooter's brains and blood flew everywhere. He dropped the dead assailant on the ground and picked up his bag. Throwing it on the front passenger seat, he quickly departed for the airport.

The pilot saw him approaching and ran down the stairs to meet him.

"Daniel, what happened? You require immediate medical attention."

Cross' endorphin rush had made him forget all about being shot. He didn't feel pain like everyone else. Blood had covered his shirt and jacket and was running down the arm.

"I met some men who seemed happy to see me," he said half smiling. "I know a local nurse. Let me call her. She is off today."

Twenty minutes later Angela arrived at the airport and cleaned him up. She insisted he needed surgery to extract the bullet but there wasn't time for that.

"Can you do it here?"

"What, wait? Are you insane? You need medical help, Daniel. I am a nurse not a surgeon," clearly upset with him.

"No, I don't have time. We can do it later. I need to get out of here."

Sitting in the Gulfstream using a local anesthetic, his friend was able to locate the bullet and remove it. A few stitches later he was done. She handed him some pain pills and antibiotics.

"Thank you. I owe you one. I will explain later," and kissed her on the cheek.

Once she was off, the door closed and it taxied down the runway.

"Hi David, I am on the way to pick up Igor and then heading to LA to see Chantelle. I have been shot but I have found Mitrovic's killer. Can you get search warrants?"

"Damn, Daniel, are you ok?"

"Thanks David, yes. I had a friend perform surgery on the plane before we left Tahoe."

"Wait, you did what?" clearly exasperated.

"She extracted the bullet and stitched me up."

"Are you insane? You need medical attention. I will have someone meet you in LA."

He had just heard those exact words. Perhaps he was. There was mounting evidence now supporting that theory.

"Ok, but I am alright. Have them meet us in Santa Monica. There are four bodies you need to pick up outside my home. At least one is still alive."

Cross put the phone down after explaining what he wanted Granfield to do next.

Verenich was picked up in Sacramento and the Gulfstream continued on to LA. Cross called Dunhill and told her where to meet and at what time.

His friend poured two whiskies and they settled in for the hour flight. Cross filled him in on events and told him about Horowitz and their attempt on his life.

"This is madness and complex. How did testing a diamond turn into this mess, Daniel? Are you ok?"

"Yes, actually I am feeling good. I sometimes wish I had validated the authenticity of it. People would still be alive."

"No, Daniel. You are about to save millions of lives."

33

The Jewish Plot

Dunhill was there to meet Cross and Verenich off the plane. So were a CIA agent and a doctor.

"Daniel, are you ok? What happened?" she said kissing him.

"I know who killed Robert, Chantelle. I figured it out on those long flights. I got confirmation this morning. I have search warrants and David is acting on them now."

He noticed she didn't flinch. She didn't bat an eyelid. He wanted to be sure she wasn't involved. But to ensure his feelings were accurate, he had Granfield get a warrant to search her home. That was being acted on as they stood on the tarmac. He still doesn't know if she is involved in the fraudulent claim for a diamond that wasn't stolen.

Just then his phone buzzes.

"David, what do you have?" he asked and then listened. "Great. And thank you. I will be ok."

He turned back to Dunhill.

"Mr. Horowitz is in federal custody on attempted murder charges. He will likely be charged with Robert's death too. That was the confirmation I needed and the reason I require medical attention. His home in Malibu also has a search warrant being acted on."

He had tears again. It was really getting to him. His life was nearly terminated a few hours ago and now the medications administered by his friend and his adrenaline were both rapidly fading.

The doctor approached and asked he accompany him to a federal medical facility. Before he did, he turned to Dunhill.

"I know the location of the diamond. I have physically seen it. I don't really know how the insurance is paid out but the diamond wasn't stolen. The FBI is now involved in this. For your sake please don't fund the loss to Romanov, Chantelle."

This part did affect her. She looked drained physically and mentally. Cross suspected she was involved in the insurance scam and wondered how much of the $25M payout she would get. He had no idea, and didn't want to know. It is very likely Kuznetsov had her involved anyway and she had no choice. In any event, her life would be free soon, he was confident.

"I need to head to the medical facility. My arm is beginning to ache. I will contact you later."

"Thank you, Daniel. You have likely saved my life," as she turned and walked away in tears.

He looked at his friend.

"I will be back in an hour or so and then I head back to Langley. Game for a ride?"

Cross followed the doctor and was taken to their medical facility.

34

Command Centre

Back in Granfield's office in Langley, it was chaos and plans were underway to terminate Brownsville's operation.

"How is the shoulder doing? You are lucky, Daniel."

"I have had better days. I slept well on the flight after the surgical medications at the hospital. I will be ok. The shoulder will require more help when this is over because the bullet splintered some bones and tore into muscle and tissue. Thank you for arranging that."

"Good to hear. You are one crazy dude," Granfield laughed.

"I have been called worse things, David," laughing along with the joke.

"How is Parisa?"

Granfield's respect for his wellbeing was heartfelt. Cross was enamoured with the man.

"I called her on the flight. She sounded in good spirits. I neglected to mention the attempt on my life for obvious reasons."

"After you two have finished your coffees, I will take you to the Command Centre. There are people I want you to meet."

"Command Centre? Holy shit."

"The diamond saga really sent the search into a mind-blowing array of madness, David," added Verenich. "This is numbing stuff."

"Thanks to your help, we are close to ending this mind-blowing array of madness, as you aptly stated. Your observations and perceptions are pretty accurate," he said smiling. "Now let us get going. The real bovine excrement is about to hit the fan gentleman, and we need to avoid a non-linear water fowl incident."

"Huh?" Verenich kind of asked.

"We need to get our ducks lined up, gentlemen," he said laughing his head off.

Cross really liked Granfield. All three entered a vast room with one huge wall full of screens. A long table sat in front of the monitors with computers and people manning them everywhere. The noise was a cacophony of endless chatter.

Granfield walked in and put a halt to activities.

"Ladies and gentlemen, this is Mr. Cross and his associate Mr. Verenich. They are responsible for starting this whole escapade we have going here. Hopefully they can help finish it."

Muffled laughter filled the room. It was best to keep spirits high.

Introductions over, Granfield then walked them over to a private room within the Command Centre. Cross recognised the two faces sitting at the small conference table. They were senators. Granfield introduced them.

Senator Watkins opened the conversation.

"Mr. Cross, it is a pleasure meeting you. Also Mr. Verenich," he said being cordial but regimented and formal. "I wish to extend my thanks on behalf of the American government, its people and the rest of humanity. You opened up a litany of immorality for sure."

"It wasn't supposed to be that way. Admittedly, it has been crazy," said Cross.

"We are impressed with your work, both of you. David has filled us all in, including the recent trip to Iran which was unprecedented. I am sorry for the attempt on your life, Mr. Cross. It seems there were a few side-bars to this shit-show," he said, being less formal. "David has assured me of your discretion because what we are about to discuss is beyond classified. Sorry I have to point out the obvious but I am legally obligated to. It comes with the territory I am afraid."

"That is fine, senator. Our continued discretion is assured, sir. We have signed contracts."

Verenich nodded in agreement.

Senator Watkins opened his talk on what they needed from Cross. He was back into the formal mode and was incredibly serious. The operation he was discussing would save the planet. Failure was not an option.

35

The Vaccine Bill

The Gulfstream was heading to Grand Cayman. Half way into the flight Granfield calls.

"Turn on CNN International, Daniel."

Cross did. He was trying to avoid news and politics for a few precious hours.

The senator from Illinois was talking about the new vaccine bill on national television.

"This bill is important for the safety of our lives, and our children and our children's children."

Cross wanted to throw up. It was all horseshit.

"We will have everyone vaccinated to prevent any future virus from spreading. As the population grows and the planet's economy gets stronger, the propensity for a virus to circumnavigate the globe undetected increases. It is vital for our survival. A virus could wipe out tens of millions before anyone knows what is going on. We will instigate a system that implants a device into the wrist of everyone who is vaccinated so we know they are safe."

Granfield had been on hold.

"This is utter garbage, David. Is this guy for real? Anyone with an ounce of intelligence will figure out that one cannot develop a vaccine for a virus that doesn't exist yet. He is an uneducated asshole."

"Well, unfortunately yes, as we now know, and some with brains are figuring this out already. They are asking that question but he is pre-empting the release of their virus. We are scanning the people around him. Some CEO's of big pharmaceutical companies are there. Many of those companies moved their Research & Development to China years ago. The chemicals you found are made by offshoot divisions of these big drug companies. We are connecting those dots too but had to dig deep. They tried to hide all this. Someone in the Chinese government helped us with the research."

"Obvious to me if they have a vaccine developed already, they must know what the virus is. I am actually curious if the virus will kill people or the vaccine, or both. If they spread the virus, how can they contain it so that the people they want alive don't get infected with it?"

Then a light went on in his head.

"Perhaps they have two vaccines. One to kill and one to save the people they deem important enough to save."

"Very clever, Daniel. Let us try and avoid learning the answers to your hypothesis shall we? Tell me when you land. The Royal Air Force plane carrying Nick Jennings from MI6 will land shortly after you. Good luck down there. You have the contact information of the UK Embassy staff member meeting you off the flight."

"Romanov will have told Brownsville about the diamond being taken."

"We thought about that scenario, Daniel. No way Romanov will halt this because Brownsville's payoff has gone missing. He will have kept that part quiet."

The call ended. Cross was livid. He was risking his own life whilst watching others die. He vowed to end this, and the senator's charade. Fuck this asshole.

36

The Bank, Grand Cayman

The flight landed at Owen Roberts International Airport and taxied to a secure location away from the main terminal. Stairs were brought up and the cabin door opened. Cross stepped out into the moistened heat. At the bottom was a new white Land Rover Discovery with government plates. A lady stepped out and greeted him.

"Hello Mr. Cross, I hope you had a good flight. I am Nichole Chapman from the United Kingdom Embassy in Grand Cayman. I will be assisting with your arrangements."

"Nice to meet you Ms. Chapman," Cross replied, shaking hands.

She was very formal and Cross was ok with that. She was English and didn't look like she came from any Caribbean Island.

"There is a private government office in the terminal. We shall wait there for Mr. Jennings who will arrive very shortly. His flight will touch down in twenty minutes or so."

"I am under your guidance, Ms. Chapman," he said smiling.

They drove to the terminal and then she led him through a secured private door and up into a lounge. There were refreshments and cookies on the table.

Half hour later Jennings arrived and they had their formal introductions. Now they headed off to the Marriott Beach Resort. They checked in and Chapman left, vowing to contact Jennings later that evening.

"Let us meet at the bar downstairs in half an hour, Daniel. Give us time to freshen up."

"I might need a few days for that, Nick," he said laughing.

"Yes, I understand. I have seen your previous travel itinerary. I highly recommend a new travel agent," he said laughing too. "How is the shoulder by the way?"

The light British banter was welcomed. Cross was exhausted.

"It is good, for now, thanks for asking. See you in half an hour. If you beat me to it after I become a horse and fall asleep standing up in the shower, a lighter local beer is fine."

Forty five minutes later Cross was down at the bar. Jennings was already there, at a quiet table off in the corner.

"Sorry, mate. I had a call I had to make involving a beautiful lady in a foreign country."

"Well that goes without saying, mate. I got you a beer. This has been quite a ride for you. I was in the office at MI6 when you were in Iran. That was amazing work, my friend," formalities now being dispensed with.

"It is pretty interesting building an agricultural research facility where one stores body bags and dead bodies. I didn't think they were mutually compatible. I admit I lost it for a while. Ambassador Butler was very gracious."

"He is an outstanding man, Daniel. The Iranian government likes him despite a lot of mitigating political bullshit. Sometimes we have to put those things aside and focus on what is important. The other stuff can be a distraction from real politics, which is human interaction with foreign dignitaries involving language barriers and cultural differences.

"Your Illinois senator is a real piece of work. I saw the feed from his speech today. The guy is an asshole."

"I may have used the same word with David at CIA. To be more accurate I said uneducated asshole," he laughed. "Yes, I wanted to throw up. People are dying already."

"Tomorrow morning we meet with the head of Cayman National Bank. I have met him before. He has to protect the assets of his clients but not when the funds come from sovereign federal institutions. There is no way he is going to protect the bank. He cannot. The fallout would be massive. I will apply some gentle persuasion, Daniel. Fuck this guy too," he laughed.

Cross was relaxing now. He had been wound up but Jennings was hilarious. He went into discussions about what he had found and experienced, including the deaths of Mikhailov and Huang and how they had shaken him up.

"No training prepares you for that mate. You can be an agent for decades and that never escapes you. Hardened or not, we are humans with souls. Worse for you I imagine. You are a scientist, a very prominent one at that."

"That is what I have been telling people. I am a scientist," he was laughing. "No one believes me."

"No one is listening to you anymore, Daniel. Clearly you have done incredible investigative work and people are admiring that and taking notice.

"The governments are cooperating. That is phenomenal progress on the world stage. Don't underestimate what you have done here. We are going to take down this moron and the dickheads who hang around him. The US and UK governments want to take down the CEO's of the top drug companies along with him. There will be massive fallout, mate."

The lovely cocktail waitress in a short summer dress came over and they ordered two more beers. It was very warm and they were overlooking the gorgeous Caribbean blue waters lapping the beaches.

"I have been here three times before. Once after massive knee surgeries and I was on crutches. Someone decided it would be good for me to share a cruise on crutches. It is funny, now. I got my Rolex watch from here."

"You are a very interesting gentleman and have some funny stories. I read your autobiography on the flight over. You should be a comedian. That was well written mate. You lived through hell."

He wanted to change subject.

"I need some food with the alcohol. Shall we order something?"

Cross waved to the waitress and she meandered over. He observed her nametag.

"We would like some special Cayman food. Please surprise us with your choices, Claudia. But I suggest not fish and chips. Thank you," and laughed.

She laughed too and skipped off.

"The Caribbean is a fascinating place. Grand Cayman has one of the highest income per capita statistics in the world but head over to another island and they are as poor as shit."

"I came here with my wife for our honeymoon. Unfortunately the demanding work at MI6 destroyed the marriage."

"I can see that. Plus you are dealing with work that you cannot take home. I can see it now. Honey, what did you do at work today? I can tell you but would have to kill you afterwards," Cross was on a roll now. He had an audience.

"Something like that," laughing his head off.

Claudia arrived with turtle, mackerel and Mahi Mahi prepared with vegetables, tomatoes, onions in a bouquet of spices and sources.

"Thank you, Claudia. This looks delicious," added Jennings.

He was a striking man. Tall, obviously fit and carried himself well. His casual white linen shirt and pants exemplified his stature. It must come with the territory, thought Cross. You would have to have this charisma and confidence to go somewhere and tell people to hand over whatever it is they are illegally doing. It takes guts.

"Have you ever been shot at, Nick?"

"An interesting and loaded question, pun intended. A few ex's would have if it was legal," now he was laughing again. "MI6 work isn't always being chased down dark alleys. A lot of the work is grunt work and desk-type stuff.

"Shall we have one more beer before we call it a day?"

"I am enjoying this, Nick. I haven't relaxed like this for weeks."

"Ok. We can have a few more. The banks don't open early here. They are on Caribbean time. We have an appointment with the gentleman at the bank at 10:30. It may be the last time he sits without a cushion with a hole in the middle," laughed Jennings.

"You are hilarious mate."

"We have to be. We deal with the dredges of society. Humour stops us putting a bullet in their heads before we ask them questions."

"I can see that. Let us ask Claudia when she comes over what else there is around here."

Claudia approached with two more beers and piled the plates ready to clear the table.

"What else is there around here other than this hotel bar?" asked Cross.

"There is a local club not far from here. Well, the beach is seven miles long so nothing is far," she laughed.

"The humour around here is contagious and everyone is a comedian."

"I get off shortly. I can take you there if you would like?"

The morning rolled around and Cross was shuffling under the sheet. Jennings called his room.

"How is the head, Daniel?"

"What head?"

"Ms. Chapman left a message last night. I guess we ignored it. I love Caribbean music when one is in the Caribbean. It makes sense and the ambiance is authentic."

"Like New Orleans Cajun music is best heard in New Orleans' French Quarter. It also sounds better dancing with local beauties. Claudia and her friend were so lovely."

"Yes they were but keeping you focused, we still have a job to do. Ms. Chapman wants to meet us for breakfast. It is 7:30 now. I suggested 9:00. She will come to the hotel."

"Oh, yes, the reason we came here," he was laughing again. "That sounds fine. It is time to shower and try to beautify myself. It may take a while this."

They took a table out under the veranda but away from the rest of the patrons. Ms. Chapman was an older lady, early fifties and still looked good. The relaxed environment and sun do that to people.

They carefully discussed the meeting with the banker at 10:30. Ms. Chapman went through the legalities of the island but Jennings didn't give a damn.

"Sorry, Ms. Chapman, but fuck the bank. I can assure you they will cooperate."

She looked startled and was taken aback. They drank some more coffee.

"I am going to make this very simple. The meeting should be no more than twenty minutes max."

Cross liked this guy. He was funny. He needed to get this done so that he could go back to the US.

Ms. Chapman drove them over to the bank and parked. The heat was rising but still manageable. All three entered the air conditioned building and were made to wait ten minutes. This already set the tone for Jennings. Out came the head of international finance. He was grossly overweight, wore glasses and looked rather pathetic in his expensive suit, thought Cross.

"Good morning Ms. Chapman, Mr. Jennings and Mr. Cross. I am sorry I had to make you wait. Please come into my office."

They followed and were seated in front of a huge expensive mahogany desk, but not before Jennings closed the door behind them. Cross scanned the room and all the furniture matched. He saw security cameras overhead. He aimed his handgun with silencer and shot out the cameras.

"We don't need those," said Cross.

Ms. Chapman was shaking.

"What can I do for you?" the wispy banker asked.

"First, call security and tell them everything is ok."

He did.

"I will keep this very short and simple, sir. I work for UK intelligence and this gentleman here works for US intelligence," he touched Cross' arm. "I brought some documents with me," Jennings placed them on the table. "It shows wired money that starts from Washington, DC and then travels to various places around the world until the final destination is your bank, in these three accounts," and placed the account information on his impressive desk. "The accounts are being accessed by three corporate entities," and placed the corporate information on his desk. "We know exactly how much has been transferred and it has been verified by the Feds in Washington. We know precisely how much each entity has removed from your bank and transferred to their respective countries, which has been verified by their banks.

"Now sir, I am going to make this very simple. I have the backing of the UK and US governments and we can destroy the transactional capability and monetary integrity of this bank, which would look really bad on your CV. If you don't do what I am about to ask, this bank will cease to exist, sir. You are fucking with sovereign money and financially supporting global terrorism. The tax payers will be a tad upset when this reaches the public domain."

The man looked frazzled. I guess Ms. Chapman neglected to inform him who we worked for, Cross said to himself.

"Am I making myself clear, sir?"

"Yes, crystal, Mr. Jennings."

"Now, I have witnesses here who will testify if need be that this was a strategic meeting to discuss global banking cooperation. You will call this number now, it is a number at MI6 in London, and you will do exactly what Derek tells you to do."

The banker called the secure number Jennings had just given him. He did as he was told and provided security information pertaining to the accounts. He was shaking. Cross guessed the guy at MI6 was telling him he knew his house, his dog's name, his children, his parents, his bank accounts, his first love, inside leg measurements. After a few more minutes, the banker put the phone down.

"Is everything explicitly clear, sir? You know what you are being asked to do when the time comes? And you will do what you will be asked to do?"

"Yes." Clearly he was shaken to the core.

"Good. Have a nice day, sir."

With that they exited the bank and climbed into the Discovery.

"This will be timed. The timing is essential. We cannot cut off funding now. It has to be exact and precise."

Cross knew why. Chapman took them back to the Marriott so they could get their bags and check out. Jennings called his office and cleared his departure. Cross called the pilot and asked he get ready.

An hour later they said good bye to Chapman and climbed aboard their respective government planes.

Cross called Parisa in Tehran.

"I finished in Grand Cayman, honey, and now heading back to Virginia. I miss you."

"God, I miss you too, Daniel. Things are hectic around here. James has been meeting with top government officials. Please be careful. I love you."

"I will honey. This is almost over. I love you too."

37

The Plan

Cross was back in Granfield's office. He was really becoming acclimated to it.

"I suggest you call Natalie. She is going into the witness protection program and then will have her identity modified. She will not be allowed to see you again. Go see her."

"I will call her this afternoon. Thanks, David. I feel sorry for her. I cannot imagine what she and Cassandra lived through."

Granfield continued.

"We have been working on a massive coordinated effort with four foreign governments. The British are involved because they are closer to the Iranian government and, of course, the banking arrangement on the Caribbean island. The morons in the White House and The Capitol screwed the Iranian relationship up. Brilliant work again in Grand Cayman, by the way."

"Nick Jennings was admirable and he is the person responsible for that. I had never seen anything like it. Poor Ms. Chapman was floored and the bank manager was shaking. He was hilarious too. A very likeable and interesting character."

"I knew you would get on. Sometimes it goes with the territory. This is almost ready to move forwards. Just a couple more days."

"Great."

"We have to keep up the pretense so we will be driving to The Capitol today. Best we do it there and not have the senator be seen coming to CIA headquarters. We need to coordinate with Senator Watkins. A car will drive us there in an hour. Go freshen up. I know you just got off a plane. Your suite is still open," he slapped Cross on the back.

They sat across from Senator Watkins in his Capitol office. Through the window Cross could see the Washington Monument. I wonder what the founding fathers would think of all this? he pondered. Accompanying the senator were Secretary of Defense and the army's Chief of Staff. They must have determined they weren't part of any coup attempt, thought Cross.

Watkins filled him in on the final phases. Confirmation filled in by Granfield.

"Mr. Tsai, Mr. Romanov and Major Hosseini all know you, Daniel. You have to be involved in this," confirmed Granfield.

"Yes, I understand, Senator Watkins. I get it," and thought carefully before adding, "I think. Two of them did try to kill me, I might remind you."

Cross was clearly very tired but he knew what is being asked of him.

"Yes, we are aware of that. We will try not have them do that again, but no promises," Granfield answered typically adding levity. "Our tactical team will go over the details but you are needed as a witness. You met these people and their entourage. Massive coordination involved and you will not be on your own this time."

"Senator Brownsville is being partly paid with a diamond. How are we going to prove this without using the real one?" Cross was just blabbering now, clearly too tired to think.

"Don't worry about semantics, Daniel. We are dealing with those. You just do what you do best," added Watkins, observing his demeanour. "Go get some rest. There is time."

Back in Langley Cross was being given the rundown of what he will be part of. It was huge and he tried to take it all in. First would be Iran, then Russia and finally Taiwan. It had to be this way and it made sense, thought Cross. Finally the senator who Cross would love to meet, would be the last person to fold.

"We will commence strategic operations the day after tomorrow, Daniel. I suggest you go get some rest."

Back in his suite, he called Mikhailov.

"How are you, Natalie? I am coming over in an hour."

Cross arrived at the same apartment complex as before. She was happy to see him.

"Your identity will be changed and you can then start your new life, Natalie."

"Thank you for everything, Daniel. You have done so much for Cassandra and me."

"I wish I could have done more."

"No, you did already. She called me when you arrived in Windhoek. She told me what a gentleman you are. She had never had that her entire life. Finally just hours before her death she found real men do exist."

The emotional shockwave hit Cross like a bullet train. His eyes were welling and Mikhailov saw it. She sourced a tissue and wiped them.

"I am sorry. I am messed up from bad experiences too."

"That is what makes you special, Daniel. You have this aura and presence and yet you are vulnerable and sensitive. Cassandra saw that and you made her happy for an instance."

They hugged and kissed before Cross excused himself.

"Thank you. I am happy I met two really beautiful Russian twins. I will not be allowed to see you again but I hope life turns out the way you always wanted it to and deserve, Natalie. I will keep an eye on you through David. I must go now."

With that he was gone. Mikhailov closed the door behind him and started to sob.

Cross returned to the suite at CIA and called Parisa.

"I miss you. I will be gone for a few days and will not be able to use my phone. See you soon, I promise."

Click. He hoped he was right.

38

The Takedown Begins

Twelve hours to countdown Cross was being briefed by top military personnel. People's nerves were being jangled and juiced and the emotional rush was on. Time to remove these bastards, was everybody's thought. The brief was repeated to ensure details were accurate and understood.

This was it. Time to head to Tehran through London. They drove to the private airport and Cross was surprised to see an American Airlines 777.

"Keeping the pretence going and the Gulfstream was too small for the contingent of Delta Special Forces unit," Winwood explained.

At Heathrow they transferred to a Royal Air Force Airbus A330, and were joined by a contingent of British SAS men. Jesus, where did my life go, mused Cross.

The pilots quickly throttled up and were hurtling down the runway soon after boarding had completed and equipment transferred. They had a timetable to stick to and were given a priority departure.

They arrived at the air base west of Tehran and were met by Iranian government and military personnel.

Karimi and Butler came over and greeted Cross.

"Nice to see you again, Mr. Cross. I wish it was under better circumstances," said Karimi.

"Mr. Karimi, can I call you Farbod? I wish it was under better circumstances also. Perhaps my next visit will be," he winked.

"James, thank you for greeting us. Good to see you again also."

"Urgency is paramount Daniel. The US Delta Special Forces and the SAS will split. Some will depart with a contingent from the Iranian military and head to the complex outside Varamin. Some will come with us. The rest will remain with the Airbus and wait for you. Major Hosseini is expecting you and Farbod. This has been co-ordinated with immense detail and care. Be careful though. Farbod was strict in who he told. However, he had to inform their president and supreme leader. They had to know. One cannot have military action using foreign soldiers on their own soil without the leaders being aware."

"Got it."

Fuck, he said under his breath.

"Exactly," replied Butler. "Let us get to the military headquarters which is twenty minutes north of Tehran. You are meeting Hosseini in his office. Some of the military in our convoy will disperse and secure other locations in and around the city."

"Is that appropriate? Do we know who his allies are in the military?"

"I understand your concern Daniel But I took care of this part," said Karimi. "The media and internet have already been shut down. We already fabricated a social disturbance so that part was easy. In an hour, Iran's internal phone network will be shut down also."

"Sorry, Farbod. I know you have. I am a little more nervous after people have tried to kill me."

"Let's go," instructed Butler.

Most of the contingent of US and British soldiers heading to Tehran were already in the unmarked buses. They would leave the airport and take different routes to Iran's military headquarters where they would park away from the property, Butler explained. Each bus would be supported with Iranian military in their own vehicles.

Cross climbed into a government supplied Land Cruiser along with Butler and Karimi and they quickly departed the military airfield, heading to northern Tehran.

"How are you going to control 650,000 military personnel? Iran's army is huge, Farbod."

"We will find out soon enough," he answered with a smile.

Cross smiled too and swallowed hard, but he loved Karimi's calmness under enormous pressure.

"I guess so."

The convoys split and headed off in different directions. Cross' adrenalin was very active again and his heart was racing. How was he going to be composed meeting Hosseini again. That man was scary.

He could hear chatter through hand held telephonic devices. They were in contact with the convoy heading to Varamin, Butler told him, and were speaking Persian through secure communication devices. He marveled at how adversaries were now working in unison to take down a common enemy.

"You look calm, James."

"Not really. I like the Iranian people. They look after the Embassy staff, particularly after the devastation in 2011. When the news eventually gets out, they will be shocked, like the rest of us are at this emerging thing put in motion."

Two hours later, they were approaching the military headquarters. Cross' heartrate jumped another notch.

Across the other side of the world progress was being monitored in CIA's Command Centre. Granfield was watching everything. The monitors at MI6's headquarters in London were working overtime also.

"They have confirmed the forces are in place at Hosseini's complex outside Varamin. The buses have arrived in strategic locations around the military facility here, and other places in Tehran. Now let us proceed to the Major's offices, Daniel. You have your gun, right? Iran's internal communication system was turned off half an hour ago."

"Umm, yes. I am ready."

Cross stepped out with Karimi and they walked towards an imposing complex. Someone came out to greet them and then were escorted into Hosseini's office. Outside things were taking place. The security guards had already been neutralised and removed. Iranian and British forces were moving into the complex.

"Good afternoon, Mr. Cross and Mr. Karimi. It is so nice to see you again."

"Thank you Major. Nice to see you again also."

Cross noticed the room was full of his entourage and recognised a few. There was a small commotion outside, even a couple of shots fired. Before anyone in the room could react, Iranian and British soldiers came charging into the room.

Hosseini was stunned and speechless. Karimi approached him as a soldier stepped behind and stuck a gun in his back.

"Major, you are under arrest for espionage and conspiring against the Iranian government and its people. As you know, these are serious charges and carry grave consequences."

Other members of Hosseini's group were being methodically handcuffed. Cross noticed an ear piece in one of Karimi's ears. He found out why very quickly.

"As we stand here I have just received confirmation multiple forces, including US and British, have entered your complex on the perimeter of Varamin and have secured it. Your people have been arrested and will be brought back to Tehran."

Karimi turned to a soldier.

"Take this man away."

Cross looked at Hosseini.

"What were you going to do with those body bags, Major?"

"One down Daniel, thank you," said Karimi. "Your people saved my country and we will be forever indebted. Now leave. You have more work."

They shook hands and Cross ran downstairs to the Land Cruiser and headed back to the awaiting A330. A bus followed them. His tiredness had evaporated. Now he was focused and energised. This was insane.

"Goodbye, James. I will be back soon," he added as they warmly shook hands and hugged.

"I figured that already."

Cross navigated the stairs and got seated. The special military units were all ready for him. The door closed and the Airbus ramped up and departed the air base. Its next destination was Moscow.

39

Romanov Loses His Head

Now out of Iranian air space, he called Granfield.

"I have never seen anything like it, David."

"No one has, Daniel. Stay focused, my friend."

Wow, Cross had never heard Granfield use endearing personal words before. He was always the quintessential professional and the epitome of a gentleman.

"Hosseini was stunned."

"Russia may not be so easy. However, the government does have control over the internet, media coverage and airwaves. This is to our clandestine advantage, Daniel"

This wasn't why Cross agreed with their order of action. He thought it was geographical. Now he realised it was who controlled the people. Who had the authoritative power. Taiwan portrays the image of a democratic country which irritates China. However, they don't have elective control like the Russian and Iranian governments do. Now it concerned him.

The Airbus touched down at Kubinka's military airbase a little under four hours later. It was conveniently located west of Moscow which would help hide their activities.

Cross stepped off the plane and walked down the stairs. He saw a black Mercedes he was familiar with and was surprised. Fedorova came over and they hugged.

"What are you doing here?"

"My job is to calm you down and keep you out of trouble, Daniel. I realise that is an impossible assignment. You have to be here, I get that, but this is a massive coordinated effort between world super-powers. I was asked to keep you up to date so I am your interpreter and protector.

"We will be involved but behind the scenes. Let them do their job. You have already been shot once. How are you, by the way?" she asked being genuine Cross saw.

"The shoulder is ok but not the best, thanks for asking. I am fine with stepping back, honestly, Alexandria."

"Russian forces are already situated outside Sergiyev Posad. There are thousands of them.

"We will be escorted discretely into Moscow City. They already know Romanov is in his building. This will be a military operation, Daniel. Force and death will occur. Putin authorised the internet, media and phone system to be disconnected temporarily. He created a reason, some social disturbance, the usual reason people are famil-iar with. No one will know what is about to happen."

With that a Russian Military General walked over and spoke to Alexandria. Obviously she mentioned Cross' name because he walked over to him.

"I speak little English, Mr. Cross. I want to shake your hand, sir."

Cross was stunned.

"You are a hero amongst the people involved in this operation. I hope I can tell you about it over a Russian beer one day," and with that he walked back to a car waiting for him.

"The General asked we follow him. We will have two soldiers with us in the car."

This was it, thought Cross.

They climbed into the Mercedes and followed what Fedorova knew as the General's car. Generals have BMW's, he asked himself. Very interesting. Fedorova read his mind.

"No, they don't drive BMW's. He also has to be discrete," she said laughing.

"Thank you for relaxing me. My heart is about to bounce out of my chest."

Cross looked around and saw a small convoy of buses. Some US and British Special Forces were on them and a few remained with the Royal Air Force plane. They were being escorted by Russian Spetsnaz Special Forces.

They left the air base.

An hour or so later, Cross could see the tall structures of Moscow City looming larger and larger. He didn't know how they could keep their approach quiet. A few minutes later the buses split off.

"They will arrange to meet at different places around Romanov Plaza," Fedorova pointed out.

"I see."

Some minutes later the Mercedes pulls up across the street from the Plaza. Cross watches as the events now begin to unfold.

Their two soldiers had stepped out and were standing guard outside the car.

One bus pulled up near Romanov's building and a Russian soldier climbed out, ran across the street and shot out the external security cameras. The rest of the Special Forces units peeled out and were wearing face masks, flak jackets and other ancillary equipment tethered to their bodies. They surrounded the entrance. Two entered the building and sprayed the security desk with gun fire and smoke bombs. The rest followed them inside a few seconds later. The occupants of the building were now running around and screaming. Cross saw a contingent of FSB offices enter and they started arresting people.

"Where the hell did they come from?"

"Lying in wait, Daniel. Keep calm," she smiled and Cross sensed she was engrossed in this too.

He saw soldiers head to the stairs and one man punch the button for the elevators. More soldiers arrived outside and he thought he heard helicopters approaching.

"Romanov has a helipad on the roof. It cannot be used anymore. Those are Russian soldiers arriving in choppers," reading his mind again.

Cross heard Fedorova's phone ping.

"Let us head inside, Daniel. The two guards will protect us."

"Let us do what? Are you joking?" His voice was high pitched.

"No, not really. Grab your gun. I have one also."

Cross somehow followed Fedorova, ran across the road and into the building. He trusted her. It was bedlam and chaos. He could see death already. Soldiers were going up the stairs. Smoke started to interfere with his sensitive eyes. Someone had cut power to the building so the elevators weren't functioning. Outside Russian citizens were stunned as the public was ushered away, most of them screaming and crying.

"Shit, running up twenty floors with my bad knee. This should be fun. I might be a casualty too," he yelled.

They followed the soldiers and started running the stairs two at a time. The soldiers were quicker and disappeared.

As they scaled the stairs a door opened on the 15th floor and Cross recognised the two men trying to escape. They were part of Romanov's guards. They were slow and Fedorova dropped them with two shots, one to each head.

"Part of my executive training and looking after you," she said.

Cross was speechless.

He walked through the door expecting more to come out of the same floor and would be ready. They heard gun shots and shouting from the floors above. Romanov appeared around the corner and was running towards the stairs. He had Kuznetsov with him. They then saw Cross and froze. The look of horror surprised Cross.

He put one bullet in Romanov's knee cap and another in Kuznetsov's head.

"Fuck Kuznetsov," he said to Fedorova who was now close behind him.

He walked up to Romanov lying on the ground and smiled. He knelt down and placed the gun on his forehead as he reeled in pain from his knee cap being obliterated.

"Natalie is a really nice Russian lady. She joined me in the shower not so long ago. She told me all about their life in Russia and how you saved them, and then abused them. The next bullet is for Cassandra who died in my arms, you fucking asshole. By the way, we have your diamond."

"Daniel, no!" Fedorova screamed as she tried to stop him.

It was too late. Cross pulled the trigger and saw Romanov's brains splatter everywhere as the back of his head blew off. He didn't care. Fedorova looked at him but now she knew. Cross had tears.

Now the head of the Romanov empire was dead, Cross' work was over for this part of the mission. He walked down the hundreds of stairs and stepped outside the building. His mind was in a fog, a haze and very distant. He sat down in the cold snow and sobbed. He was inconsolable. Fedorova had followed him and held him tightly.

"I didn't know how emotional this has been for you," she said.

"I promised Natalie I would get revenge for Cassandra's death. I am so sorry. The emotions got the better of me."

The General saw Cross and came over. He spoke in Russian to Fedorova. Before he left he bent over, grabbed Cross' hand and shook it again. He patted him on the bad shoulder not realising and Cross screamed. Fedorova explained his recent near-death altercation with a bullet.

The General stood in admiration and saluted him. Cross hauled himself to his feet and returned the mutual respect.

"The complex outside Sergiyev Posad has been neutralised," said the General and hurried away.

"Who are you, Alexandria?"

"We knew about your first mission here a few weeks ago. I am an ex Russian military girl trusted by Putin's government. I do not work for the American Embassy. I was contracted by them for your arrival. Despite adversarial bullshit the media propagates, the Russian and American governments do cooperate on some limited level. They had suspected for some time that Romanov was up to something but they couldn't find concrete evidence. They do in fact want some scientific equipment in Russia. That part was real and will work with you on that when this crap is over. But they knew Romanov was dangerous so they assigned me to protect you. Now let us go. You have another job. Two more I believe."

Cross was speechless, for a second time.

They climbed into the Mercedes and headed back to the military airfield.

"Goodbye, Daniel. It has been a pleasure. Stay in touch. You have my contact."

"Thank you. I will call you," as he climbed the stairs.

The SAS commander on the Airbus was ready.

"We might need more men in Taiwan, Commander."

"We know, sir. They are on their way. The US has personnel already stationed at the Military Air Force Base in Okinawa. We will be coordinating with them.

"Take a seat and make yourself comfortable. This will be approximately fifteen hour flight. The plane is a modified A330 and we will be refueling midair."

The Airbus reached rotation speed and it started to lift off the tarmac. Cross felt the plane make a turn as it headed back east towards Taiwan.

He called Granfield.

"Mission accomplished in Russia but it was a military exercise, David."

"Yes, we heard but knew it would be. No way to get enough people into that building quick enough. I had to keep that part quiet but you know why. Get some sleep. Taiwan will be difficult also. We are working on compromising our illustrious Illinois senator. I asked James to let Parisa know you are ok. Please get some rest."

The call ended. Cross was handed a glass of aged whiskey and he downed the whole lot in one shot. The attendant brought back the half empty bottle and gave it to him.

40

Wu Vanishes

Some fifteen hours later, accounting for airborne refueling, the Royal Air Force A330 landed at Ching Chuan Kang Air Base located in Taichung City. It was Taiwan's military base shared with the city's international airport and conveniently located in the middle of the country. The last time Cross was in this city his client was chasing a truck through the streets.

The Special Forces disembarked first and were met with Taiwan's military. Cross followed. Granfield had filled him in so he knew who to expect.

"Hello Mr. Cross. I am Mr. Ma from the Taiwanese government. Ms. Li is from the British Office in Taipei. She will be here to help you with translational services and strategic expertise."

"Hello Mr. Ma and Ms. Li."

They shook hands and added some pleasantries.

"This will be a military operation, as you know, Mr. Cross. However, we understand you will be needed to be a formal witness to the proceedings. My government is very grateful for your services. We are sorry about Ms. Huang's death."

"I am sorry too, Mr. Ma. She was a lovely lady. I still don't know why they were after me."

"Perhaps it was her husband, Mr. Cross."

Cross was not expecting this level of humour. He was almost floored.

"Well, I never thought of that. Perhaps indeed."

"Our job is to make you relaxed as possible. Ms. Li is here to see to that. I know what you have been through. We were informed through private government channels. We don't even know who is involved with this agricultural research project in Taiwan with regards to government people, both here and in China. We have been treading very carefully. We believe the virus and vaccines were to hit mainland China rather than Taiwan. Some officials in China had to know about what is going on here."

"That is our intelligence conclusion also, which would jeopardise the current tenuous relationship you already have with Mainland China."

"Indeed, Mr. Cross. That is why this is serious. Let us step into a government vehicle and we can talk as we drive south to Kaohsiung's dock area. I will be dropped off prior to you heading to GreenSea Enterprises. You do understand my position as an important government figure."

"Yes, Mr. Ma."

They stepped in the back of a black Audi Q7 and were on their way south.

"The Special Forces from US and UK are heading to the three main locations you found in your last visit here. They are being accompanied by Taiwan's Special Forces also. As you can see, a bus is in front of us as we proceed south on Highway 1. There is also a military vehicle behind us."

Cross looked around to make sure he was right. Mr. Ma laughed.

"You British," he said smiling.

"No, I believe you," Cross smiled too. "The head of this operation is Mr. Wu. I never got to see him when I visited his facilities."

"Mr. Wu is very elusive. However, we have been monitoring him for some time. The surveillance was adjusted and increased after your findings and it has captured him at the facility in Kaohsiung. We haven't seen news of the Iranian or Russian operations yet. It seems those governments control the media and internet which is good."

"That was the reason behind the operational and strategic technicalities, Mr. Ma. I thought it was geographical at first."

"Yes. Your government," he coughed and laughed. "Which one do you represent, Mr. Cross? Your government had a representative fly to Taipei to brief us. Let us hope we have surprise on our side.

"The facilities at the docks have surveillance. We have people there. As far as we know, Mr. Wu is still there," repeating himself to reassure Cross.

He presented Cross a picture of him and he was shocked.

"I have seen this man. Let me think now. Yes, that is it. I saw him arrive at the grow farm up in the hills. He was masquerading as a security repair man. I saw him arrive. No wonder the guard looked a little flustered," Cross remembering.

Wow, he sat back in the Q7's back seat and pondered for a moment.

"Did he know I was there? Is that why they tried to shoot me?"

"No, I am still going with Huang's husband shot at you."

Ms. Li chuckled.

Cross was mesmerised. He didn't know if Mr. Ma was told to relax him or if the gentleman was just doing it because that is who he is. Or perhaps he knew what Cross was heading into. Whatever the reason, Cross was relaxed and enjoying the humour. Unfortunately, he needed to focus. He checked his weapon by his ankle. Ma watched him.

"You may need that, Mr. Cross."

Cross' phone buzzed but he ignored it.

"I have used it already. I don't like using it but sometimes it is a choice between me or them."

Ms. Li looked at him.

"I am sorry, Mr. Cross. I didn't know," she added and looked sad.

"I didn't either. That wasn't part of my CIA contract when this started."

The Q7 took a few side streets and was now downtown Kaohsiung. Cross recognised the area. It pulled up behind another Audi. Mr. Ma shook his hand, stepped out and walked around. Cross got out also.

"Be careful, Mr. Cross. It was a pleasure meeting you. I gave you some instructions in between the levity. I also enjoyed that. We are nervous here for obvious reasons. You helped with my release. Here is the General's contact info. Ms. Li has it also. He has been instructed to wait until you arrive.

"Ms. Li has my contact info but here it is. Please keep me informed. I would like to see you before your departure. I can ride with you back to Taichung City."

"Thank you so much, Mr. Ma. Hopefully this madness will end positively."

The Q7 left downtown and headed to the port area. Ms. Li was talkative now. Perhaps the culture in Taiwan kept her quiet or it was just the hierarchy structure.

"We have instructions to stay back when the final phase starts. The General will advise once we get closer."

As they approached, they took an early exit and entered a different dock area.

A military officer approached as they entered an artificial makeshift security check point. As soon as he knew Mr. Cross was in the rear, he waved the driver forward. They headed towards a building that had been covertly converted into a military post.

"Hello Mr. Cross. Nice to meet you. I am the General in charge of this operation," his English was good.

"Nice to meet you General," as they shook hands.

"Please come inside and help yourself to a coffee. Ms. Li, what would you like? We have thirty minutes yet while the other military posts are in place and accounted for."

He knew Li even before being introduced. Another military officer, Cross thought as he remembered Fedorova.

They sat down at the mini conference table. Papers and maps were everywhere.

"Soon the research facility will be overtaken. That will be easy to get in since they don't have much armed security there. We have military personnel in hazmat suits because of the biological weapons. We don't really know the volumes of virus and vaccine vials they have produced. It is a very dangerous and risky operation though. We know they haven't shipped them to Russia or Iran yet. We were monitoring that.

"The grow farm may be the easiest operation to stop. There are unknowns there also.

"We believe Mr. Wu is in the warehouse building with Mr. Tsai, whom you have met. That is the surveillance information we have been given anyway. As you can see, there are unknowns, Mr. Cross.

"We will go in first and you and Ms. Li will follow. Keep your heads down," he looked at Li also. "We expect this to be a military-style cease-and-desist order. What that means is they won't cease-and-desist until a gun is put to their heads or their hearts stop pumping," he said the latter part smiling.

"Thank you, General. I am being asked by the US government to confirm Mr. Tsai."

"Yes, I know. Your laws protect perpetrators. Something about being innocent-until-proven-guilty shit. We in the military see things differently. We negotiate using more convincing methods."

"The US military gets into trouble doing that," he said chuckling.

"Ten minutes, Mr. Cross. Finish your coffee."

Cross' heart was beating so hard he could likely see his chest move. Just then his phone buzzed and he nearly leapt out of his skin.

"David, I nearly had a heart attack."

"We have the information we need for Senator Brownsville's arrest. We will wait until you get back. The Taiwanese government has assured us they will control the news feeds coming from their island and filter the internet but, unlike Iran and Russia, they cannot guarantee that. Iran and Russia have done masterful jobs of shutting that down. Be safe and get back here as soon as possible. I tried to call earlier but you didn't answer."

Shit, he was talking with Mr. Ma and ignored the buzzing phone. "Got it."

"Let's go," shouted the General.

Li and Cross leapt into a military vehicle which started rolling. They were following other armoured-class vehicles and heading towards GreenSea Enterprises, he guessed. He didn't know. There were no windows in the rear of the personnel carrier.

He started hearing gun fire as they approached. They stopped and the doors opened. The men jumped out first and started running towards known cover targets. Cross and Li followed.

He could see the building now. They were in front of the security gate Cross was familiar with. The guard was already on the floor in the guard-shack doorway. Cross could see blood. The multinational Special Forces were heading in their vehicles towards GreenSea's warehouse off in the distance, using anything to keep them covered and safe from any shots coming at them. This was a surprise attack.

Suddenly Cross could see the flash of gun fire from the warehouse building. Shit. He pushed Li to the floor and helped to cover her. They got up and continued on, following other soldiers towards the building. There was an explosion and a small incendiary device went off by the secured front entrance. It blew a hole in the wall and the door no longer existed. Now Cross could see Special Forces at the back of the property as they surrounded it. Where did they come from? he muttered. Men in camouflage had exited the military vehicles and ran inside firing. Cross and Li followed. Finally he was in the building and he heard screams and the sound of gun fire. He saw bodies scattered around the office areas. Eventually the noise subsided and the sound of bullets being fired came to a halt. Cross walked further in, past the areas he had visited only a few weeks ago and into the warehouse.

Taiwanese security police were now swarming the area and had started to handcuff GreenSea employees. Then he saw Mr. Tsai in handcuffs and walked over.

"Yes, that is Mr. Tsai," he told the security officer. "Nice to see you again."

Cross mustered as much energy as he could and punched him in the face. He felt his cheekbone shatter. Tsai wasn't expecting it and the big man keeled over. More security people came over along with the General, who spoke in Mandarin, and they picked up Tsai and walked him outside.

"That was for Ms. Huang, General. I am sorry. We are not supposed to bring personal emotions into battle. I did in Moscow too."

"I think quite the contrary, Mr. Cross. I would have put a bullet in his head but you don't know the laws here or me. We would have all defended you. It was self-defense."

He shook his hand.

"Thank you General."

"No. Thank you, Mr. Cross. The people of Taiwan all thank you. Before I gave the order to go in, I received confirmation the research facility had been secured with little resistance. Everyone is safe but they were ready to ship large pallets of whatever it is. Enough for tens of millions of deaths I was told. The grow facility was also entered and we secured that too. Mr. Wu was not found at any of those locations. We don't see him here either so our intelligence was wrong."

"That is interesting."

Cross found Li and they exited the building.

"Are you ok?" he inquired.

"Yes. I am a member of the Taiwan military, Mr. Cross. You didn't have to toss me to the floor," she said laughing. "You could have done damage. A bullet would have been safer. Perhaps you watch too many Hollywood movies."

Cross was now laughing too. Damn, he needed that.

Cross called Granfield.

"David, it is all secure here but we didn't find Mr. Wu."

"Ok. Get yourself home. The British are allowing you to use their A330. Great work."

Next call.

"Mr. Ma. It is secure."

"Yes, the General called me. Good work. Take the Audi and ask the driver to meet me downtown."

An hour later they were on the way to the air base, ready for another long flight back to Langley. One final act to go for Cross.

"They walked through each location and couldn't find Wu. We are monitoring airports and other possible exit routes. However, this is an island and anything is possible. We have the navy searching also. He could even have a submarine."

Damn, Mr. Ma was funny.

"Thank you for your help, Mr. Cross. You saved countless lives and the security of the planet, in essence."

"Please, many people were involved in this. I have one more unpleasant operation and then it will be over."

The Q7 pulled up to the bottom of the stairs leading to the A330. Cross got out and shook hands with Ma and Li.

He walked up the stairs and planted his tired body into a seat ready for the flight. Some US and British Special Forces had waited for him and were also now secure in their seats.

The Airbus thundered down the runway and took off. He wanted to call Parisa but couldn't. He was still under CIA and military operations.

He called Granfield.

"We just left and will be there in about fourteen hours."

The same attendant knew him by now and brought a full bottle of aged whiskey. She smiled at him.

"Compliments of the flight crew. Just drink from the bottle. No one cares and you have earned it, Mr. Cross."

41

The Final Curtain Call

"We have arranged for you to meet Senator Brownsville in a hotel room in the suburbs of Washington, Daniel."

Cross was back in Granfield's office in Langley. He was drinking coffee and spilt it all over himself when he heard what he said.

"Wait, you have done what?" his eyes were wide open.

Granfield was laughing.

"You are the mastermind behind this whole circus operation, Daniel. This is now the final pinnacle, the final curtain call if you will, of what you have achieved. We will have news cameras waiting. Senator Watkins has agreed.

"You will be presenting the diamond to Brownsville under the guise of a trusted associate of Romanov's. We will provide you information, courtesy of the Russian federal government that only Romanov would have known. Brownsville we know will ask specific questions to confirm your identity."

"This sounds crazy."

"Crazy is your definition. We wanted to call it Operation Insanity ourselves," he said laughing.

"Damn, why is everyone a comedian nowadays? Even Mr. Ma was hilarious," Cross was laughing too. "What diamond?" he added.

"Well, that is the kicker. He doesn't need to know there isn't one. We just present him a mahogany box that looks like one. The perception is he is accepting a gift from a known oligarch. He was planning on becoming the US president with help from the criminal element in society. The fact he was going to annihilate tens of millions of people was secondary and a necessary nuisance."

How did Granfield know it was in a mahogany box? Cross asked himself.

"How did the bank in Grand Cayman work out?"

"You were spot on about the Brits' illustrious Mr. Jennings. Quite a reputation he has. Someone known as Derek, perhaps a pseudo name, at MI6 had the information to shut down and transfer each bank account just before the respective operations hit each enterprise. It was genius."

"Yes, he was good down there. I was impressed. Poor Ms. Chapman from the UK Embassy didn't know what to say. In fact she didn't. She drove us from the bank, to the hotel, to the airport without uttering a word. Jennings and I laughed about it on our flights home.

"How is Natalie?"

"I knew you would ask. She is fine, starting her new life in the US. She has been given monies to buy a house and find a real job. She could even work for the US government. That is her choice. Now that Romanov and Kuznetsov are dead, you will be able to visit her. We also flew Igor back to Sacramento. He is a fascinating character and we will use him again in the future."

"Great. You are a man of your word, David. If it involves diamonds, don't have him call me. When do I meet the infamous Senator Brownsville?"

"That is arranged for tomorrow afternoon. Go get some rest."

Cross seemed relaxed now. Granfield had helped tremendously on this portion of his work. He had been well supported and trusted.

Granfield put his career on the line to surreptitiously implant Cross into this operation.

It was late and he headed down to his suite, poured himself a drink and fell asleep.

42

Senator Brownsville and the Diamond

Cross was up around 8am and meandered upstairs to Granfield's office. Damn, did this guy ever sleep?

"Good morning."

"Good morning, Daniel. Grab a coffee and I will be right back. Then we will head over to The Capitol."

They entered Senator Watkins office and sat down. The senator versed Cross on some details and facts about Brownsville. This has to be an open, relaxed forum in the hotel they were planning to meet. The room would have CIA cameras installed. Cross had to be involved in general conversations to make the senator trust him. Romanov had been in contact the day before his demise and Putin hadn't restored systems yet in Russia. It had to be this way. They had infiltrated the telephone network and used someone who sounded like Romanov. The Russian government had even secured his private line, so that anyone who called it could still reach Romanov's imitator. It was very clever.

"Here is Brownsville's number. Call him," said the senator, "But use this phone, and it is being recorded," as he handed him another secure phone.

"Hello Mr. Mulligan. Romanov told me you would be calling."

"Hello Senator Brownsville. How are you? Everything is in place for this afternoon. I will be bringing the merchandise we had discussed."

"Excellent. I will look forward to meeting you."

Click.

"Who is Mr. Mulligan, by the way? And who decided an Irish name would be good with an English accent?"

"It is ok. We created a fictitious name that even includes a Facebook page, a website for your business. Something about you being a strip club owner, with felonies for child pornography. Nothing outlandish," Granfield interjected. "The irony of mixing Irish and English was brilliant, right? It just added to the arrogant stupidity of all this."

"How can I say this? Umm, you should be on stage," and laughed.

"I was serious about part of that. Here is the FB page and web-site. Just go and look at them later. Nothing exciting, except for the strip club ownership," he said smiling.

Cross was ready, and so was Granfield. Brownsville had selected the hotel and room number. CIA had to work incredibly quickly to get the gear set up. This was it.

Granfield drove him across to the hotel just outside Washington, DC. They parked several blocks away just in case. Granfield gave him advice before he jumped out.

"Keep the conversation simple. Don't go off topic or meandering on about your strip club virtues," he was trying to relax him and smiled.

There was a car for Cross to take and park at the hotel parking lot. Granfield knew the senator would be prepared. They had to be too.

A CIA van was parked down the road and was monitoring the room and hotel. It was full of electronic gear just for that purpose.

Cross was nervous. He had done incredible things so far. This shouldn't even be on his radar screen but it was. He had never met anyone who wanted to control the world.

He entered the hotel and took the elevator to the 10th floor. It was the top suite, of course. Nothing but the best for this corrupt senator. He knocked on the door and a young lady opened it. Cross walked in.

"Hello Senator Brownsville. It is really nice to meet you."

"Hello Mr. Mulligan. Thank you for coming."

The guy was a sleazeball if ever there was one. He had this aura of arrogance and narcissism. His suit was expensive and he smelled like a whorehouse. His sun bed tan was obvious. He had a firm grip as they shook hands but he was greasy, like he had lathered in moisturising cream beforehand. He likely had. The people in the room obviously were his ass-lickers, as Granfield termed them. They were all looking up to this asshole.

Cross carried a leather satchel. The diamond box was too large to accommodate a briefcase. He wanted to be as casual as possible, but fuck this guy. He wore an Italian suit and silk neck scarf. Cross knows how to dress too.

They chatted for a while. Brownsville even brought up Mulligan's fictitious strip club in Florida. Bloody Granfield. He was going to make him pay for that.

Finally, after twenty or so minutes of chat, Brownsville led him off into a quiet corner and asked about the diamond. It had to be the senator that brought it up first. Cross wished it had been the first question. He lifted the satchel and opened it. Inside was the mahogany box. It was obvious Brownsville was prepared for the packaging. He lifted it out and unlatched it, his face corroborating expressions a poor child would make upon receiving a gift. A fuzzy round black and white soccer ball was on the plinth.

Immediately the suite door was shattered and FBI people came crashing in. News camera crews swarmed in and Granfield and Senator Watkins followed. Brownsville was motionless and had fear in his eyes.

Cross stared at him.

"You narcissistic, megalomaniacal prick. You had people killed around the world to satisfy your growing ego and greed. I think the electric chair isn't good enough for you."

It was all being broadcast on national news stations. Cross was the hero. Brownsville was cuffed and marched out the door but not before Watkins joined in.

"You were elected and trusted by the people of Illinois to carry out your civic and legal duties. You are a disgrace. I hope you rot in hell."

The FBI removed him and Watkins took the news mic and filled people in. It was a developing story that included five countries and five foreign governments. Before Cross was asked to join in, he walked out the room. Granfield followed.

"Let's go immerse ourselves in a drink or two, Daniel. I know a strip club around here, since you are now educated on such establishments," he added, laughing so hard.

Several hours later, Granfield had a driver arranged to take Cross back to Langley.

"Stop by my office in the morning before leaving. I need to talk to you. I was also given special permission from the British government to hold their A330 here for a few days. I am guessing you have someone to go see."

Cross was speechless and hugged Granfield. He didn't know what to say.

Once back at his suite, he called Dunhill.

"Hello Chantelle. I just want to let you know you are now free. No more being controlled by your ex-husband. He is dead."

"Come and see me when you get back. I will buy you dinner."

Click.

The following morning Cross entered Granfield's office.

"Coffee and breakfast are here already, Daniel."

"Thank you for everything, David."

"Wait a minute. You are thanking me? Don't do that again, my friend. You got the world together. You have governments who have never cooperated before now cooperating. You have an open ticket to anywhere you ever want to go."

"I will only ask for one thing, David. Are the legal documents being handled?"

"Yes, Daniel. They are being handled by Senator Watkins personally and you have my assurances. I have one more matter to discuss. Natalie left a key and a security code number for you. I am going to give them to you and then exit the room. The box in question is in the cabinet over there." as he pointed. "I know nothing about the contents nor do I ever want to know. Don't bring them up to me, you promise, ever?"

"I don't know what you are talking about."

"Precisely my point."

"No, I was being serious."

"Me too. The Royal Air Force Airbus is ready for your departure. I have a car waiting downstairs."

With that, Granfield left the room and Cross walked over to the cabinet. He opened the door and behind it was a mechanism to open a safe of some sort. Cross typed in the access code and then inserted the key he had been given. The door opened and revealed a mahogany box. Cross knew what it was. Placing it on the desk, he opened it and there was a hand-written note inside.

'This is my gift to you. You saved my life and gave me and my sister Cassandra hope. She didn't know men like you existed. She was happy in Namibia, even if only for a fleeting moment. With my love always, Natalie. P.S I hope to see you again and don't be shy'

Cross slumped in Granfield's office chair, holding the note. He was finally too overwhelmed and needed the emotional release. He put his head in his hands and sobbed like a baby.

Cross was relaxed as the A330 left Heathrow. He turned on BBC World News and saw the President of the United States at the podium on the lawn of the White House. It was now major world news.

"Over the last few weeks the CIA in unprecedented cooperation with Taiwanese, Russian, Iranian and British governments thwarted a plot that would have killed tens of millions of people around the world and changed life as we know it."

The feed showed a video of Brownsville being arrested in the hotel room and escorted out. The feed included Watkins giving his speech for the media. He saw himself and Granfield in the background exiting the room.

Then the video feed went to vast warehouses filled with crates Cross had seen in Taiwan and Russia, only these warehouses were located in the US. The President continued.

"Senator Brownsville of Illinois has been arrested and faces espionage, felony and other serious crimes against the state. CEO's of major pharmaceutical companies have been arrested on conspiracy and other related charges.

"The person responsible for exposing this plot is Dan…"

The TV went blank. Cross had heard enough and was done. He didn't care anymore.

The A330 landed in Tehran. The stairs were pushed forwards and the main cabin door opened. As he exited the plane he saw the white Range Rover with Parisa standing there waiting for him. He had his bag and ran down the stairs and into her waiting arms...

═══ *Also by* ═══
GEOFFREY BOTT

Uphill

Born in England to a middle class family, Geoffrey Bott excelled at school in most sports. A tenacious and unbridled drive to succeed that he didn't know would be required in order to survive later in life.

Armed with a degree in engineering from the University of Sheffield, Geoffrey moved to California to reap his American Dream.

Uphill is incredibly emotional, vivid and detailed about the rise and fall of a gifted and talented engineer. An innocuous knee injury playing rugby for his city would develop into a grim prognosis a few decades later. A month after rejecting a second groundbreaking knee rebuild procedure, his wife files for divorce and the life he had attained started to unravel.

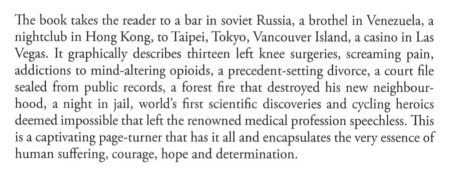

The book takes the reader to a bar in soviet Russia, a brothel in Venezuela, a nightclub in Hong Kong, to Taipei, Tokyo, Vancouver Island, a casino in Las Vegas. It graphically describes thirteen left knee surgeries, screaming pain, addictions to mind-altering opioids, a precedent-setting divorce, a court file sealed from public records, a forest fire that destroyed his new neighbourhood, a night in jail, world's first scientific discoveries and cycling heroics deemed impossible that left the renowned medical profession speechless. This is a captivating page-turner that has it all and encapsulates the very essence of human suffering, courage, hope and determination.

An inspirational, entertaining and riveting story that will leave the reader stunned and emotionally drained.

Learn more at:
www.outskirtspress.com/uphill